Ransomed
Heart

BOOKS BY SARA MITCHELL

Available from Bethany House Publishers

Montclair
Ransomed Heart

SHADOWCATCHERS

Trial of the Innocent
In the Midst of Lions

Ransomed Heart

Sara Mitchell

BETHANY HOUSE PUBLISHERS
MINNEAPOLIS, MINNESOTA 55438

Published by Bethany House Publishers
A Ministry of Bethany Fellowship International
11400 Hampshire Avenue South
Minneapolis, Minnesota 55438
www.bethanyhouse.com

Printed in the United States of America by
Bethany Press International, Minneapolis, Minnesota 55438

ISBN 1–55661–499–3

Author's Note

EXTENSIVE RESEARCH WAS incorporated into the writing of *Ransomed Heart* to insure as much authenticity as possible. For that reason, I feel compelled to explain a couple of historical *in*accuracies—liberties I took because, after all, this is a work of fiction.

The personnel filling the Denver office of Pinkerton's National Detective Agency are all fictional; the actual superintendent and several operatives during the 1890s bear no resemblance whatsoever to any of the characters in my book.

Cripple Creek also suffered a major fire in 1896 that destroyed a goodly portion of the town. I make no reference to such a fire, much less indicate that it ever happened, since it had no relevance to the story.

There *are* many abandoned mines and doubtless long-filled entrances and holes peppering this region. But (to the best of my knowledge) none of them contain the remaining sacks of Booker Rattray's hoard!

SARA MITCHELL is the author of numerous popular novels published in the CBA market, as well as several musical dramas and skits. The wife of a retired U.S. Air Force officer, Sara spent twenty-two years traveling, visiting, and living in diverse locations from Colorado to England. This wealth of cultural experience finds its way into all her works. She and her husband currently live in northern Virginia. She enjoys hearing from her readers. You may write to her at the following address:

Sara Mitchell
%Bethany House Publishers
11400 Hampshire Ave. South
Minneapolis, MN 55438

Contents

Author's Note   5

Prologue   9

PART ONE: Rebellion   11

PART TWO: Retribution   119

PART THREE: Ransom   201

Epilogue   280

"The wicked become a ransom for the righteous,
and the unfaithful for the upright."

Proverbs 21:18, NIV

Prologue

Front Range mountains, Colorado
September 1896

"JED, HOW MANY TIMES DO I have to tell you we need to leave?" He shifted restlessly on his cot, frustration and helplessness killing him as surely as the festering wound in his right leg. "You tell me nobody ever comes to this shack."

"They don't. Rest, Isaac." The old man called Jed patiently tucked a moth-eaten blanket around him.

Rest? How was he supposed to rest? "Nobody's had a reason to come looking . . . until now. Don't know what kind of game Booker Rattray's playing, but I must have transferred several hundred thousand in gold . . . not to mention two sacks of bearer bonds. Those jewels alone would ransom an entire country." Once more he struggled to rise, fell back panting.

"A disturbing secret, to be sure," Jed allowed. His hand closed over Isaac's shoulder and gently squeezed.

"Got to get word to my sister . . . in Denver. Rosalind's smart—she can help us, Jed. I'm not safe here anymore—*you're* not safe. Not since you played the good Samaritan and took up with the likes of me. Why can't you get that through that mule-thick skull of yours?"

The wise old eyes never flickered. "Insulting Sheba's a waste of time, my son. Besides, she's the one who carried you to safety without even a bray of complaint."

The burly preacher rose, poured another cup of weak tea

into a battered tin cup and brought it back to the cot. "Here. Drink this." He held Isaac's head and pressed the cup to fever-cracked lips. "I've been tramping these mountains for three decades now. I know the people, know just about every rock, tree, and stream in these parts." The gravel-pit voice washed over Isaac in a relentless, steady flow. "You stumbled onto that needle-eye crevice. Chivvied all those bags halfway down the ravine—an amazing feat in itself. Through the mercy of the Almighty, I found you before Booker did."

The old preacher paused. "Just remember, the same God who's been watching over me all these years is also watching over you."

Isaac Hayes finished the bitter tea and lay back with a groan. "Don't know about God, but I do know my sister. Gotta write to Rosalind, Jed. Then we're leaving." His trembling hand closed around Jed's wrist. "If we don't make it to Denver before Booker Rattray finds where we're holed up, that God you're always talking about will be watching over us face-to-face. We'll both be dead."

PART I

REBELLION

1

Denver, Colorado
October 1896

THE FIRST THING ROSALIND HAYES noticed about the stranger was his hair. At nine-thirty in the evening, the gala welcoming fete for the earl of Sussex and his New York bride was in full swing. Light from gleaming brass sconces and Austrian crystal chandeliers bathed the marble and wood-paneled rooms in mellow gold. From the back of the ballroom a string orchestra played a succession of tunes, the dancing notes a counterpoint to ceaseless conversations.

Over two hundred guests—the elite of Denver society—mingled with genteel confusion throughout the ground-level rooms of her sister and brother-in-law's mansion, which perhaps explained why Rosalind hadn't encountered the man any earlier.

"I beg your pardon?" Distracted, she turned to Mr. and Mrs. Hildebrand. "I'm afraid I didn't hear you."

"Noise is dreadful," the older woman agreed, lifting a languid hand to stroke the diamond choker adorning her plump neck. "But it does offer a suitable showcase for my anniversary gift from Archibald. Miss Hayes, what *are* you gawking at?"

Rosalind jerked her gaze away from the man on the opposite side of the room. All the gentlemen sported white tie and tails . . . but he was the only male guest whose hair streamed past his shoulders and down his back. The jet black strands were neatly tied with a length of black satin ribbon so that the queue all but disappeared against the formal coat.

"Probably the entertainment Driscoll promised when I talked with him at the club last week," Mrs. Hildebrand's husband offered, looking faintly amused. "It's . . . ah . . . headed this way."

"The string orchestra?" Mrs. Hildebrand queried, lifting her lorgnette to study Rosalind. "Surely not. They're good, to be sure, but if I may say so, Miss Hayes, your brother-in-law's selections are . . . somewhat bourgeois, aren't they?"

"I've always enjoyed Mr. Sousa's music," Rosalind responded almost absently, "though perhaps Oliver should have brought in a few horns for those selections. But the strings are perfect for 'Sweet Rosie O'Grady,' wouldn't you agree?"

Beside her, Mr. Hildebrand brought a gloved hand up to hide a smile. Chagrined, Rosalind realized she had just broken her promise to Alberta to be on her best behavior. Unfortunately, after three hours of social discourse, her good intentions were fraying rapidly. The tall stranger with the hair of an Indian warrior hadn't helped. . . .

Mesmerized, she followed his progress through the crush of guests in the entry hall. Surely Oliver hadn't invited an Indian—he and Alberta were far too conscious of social convention. Not to mention their reputation.

It was time to execute a discreet retreat. Better yet, perhaps she would—

"Good evening."

Rosalind started, then hastily composed herself. "Good evening." She focused a hopefully serene gaze over the man's broad shoulder. My, but he was tall! *It isn't polite to stare*, she reminded herself.

"I don't believe we've been introduced," Mr. Hildebrand remarked with chilly aplomb, as though the man with the queue had singled him out.

"No." The stranger's own voice was equally chilly. "We haven't."

He towered above the three of them—even Rosalind, who at five-five was taller than most ladies and many gentlemen. She slid a glance toward Mr. Hildebrand, wondering if his wooden expression disguised the same blend of intimidation and affront that she felt toward this . . . this annoying unknown guest. Then she looked directly at the stranger.

His gaze was fixed on her with the unblinking watchfulness of a tiger. An apt metaphor, Rosalind realized, her throat strangely tight. Amber-colored eyes gleamed with the same golden brilliance as those of a giant cat—alert and patient. And just as dangerous. Disdain and arrogance were stamped in the hard cheekbones and firm, unsmiling mouth. He looked—and acted—as if he didn't care a flying fiddle what any of the two hundred guests thought of him, Rosalind concluded.

Without a word, the Hildebrands retreated into the crowd, leaving her at the mercy of the tall stranger with his unorthodox appearance and daunting manner.

Unnerved, she fell back on the etiquette drilled into her for years by her mother and older sister. "So nice of you to come," she recited dutifully, offering her hand. "We haven't been—" The words stuck in her throat as she caught sight of the man's hands.

Not only were they bare, but his left one rested on the pearl handle of a wicked-looking knife. The weapon was strapped to his trim waist, and Rosalind couldn't have been more taken aback if a snake had slithered from beneath his waistcoat. Two decades of training in the social graces shattered. She gaped, her hand suspended in midair.

Without warning a waiter bumped her shoulder, propelling her toward the stranger. In a swift movement that left Rosalind gasping, the man's bare hands closed over her waist, lifted her aside, then set her down next to one of the marble columns gracing the entry hall.

"Forgive me," he said. "I thought you'd prefer an inappropriate touch to an impromptu embrace."

"I—" *wouldn't have minded that either*, she almost said, shocked by the impulsive thought. Her face heated, and she wanted to dive behind a pillar.

The unusual amber eyes narrowed. For a long moment he searched her face. Then he smiled, a slow, pleased smile so loaded with unexpected charm, Rosalind's blush scalded her skin. The man's smile deepened, and his right eyelid slowly closed in a mischievous, deliberate wink.

By the time Rosalind untangled her wits and her tongue sufficiently enough to reply, he had disappeared down the long hall leading to the music room.

Her pent-up breath escaped in a long quivering sigh. Moving in a daze, she gravitated down the hall, not realizing she'd subconsciously followed the man until her wandering gaze caught a last glimpse of the back of his head. Between the powerful shoulders his long queue danced a sinuous sway as he walked, with the crowd parting like the Red Sea at his passage.

A monkey in tie and tails. That's what he felt like—had felt like since donning the unaccustomed evening wear some seven hours earlier. Throughout the evening, Pinkerton's National Detective Agency operative Adam Moreaux had resisted the urge to rip off the preposterous outfit. No doubt Maxwell Connelly, the agency's Denver superintendent, was enjoying a hearty laugh at Adam's expense.

He lifted a hand to his side, his surliness mollified by the presence of the bowie knife. If Max knew about the small rebellion, it would be Adam enjoying the laugh instead.

Pinkerton's had been retained for the evening by Oliver Driscoll, who categorically refused any security measures other than a lone undercover operative, unobtrusively mingling with the guests. Driscoll's obstinacy was infuriating. Some of the wealthiest people west of the Mississippi were in attendance at his fancy soiree, all of the women draped in dazzling gems.

The circumstances begged for enterprising criminal minds. Especially, Adam knew too well, one with the sophisticated tastes of the society thief known as the Catbird. The notorious jewel thief had eluded capture for two decades now—a persistent blot on Pinkerton's reputation, battered in recent years, especially out here in the West.

Regrettably, the undercover operative assigned to the Driscoll reception had fallen ill.

"Good thing, to my way of thinking," Connelly had maintained. "Much better actually, your being in town. Your . . . ah . . . very *visible* presence will provide an effective deterrent to a robbery."

Frustrated, Adam had argued, "If the Catbird doesn't show at all, he still escapes, making us look like incompetent bunglers. You've plenty of undercover operatives, Maxwell. Send another man—someone who thrives on hobnobbing with the society crowd. Tell you what—I'll prowl the grounds, stay out of sight, keep watch from the background."

"You're the best operative west of the Mississippi" was the impatient retort. "You're one of the best, period, regardless of your . . . peculiar views. I don't want you in the background. You're here, and I plan to take advantage of it. So stuff yourself in white tie and tails, Mr. Moreaux. You certainly can't wear *those*."

Shaking his head, the superintendent had eyed Adam's buckskins. "And hopefully, if the Catbird is about, seeing you should make him keep his sticky fingers in his pockets, at least for this affair."

He clapped a hand on Adam's shoulder. "Just for tonight, Panther. That's all I ask. Keep the blue bloods and their jewelry protected, and tomorrow you can resume tracking the Simpson brothers. You say they headed for Cripple Creek?"

A burst of laughter returned Adam to the present.

Grimacing, he ran a hand beneath his too-tight, too-starched collar. So far, enforced guard duty had netted nothing but physical discomfort, multiple frosty acknowledgments, and a few fascinated glares—mostly from the ladies. Except, he remembered with a faint grin, for the young woman with expressive eyes and regal bearing. Her snootery had unexpectedly dissolved when she was caught off guard by an "impromptu embrace," he remembered calling it. Thus far, that amusing incident had provided his only smile of the entire evening.

His prowlings had brought Adam back to a small dark room, deserted two hours ago. This time, he surprised a couple wrapped in a passionate embrace on a striped fainting couch. Gasping in fright, the red-faced girl turned her head into the cushion while her erstwhile lover, equally red-faced, struggled to his feet.

"Next time, you might try to be more discreet." He studied their faces, young and scared, neither of them the profile of an infamous thief.

Without another word he retraced his steps and padded silently down the hall, his thoughts returning to the brown-haired, green-eyed girl. In Adam's opinion, *she* bore serious consideration. Intelligence had shone like a beacon out of those eyes once the supercilious mask of her face had crumbled. Intelligence, along with a refreshing lack of artifice. Adam's interest had been snared for the first time all evening.

While he was convinced that the Catbird was a man, he was equally convinced that a shadow partner must exist somewhere—and that it might easily be a female. Oddly, he found himself hoping it wasn't this particular woman, if only because of her blush. He'd wondered ever since what retort she'd almost let fly.

Definitely an intriguing young woman—altogether rare in this crowd of plaster-faced peacocks. Too bad he could only pursue her on a professional level, as a potential accomplice.

2

IT WAS A LITTLE PAST MIDNIGHT. Guilty but unrepentant, Rosalind crept down the deserted hall on the third floor. Over the past hours she had had enough partying to last until the turn of the century. Her face ached from hours of forced smiles; her feet hurt from the cramped evening slippers. Even the soft rustling of her satin brocade skirts annoyed her ears. On the noise level at least, she agreed perfectly with Mrs. Hildebrand.

After massaging the back of her neck, she withdrew a long hairpin to scratch a persistent itch deep within the pile of curls arranged on top of her head. She seriously debated whether or not to remove her shoes; she certainly didn't plan to return downstairs until the last guest had departed.

Parties—how she detested them. For that matter, she disliked any large social gathering whose only purpose seemed to be self-aggrandizement.

Grumbling to herself, Rosalind marched down the hall to an unused servants' quarters, opened the door and slipped inside, shutting the door behind her. Across the room, the dormer window with its outside balcony beckoned. Seconds later she was climbing through the window as though dressed in dungarees instead of an elaborate evening gown.

Outside, the vast starlit sky stretched across the canopy of space. A serene harvest moon backlit the city and the jagged profile of the mountains some twenty miles to the west. *The mountains* . . . rising from the plains in endless stone waves, luring wandering souls with their mystery and magnitude.

Rosalind propped her elbows on the stone balustrade, oblivious to the crisp autumn wind, and the height, and the ensuing lecture she was sure to receive from her sister. Closing her eyes, she lifted her face and drank in the night, wishing with a fervor so profound it squeezed her heart that she could be anywhere but *here*.

After a few more moments, she turned away and ducked back through the window. At the opposite end of the hall was a small salon, where she often read stories to her nephews, George and Gregory, all three of them cozily ensconced on a cushioned settee. Smiling at the memory, she strolled back down the hall, thinking idly how dark it was up here. The servants had neglected to turn on any of the hall lights, probably because the boys had been farmed out to their grandmother, and all the guests were two floors below.

The moment she entered the salon Rosalind turned on a lamp. Only then did she realize that the deserted hallway had made her nervous. Strange. As a child she'd never been timid in the dark. Many nights over the years she had slipped outside with a quilt, fearlessly making her way to the open spot at the corner of their yard. There she would lie on her back, wrapped in the warm quilt, count the stars . . . and talk to God.

Jabbing a loose hairpin into place, Rosalind scanned the room. Doubtless her fleeting anxiety was the product of an overactive imagination. The previous month a robber had broken into the Wilkinson home, only five blocks away. A housemaid had been murdered. . . .

Shaking her head, Rosalind reached for an afghan folded across the arm of the settee—and, from the corner of her eye, she detected a slight movement in the shadows near the windows. She froze in midreach, her gaze fastened on the window.

Nothing. There was nothing. Impatient all over again, Rosalind stepped forward, eyeing the heavy drapery folds flanking the windows. The gentle ripple in the lace curtains covering the glass was only air currents, she told herself. And yet—

Eyes narrowed, she stared harder, torn between caution and curiosity. Her gaze settled on an elongated shadow staining the floor beneath the window.

"Who's there?" she demanded, snatching up a small marble bust displayed on a brass stand.

Behind her, something fell with a light clatter onto the parquet floor. Rosalind whipped about, almost dropping the bust.

A tickling chill feathered the fine hairs at the nape of her neck. She whirled back toward the window. Less than a yard away stood a slender man, dressed to the nines in formal attire. He had materialized with the speed and soundlessness of a ghost, though he was clearly no apparition. His gaze met Rosalind's, and for a moment they stared at each other in utter silence.

Then he glanced at the figurine, and a slow smile spread across his face.

Rosalind half lifted her makeshift weapon, but he merely stood there, that humorless smile unwavering, as though he realized neither she nor the figurine constituted a serious threat.

Dreamlike, Rosalind set the bust back down.

To her horror, the man took a step forward, then another, until he was so close Rosalind could feel the heat emanating from his body as he brushed past. Without breaking eye contact, he stooped and felt along the floor. Then he straightened and pressed a small, hard object into her hand, closing her fingers around it.

She gasped and jerked her hand away.

The intruder's mouth twitched, and a strange expression briefly stirred in his dark eyes. Turning, he threw open the sash, climbed over the sill—and disappeared into the night.

Only at that moment did Rosalind remember that they were three stories aboveground. She stared blankly at the billowing lace curtain, then opened her fist and looked down at the jewel-encrusted brooch resting in her palm.

3

AT FORTY MINUTES PAST MIDNIGHT, Adam tracked down Oliver Driscoll. His host was holding court in the music room, listening with several other guests while the earl of Sussex compared his summer estate in Scotland to Queen Victoria's Balmoral.

Adam's sudden appearance plainly annoyed both the earl and his host. Unfazed, Adam addressed the latter. "I'd like a word with you," he murmured, keeping his voice low but firm.

"I'll meet you belowstairs—in the servants' hall. Fifteen minutes." Driscoll's brusque tone was almost insulting.

Adam lifted his hand to fondle the bowie's pearl handle. "*Now*," he said. "Either here, with your guests listening in . . . or in that parlor across the hall."

A muscle jerked in Oliver Driscoll's cheek. Beside him, the clutch of equally tight-jawed men stirred, wavering between strategic retreat and a verbal show of support.

"Saw you earlier," the earl abruptly announced. "Heard about you as well." He lifted a gold quizzing glass to his eye for a closer inspection. "Indian, are you? Wouldn't know which tribe, of course—all the same, don't you know. You wear clothes well, my good man, but your manner leaves—"

"He's not an Indian. He's a—never mind," Oliver snapped. "We'll retire to the parlor." He took a breath and turned to the earl. "If you'll excuse us, Your Grace."

"Good choice," Adam agreed, sending the earl a look that caused the pompous windbag to drop his monocle. Utter silence followed Adam and Oliver Driscoll out of the room.

"Maxwell Connelly insists that you're the best operative Pinkerton's has to offer," Driscoll began the moment he had shut and locked the door of the parlor. "Unfortunately, so do the mayor, the chief of police, and William Pinkerton . . . which leaves me with little alternative but to go along with the arrangement."

Adam kept his mouth shut until Driscoll's complexion resumed its fashionable pallor. "Tell you what," he offered. "Why not just pretend I'm another guest."

"You're not a guest. You're a paid guard," Driscoll muttered. "But . . . you're right." He stiffly inclined his head. "I apologize, Mr. Moreaux."

Adam chose to respond to the note of grudging respect rather than the reluctance. "Apology accepted," he said. "Now . . . I've singled out a half dozen men and three women who may or may not be whom they appear to be. If you like, I can describe the individuals, or we can stroll through the crowd again." He smiled. "Whether it's due to my presence, or because all the thieves took the night off, it does appear as if all the talk around town tomorrow will be about your social success instead of a daring robbery."

He'd scarcely finished speaking when someone rattled the doorknob, then pounded on the thick oak panel. "Mr. Driscoll! Sir! Are you in there?"

Adam took two steps, turned the key, and flung the door open. A harried servant—one of the coachmen, Adam judged—stared wildly from one to the other, crushing his top hat in his hands. "Forgive me, sir, but there's a problem. Two witnesses claim they saw someone . . . that is, a man was spotted climbing—"

Driscoll's temper flared anew. "Spit it out, man!"

Calmly Adam gestured the flustered coachman into the room and shut the door. "Now, just what is it you saw? Someone climbing through a window?"

The agitated man shook his head. "Dunno," he sputtered. "The woman—she were a young gal, actually—she started screaming. Durn near spooked the horses. Her escort ordered me to fetch you, sir. But I had to settle the team first, you understand, Mr. Driscoll, sir—"

"Easy—you've done well," Adam inserted before Oliver Driscoll could launch into a tirade. "What's your name?"

"G-Godfrey, sir. Josiah Monroe's coachman. Sir?" A stolid man with slicked-down gray hair and anxious brown eyes, Godfrey's gaze darted from Adam to Driscoll and back again. "You—you're Panther, aren't you?" he breathed. "Crackerjack! That blade you carry—it's a real bowie?"

"Yes. Godfrey, where is the couple now? Time is of the essence here."

"Bungling incompetent," Driscoll muttered, and poor Godfrey's ears turned bright red.

"They was hiding in Mr. Kirk's carriage. I left them there, shivering in their shoes."

"Good fellow." Adam clapped the old man on the shoulder and sliced a glance at Oliver. "Mr. Driscoll here will see that you're properly compensated, I'm sure. Now, I'd best check this out before any more time passes."

Sure enough, it was the young couple Adam had surprised in the receiving room. The raw young gentleman, his voice shaking with excitement and embarrassment, told Adam that a dark figure had climbed down a rope, all the way from a window on the third floor. Adam determined which window, then sprinted across the dew-drenched lawn.

Beneath some freshly planted shrubbery, he discovered multiple footprints in the soil. The rope still dangled a foot above his head. So. The miscreant had been in a bit of a rush, had he?

Adam shucked off coat, vest, and tie, tossing them onto the ground. Then he reached up, grabbed hold of the thick hemp, and started climbing.

Far below, shouts followed his ascent, and Adam grinned. He was still smiling when he reached the small window on the third story and cautiously parted the curtain. A single table lamp spilled a pool of yellow light into a hexagonal chamber, seemingly deserted.

With a grunt of exertion, Adam heaved himself over the sill and dropped noiselessly onto the floor, taking in every detail of the room. Nobody spoke. Nobody moved to attack or flee.

He flowed across to the door, looked out into the hall—and glimpsed the shadowy form of a woman disappearing down the staircase. Adam caught up with her halfway down, on the landing of the second floor.

He jerked her to a halt and spun her around. "So. It had to be you."

"Let *go!*" Twisting sideways, she wrenched her arm, then kicked him, her stockinged foot making little impression on Adam's shin.

"Quit struggling, you little wildcat," Adam growled, but he gentled his hold.

The green-eyed society belle who had so charmed him pulled free, then hauled back and let fly a blow that might have broken his jaw had Adam not recaptured her fist an inch before it connected. He quickly secured her other hand, holding both hands until she opened her mouth—to scream, Adam instantly divined.

He shifted, manacling both her wrists in his larger hand and clapping his palm over her mouth to stifle an enraged shriek. "Who are you?" he demanded, shaking her a little. He lifted his hand. "Keep quiet now. My name is Adam Moreaux. I'm an operative with the Pinkerton National Detective Agency, and I really have no intention of harming you."

Gray-green eyes narrowed. "I don't believe you," she fired back. "And you *are* hurting me!"

Cries of alarm and confusion erupted from the floor below. Adam stared down into the flushed, angry face so near his own—and realized with a prick of shame that she was also afraid. "Sorry." He released her and stepped back, making sure his body blocked her escape into the throng. "Some guests witnessed a man climbing out of a window on the third floor. I thought you might be his accomplice."

She stopped rubbing her wrists and glared. "I'm still not convinced *you're* not his accomplice. In fact—"

All his muscles tensed. "You knew that a thief—possibly a gang of thieves—was in the house?"

"I . . . yes. I surprised him, in the governess's sitting room. The one on the third floor." Her mouth dropped open. "Wait. How did you—you came up behind me. . . ."

"Whoa, there," Adam murmured, reading the panic in her eyes. "I climbed up the rope myself."

Her gaze swept over him, widening as she noticed his disheveled state. Seemingly stunned, she stood without moving, and Adam read every emotion in her face as easily as though she were a child. "Who are you . . . really?" she whispered.

"Just as I told you—Adam Moreaux, Pinkerton operative." He heard footsteps pounding up the stairs and swiveled, automatically shackling the young woman, both to protect her and to prevent her from fleeing—or coshing him over the head.

A young man with close-cut blond curls and a pencil-thin mustache stopped dead at the head of the stairs. "He's up here!" he yelled.

Adam relaxed. "I've caught either an accomplice or a guest who happened to be in the wrong place at the wrong time," he announced, slanting the young woman a dry look. She was tall for a woman, he realized, her head almost reaching his shoulder. But her frame was slender, though she was supple rather than delicate. An elusive fragrance teased his nostrils. For the third time he released her and stepped back, alert to every movement if she still chose to run.

"An accomplice?" the blond man echoed. He snorted. "That's Rosalind Hayes. Who are *you*?" He eyed Adam's hair before his gaze dropped to the knife. "Say—is that a bowie knife?"

"Where's Oliver Driscoll?" Adam demanded in response. He turned to Miss Hayes. "Your brother-in-law, right? And the hostess, Alberta Driscoll, is your sister?"

"Yes."

Adam heard more footsteps ascending the stairs, more cries of alarm. Reluctantly, he steeled himself for the inevitable. "I'll need to question you about what you saw. Would you mind

26

waiting in that room on the third floor for a little while?"

She shook her head.

Adam nodded, then turned to face the oncoming herd, led by an outraged Oliver Driscoll.

4

HEART THUDDING, ROSALIND STOOD in front of the tall window, shivering as the cold wind swirled outside. How could they climb a flimsy rope, *three stories* from the ground? Leaning out, she watched the beehive of activity. Directly below stood a stout policeman, his hands clasped behind his back. Keeping the curious away, Rosalind decided. Departing guests scurried into their carriages like rats fleeing a fire. Dozing horses snorted awake, their breath pluming in the frosty air.

Rosalind watched for a moment longer before turning again to the rope. She cast a furtive glance backward, then tugged off her gloves so she could feel its texture.

"Thinking of taking a shortcut?"

Rosalind turned, barely suppressing a groan at the sight of Detective Moreaux, Oliver, and an officious-looking policeman striding across the room. She shrugged. "I might. But I have a feeling I'd end up splattered all over the bushes Alberta planted a month ago."

"Rosalind, please." Oliver ran his hand through his hair as he came to stand beside her at the window. "Mr. Moreaux tells me you surprised the thief in here."

Sighing, she inclined her head.

"You slipped away, forgoing your social duties, abandoning your sister when she needed you most."

"How is Alberta?"

"Practically hysterical." A vein jumped in his forehead. "The evening's ruined—an utter disaster."

"How many of your guests lost valuables?" Detective Moreaux inquired, the deep voice sounding both calm and cold.

"Only the overnight guests who left jewelry in their chambers—most from the second floor."

"Don't be beatin' yourself up over them paltry bits, Mr. Moreaux," the policeman chimed in. "He's a slippery shadow, is the Catbird. Leastways, you foiled his chance to work the crowd."

"We haven't determined that the robbery was the work of the Catbird," the detective corrected with quiet but unmistakable warning.

Still smarting from their earlier encounter, Rosalind darted a surreptitious glance in his direction. Wariness mixed with fascination. Never had she been so close to a man like Adam Moreaux—except for the intruder. The detective intimidated her, and she instinctively knew that he either didn't like her or he didn't trust her. But she was far less certain of the robber's intent.

Stiffening her spine, she forced herself to meet Mr. Moreaux's gaze. In spite of the predatory gleam in his eyes, he had not truly hurt her, for all her heated accusation. She still grappled with the knowledge that he was a detective instead of an exotic Indian warrior or a wealthy eccentric whose entrée into Denver society she had missed. Detectives, to her way of thinking, were nasty little men who crept about the underbelly of society, performing a necessary service, almost indistinguishable from the very criminals they were hired to track.

Like the thief who had pressed a brooch into her hand and vanished.

"Rosalind!"

She blinked, turning to Oliver. "I'm sorry. What did you say?"

"Sergeant Johnson and Detective Moreaux need to ask you a few questions."

Rosalind tugged her gloves back in place, concentrating on

the mundane task. "Certainly." She produced an empty smile. "Ask away."

The officer stepped forward, his chest swelling with self-importance. "Exactly why were you in this part of the house at the precise hour the thief made his appearance? We'll need a description of his features, of course. Also his clothing, the—"

He halted in midsentence when Detective Moreaux lifted a commanding hand. "Miss Hayes has endured a shock." He divided his gaze between both men. "Why don't we sit—" He paused, looking thoughtful. "Better yet, Sergeant Johnson, if a room were set aside on the main level where the guests who were robbed could assemble, perhaps you could record a description of the missing pieces. I'm sure Mr. Driscoll would be happy to see to it."

Rosalind never knew quite how it happened, but soon she and Adam were the only two people left in the room. A fine tension filled the air, somehow different from the defensiveness she always felt around Oliver. She smoothed her hands over the Brussels lace on her gown, wishing she knew what to say. Wishing with growing disgruntlement that Detective Moreaux would do something—*say* something, instead of just standing there.

The unwelcome realization crept over her gradually: he was toying with her, mentally stalking her, waiting until the silence was uncomfortable enough to force her to speak. Rosalind almost smiled. Far more brutal tactics had been employed over the years to gain her compliance. Consequently, she had developed an inner resolve as impenetrable as the shell of a hundred-year-old tortoise . . . when she chose.

Head high, she meandered toward the settee and picked up the afghan she'd dropped earlier. With painstaking neatness she folded and draped it across the back. Then she sat down, leaned back, and, as though she were alone, picked up the book of Christina Rossetti's poems she'd been reading to the children the previous week.

Adam Moreaux laughed.

And dropped down beside her.

5

"YOU'RE AN . . . UNUSUAL YOUNG WOMAN," he announced, twisting so as to peer directly into Rosalind's face.

"So I've heard," she murmured, folding her hands in her lap. Except the adjectives were usually less complimentary. And since Oliver had left her unchaperoned with a strange man, likely she would be the recipient of several more. "And you, Mr. Moreaux, are an unusual man."

"So I've been told. Well?" He sat back, and the queue spilled down the front of his chest. "Go ahead. Ask me whatever's burning a hole in your tongue. Then I'll ask you whatever *I* choose."

Rosalind pursed her lips. "Clever." Was he trying to trap her? It was disconcerting to realize how much she wanted to understand this large, powerful man, who moved with the silent grace of a hunting cat. "Um . . . could you at least tell me how difficult it is to climb a rope up the side of a house? And if I—"

"If you what?"

"Nothing. Perhaps I should tell you what I know about the thief."

"Perhaps you should first finish your sentence." He stretched out his long legs, then ruefully examined his scuffed boots. "I wouldn't recommend scaling a wall in formal evening wear." He chuckled.

"Did the rope burn your hands?" Rosalind blurted. In a remote way, Adam Moreaux's extraordinary unconventionality reminded her of Isaac, the black sheep of the Hayes family.

The detective laughed again, a deep-throated, surprisingly appealing laugh. "Without a doubt you're a strange one," he murmured. "I confess I never expected to meet such an—" He paused, his gaze sweeping over her, "—an *un*inhibited young woman in a place like this. Not at all the proper young debutante."

"I'm far too old to be considered a debutante," Rosalind returned stiffly. "And I've heard enough about my . . . character flaws to last three lifetimes." She started to rise, then froze in shock when Mr. Moreaux's hand closed over her forearm, restraining her.

"Tell me about the thief." His voice, though whisper soft, communicated an unmistakable order. Almost a threat.

Rosalind's scalp prickled and her head came up. "Please remove your hand. And—" She took a deep breath before deliberately adding, "—you're sitting too close. It's unacceptable."

All warmth vanished from the detective's face. "Certainly, Miss Hayes. We wouldn't want to further tarnish your reputation, would we?"

"My reputation is not your concern."

"No, it isn't. Tell me what you saw."

Rosalind stifled the impulse to prolong the verbal duel. It was plain as white paint which of them would suffer, and it was not the Pinkerton detective. "I came up here to—" She bit her lip, then shrugged, "—to escape. When I turned on the lamp, I thought I saw something behind the drapes." She pointed. "Those behind you. Then, obviously as a diversion, the man threw—oh! I forgot."

She thrust her hand inside the hidden pocket in her gown, retrieved the brooch, and held it out. "He threw this pin onto the floor. When I turned toward the sound, he came up behind me. He—" Without warning, a wave of nausea rippled through her. He could have murdered her! At this very moment, she could have been sprawled on the parquet floor, lifeless, blood pooling—

"Miss Hayes!" Mr. Moreaux's insistent voice shattered her gruesome speculations.

Rosalind blinked. Beneath the constricting bodice of her gown, her heart was racing. Her lips and the tips of her fingers were numb, as though she'd been stung by an angry wasp. "You don't have to shout. . . ."

"Easy now. You're a little pale. What—"

Alberta burst through the doorway. "I came as soon as I could." Her horrified gaze darted between Rosalind and Detective Moreaux. "I'll have a word with Oliver later, about leaving you alone and unchaperoned with this . . . this . . ."

"He's a detective, not a barbarian." Rosalind pressed her fingers against her temples. She knew she was contradicting her own sentiments, but her sister's reaction shamed her into defending Mr. Moreaux. "I'm perfectly safe, Berta."

"Do *not* call me 'Berta.' Come with me, Rosalind. I need you downstairs. It's chaos down there. The evening is ruined. *Ruined.*"

Lazily the detective rose to his feet. "Mrs. Driscoll, I'll escort your sister back downstairs in a few minutes—after I've finished interrogating the witness."

Alberta bristled, but instead of arguing, she closed her mouth after an angry sniff.

First Oliver, then Alberta. Apparently *nobody* was a match for the impertinent Pinkerton detective. "It's all right," Rosalind promised her sister. "Nobody who matters knows I'm up here anyway."

"But—why does he want to talk to *you*, Rosalind?" Alberta fixed a commanding glare upon an indifferent Adam Moreaux. "You, sir, should be chasing down the thief. That's why my husband hired you. Disgraceful enough that your outrageous appearance almost spoiled my reception. Now it's a disaster anyway, and for what?"

"Alberta . . ." Rosalind began, but Adam Moreaux cut her off.

"You and your husband refused the services of posted guards, Mrs. Driscoll." His voice dropped to the deadly quiet tone that was more effective than all of Oliver's angry diatribes.

"This event has been highly publicized for weeks—an open invitation to every burglar from San Francisco to Kansas City. When one flaunts wealth, ma'am, one sometimes pays the price."

After a moment of unpleasant silence Alberta turned to Rosalind, two dots of angry color staining her cheeks. "I'll send a maid . . . but if you want to go downstairs with me—"

"Don't worry. I can take care of myself."

"I know you think so." Alberta looked pained. "That's what concerns me." After a last glare for the imperturbable detective, she retreated, leaving behind a thick silence.

Mr. Moreaux sat back down. "You were about to tell me what happened after the thief tossed this brooch on the floor," he said as though there had been no interruption at all. Idly he examined the stone, glittering in the lamplight like drops of crystal blood.

"Um . . ." Rosalind watched him handling the jewelry with the skill and delicacy of a jeweler. She found it difficult to concentrate. "He . . . ah . . . well he just appeared behind me—he moves as quietly as you, Mr. Moreaux, and I did wonder if you could be an accomplice."

The detective raised one thick black brow. "Go on."

"He never spoke. Just looked at me. Then he picked up that brooch and pressed it into my hand." She swallowed, remembering with a sting of shame that she'd been almost as fascinated by the thief as she was by the man intent now on capturing him. "He . . . smiled. And then he went out the window."

"What did you do then?"

Rosalind hesitated. "I ran over to the window and looked out." She met his gaze. "I thought about trying to cut the rope, but there was nothing here to—"

She glanced at his knife, then jumped when he emitted another of those deep chuckles. A shudder of relief quivered through Rosalind's body, and she relaxed against the cushion.

"I'm sorry you didn't have my knife," he murmured. "Would have made my task a lot easier."

"Do you read minds as well, Mr. Moreaux?"

"I read people, Miss Hayes." The dark winged eyebrow lifted

again. "And I track them. You learn a lot about human nature that way."

"Oh. I suppose you would." She smiled faintly. "Well, even if I'd had your knife, I probably wouldn't have used it."

"Describe him for me now, if you will." The detective leaned closer. "Close your eyes; picture him in your head, if it's easier to concentrate that way. Any detail might help us catch this man."

Rosalind obeyed, mostly because she felt so uncomfortable with Mr. Moreaux's proximity. She could practically count the lashes that framed his eyes. Irritated with herself for noticing, she concentrated instead on describing the thief. "His hair was dark—like yours—but he wore it fashionably short, parted in the center. Some strands of gray at the temples. None in his mustache, as I recall."

"What kind of mustache?"

"Thin, straight, with waxed ends. I'm not sure about the color of his eyes—dark, I think, but the light was behind him, so his face was in the shadows."

"Height?"

"A little taller than I . . . but he moved a lot like you. Quick and quiet. Like a cat."

Her eyes widened at the sound of his soft laugh. "Thank you."

"You're welcome." She took in his disheveled condition. Torn and soiled shirt. Collar and tie missing, along with one of his cuffs. "The thief either entered with other guests and placed the rope earlier in the evening," she said, "or else he's had plenty of practice in breaking into other people's homes."

The detective's smile faded. "Miss Hayes," he began, appearing for the first time as if he weren't entirely sure of himself, "I'm afraid you've inadvertently placed yourself in grave danger."

"Because I saw the thief? Surely if he were a murderer, he would have killed me on the spot, realizing that I could identify him—" Easy to say *now*, Rosalind mocked herself silently, wishing her bravado had not deserted her earlier in the evening.

Mr. Moreaux held up the ruby brooch, studying it for a long moment before switching his gaze to Rosalind. "The Catbird," he informed her, "isn't a killer by nature. He's a thief. An extraordinary one, to be sure. But he confines his crimes to the theft of expensive, ofttimes untraceable jewels. To my knowledge he—"

Rosalind didn't notice the pause. "The Catbird?" she echoed. "What makes you think this was the Catbird?" Her pulse pounded in her ears as a surge of contradictory emotions roiled through her.

"Well . . . I wouldn't have known for sure until I saw this." He casually tossed the pin up and down. "This particular piece is part of a job he pulled in Chicago seven months ago—classic Catbird. This brooch is part of a set—ninety-year-old heirlooms. Belongs to a family named Burrows."

"I remember." Stunned, Rosalind lifted her hand, dropped it back to her lap. "My oldest brother Charles and his wife were guests at that party. They said the Catbird stole not only jewelry from safes and bedrooms, but managed to steal a half-dozen pieces people were wearing. Gladys—that's Charles' wife—babbled for weeks about how fortunate for her that he didn't take her pearl choker." She gazed at the brooch as if it were a live coal. "And nobody noticed until after the party."

"That's why he's not been caught in twenty years."

"But why was he carrying that brooch then? You say he stole it seven months ago."

"One of his trademarks. He likes to annoy the authorities, every so often leaving behind a piece from another job—something like a calling card."

An unwilling tingle of admiration set Rosalind's mouth to twitching again. "An arrogant sort, isn't he?"

"Hmm. More so every year he escapes detection and capture." He studied her a moment. "You threw him a bit, I'd guess. Usually he leaves behind a piece of less value. This"—he held up the brooch, inspecting the dully glittering stones—"is worth a bit. He might have been holding it to sell, or for sheer enjoyment. Who can say? I know his habits, but not the inner workings of his mind."

Rosalind shook her head. "Does he know you, Mr. Moreaux? Is that why you were here tonight? As a deterrent?"

"You're a lot quicker than most society ladies, I'll say that for you. At least the ploy worked, as far as lifting pieces from the crowd. Unfortunately, as we tried to tell your brother-in-law, a single operative can't protect an entire mansion." He scowled. "He should have listened."

"Oliver doesn't listen to anybody but himself."

"A mistake, as he has discovered to his cost." Mr. Moreaux paused, then added, "But the Catbird made a mistake as well—highly uncharacteristic, but like I said"—his gaze swept over her in mocking amusement—"I've a feeling your presence was as disconcerting to him as it has proven to be for me."

Rosalind ignored the observation. "According to all the newspaper accounts, nobody even knows what the Catbird looks like," she said. "He always blends in—like a catbird laying its eggs in the nests of other birds. They raise the babies as their own."

"Mm. Until the catbird fledglings knock the duped birds out of the nests. This man is far from stupid, Miss Hayes, and obviously has a warped sense of humor. But everyone makes mistakes eventually. Pinkerton's has been chasing the Catbird since the late seventies. After he pulled off the theft of the Petrovna jewels last spring, we've been slowly tightening the net." He smiled thinly. "Laying a few false eggs in nests of our own."

"*I'd* recognize him again," Rosalind murmured. Beneath her gloves, her palms were perspiring again. "Mr. Moreaux . . . I didn't see him for very long, or in good light, but I would recognize him again."

"I know." With the silent, swift grace she was coming to associate with this man, Adam Moreaux stood. "And that, Miss Hayes, makes you the only living person who can."

6

BREATHING LIGHT AND FAST, Napoleon LaRue sat huddled in the darkest corner of a small balcony. For the first time in years, he'd barely escaped being caught. First by a stunning woman who should have been mingling with the guests, then by a young couple who also should have been inside with the rest of the crowd instead of dallying in a carriage. LaRue's fingers balled, and he fluently cursed the pair who had sounded the alarm. Oddly, he didn't feel like cursing the frightened woman who had forced him to cancel his well-laid plans for the Driscoll reception.

A bitter northwest wind gusted around his head, bearing with it the amusing sounds of panic and confusion. Idiots, LaRue thought, wrapping his long black coat more tightly about his body.

Earlier, he'd left his satchel on this dark ledge, whose only occupants until LaRue slipped through the narrow window had been a couple of pigeons startled from their roosts. The front entrance, facing the street, and the porte cochere where the carriages stopped to drop off guests, were on the opposite side of the mansion, making his job a lot easier—and now ensuring his escape. It would never occur to any of the frantic constables scouring the house and grounds below to search the nooks and crannies on the *outside* of the mansion.

Too bad about the rope. It had been one of his favorites, and he would have mourned its loss if he hadn't been so furious over his thwarted plans. Shifting a little, LaRue leaned back against the cold stone balustrade. He probably shouldn't have gone through with this job in the first place, especially after spotting his black-haired nemesis. Panther, they called him. LaRue sneered. Some moniker—the Pink was just another in an endless succession, none of them equal to the Catbird.

His thoughts turned to the interfering woman. Originally he'd planned to cosh her on the head, leave the brooch in her hand—a nice touch—then finish his business on the main level. But she'd turned around, and with those big eyes shining above a swanlike neck made for jewelry, LaRue hadn't been able to follow through. She'd been afraid, of course, but she'd also been fascinated. If he'd been of a mind, he could have stolen a kiss, along with the tidy bundle of jewelry and whatnots he'd lifted from the bedrooms.

On the other hand . . . she'd seen him. Close enough and long enough to provide a description.

LaRue peered between the stone spindles, thinking while he listened. He didn't want to risk a murder charge at this point— not when he was days away from being able to hold his lifelong dream in his hands again.

The Petrovna Parure. The most exquisite pieces of jewelry he'd ever seen—an entire five-piece collection, from the diamond-and-emerald choker to the matching stomacher brooch, commissioned by the daughter of Peter the Great a hundred years earlier.

Smuggled out of Russia, they'd first been bought by a corrupt British duke but had found their way back to the Russians in the 1860s.

Now they belonged to *him*—a former orphaned brat with a big name he'd learned to hate. Napoleon LaRue might be a middle-aged nobody, but as the Catbird, he'd pulled off the heist of the century this past spring at the Russian embassy in Washington.

When Booker met him in New Mexico to hand over the haul, LaRue planned to take a long vacation. No jobs. No plans.

Just uninterrupted hours of pleasure, admiring the Petrovna Parure.

His to treasure. His to hold, to bask in the sparkle and shine of their perfection. His to—

—lose forever if that girl gave the authorities an accurate enough description of him!

Gloomily, LaRue flexed his fingers, shivering when another blast of wind moaned through his cloistered perch. The vacation might have to wait, because after he and Rattray parted in Raton, he would have to return to Denver and take care of the girl. The thought gave LaRue no pleasure. Women had been created to display jewels. Without those long, graceful necks and slender hands, he would have been nothing but a two-bit burglar.

Nonetheless, to protect his most prized possessions, the Catbird would accept whatever challenge fate tossed his way.

Even if it required the sacrifice of a woman's life.

7

Mountains below Cripple Creek, Colorado

ADAM REINED HIS HORSE IN and dismounted, giving the tired animal a fond pat before removing the saddle and bridle. "One hour only, Biscuit," he warned his faithful companion, smiling when the animal rubbed his nose against Adam's chest. "All right, all right." He scratched beneath the sweating forelock, where the bridle's headband had left a faint mark, then sent the horse off with an affectionate whack.

They had stopped on the rim of a rocky gorge, choked with Gambel oaks and a sprinkling of stubborn juniper. A half mile away Adam heard the shrill whistle of a train, chugging its way toward Cripple Creek. He probably should have taken the train—he would have made the trip in a lot less time. But his skin still twitched from the debacle two nights ago at the Driscoll mansion, and Adam had headed for the mountains to lick his wounds. Sighing, he stretched out beneath the branches of a stately ponderosa pine, propped his back against the trunk, and closed his eyes.

Moments later he caught a whiff of Kat's distinctive musky odor just before the cougar collapsed bonelessly beside him. "At least you weren't there to witness the fine mess I made of things," Adam confessed, not bothering to open his eyes as his hand easily found the big cat's belly.

Kat's favorite pastime, on those occasions when Adam took

time to ponder and pray, was to lie on her back next to him, belly up. This supreme gesture of trust never failed to bring a lump to his throat. He had raised the cougar from the moment she'd been born, the runt of the litter, later abandoned by her mother. A wild animal, yes—but over the past twelve years, also Adam's faithful companion, partner, and . . . well . . . his friend.

"Need to run Booker Rattray to earth pretty quick," he said after a while. "I barely got out of town with my hide intact, after Max finished chewing it up for botching things." His hand burrowed into the rough fur, and he felt as much as heard the cat's rusty purr. "Should have brought you along, sweetheart— maybe the Catbird wouldn't have flown away, leaving me with nothing but a feather or two." A single brooch—and a witness.

Divine justice—or heavenly humor, he wondered, remembering his interview with the vexing woman. The presence of the brooch had elated him, because it offered the most damaging piece of evidence to come the Agency's way in over a year.

Then there was Oliver Driscoll's sister-in-law. "Rosalind Hayes . . ." He pronounced it out loud. Even her name was contradictory—feminine yet condescending. Just like the woman herself.

Adam had spent the better part of the past twenty-four hours learning everything there was to know about the Hayes family. None of it had been a surprise, except for Rosalind. Old family, Virginia roots. Emigrated to Denver twenty-odd years ago, a move apparently prompted by Edward Hayes' wanderlust. He'd made a tidy fortune in the hardware business, selling supplies to miners, storekeepers, and incoming settlers. Along the way, he'd earned a reputation for scrupulous honesty.

"'Course he could have bought the reputation," one of the other operatives had observed cynically. "Out here, fling enough money around, and folks will call Jack the Ripper 'Saint Jack.'"

Suddenly restless, Adam pulled out his bowie. Vast material wealth irritated him. Brought out the worst in him, frankly. Always had, ever since he learned that his mother's family had disowned their daughter for marrying a no-name agent from the Bureau of Indian Affairs who had rescued her from a band of renegade Utes.

Rosalind Hayes isn't to blame for the sins of your mother. . . .

"Don't preach at me. I'm not in the mood," Adam growled to his annoying conscience. He jackknifed forward.

Kat's ears flattened, her black-tipped tail swishing in warning.

"Sheathe those claws, you ornery varmint." He rose to his feet in one lithe motion. A plump pinecone dangled from the branch of a tree a hundred feet away.

A faint smile tickled the corners of his mouth. Just to test himself, Adam swiveled about, counted to twenty, then whirled, drawing and throwing the knife with an exhilarating speed that had caused more than one trigger-happy gunman to back down without a whimper. The knife thudded into the trunk of the tree with a muffled thwack, and the severed pinecone fell to the ground.

"Wanna fetch?" Adam asked Kat, who replied with a bored yawn.

Adam laughed, then whistled for Biscuit as he loped across the rocky earth to retrieve his blade. Five minutes later the three of them were on their way to Cripple Creek.

❖

Denver

Three days had passed since the robbery. For Rosalind, three endless days.

Before the Catbird's disruption of her life, she had at least enjoyed a modicum of tolerance on the part of family and friends for her occasional lapses of decorum. Rosalind made a face. Ever since the robbery all the mundane details of her life seemed to provide nothing but fodder for the town gossips.

Today, grateful for the excuse, she was at home helping her mother fold freshly pressed linens. Outside, a cold, rain-scented wind rattled the shutters, and Rosalind made a mental note to ask Zeke to take a look at them.

"Have you reconsidered your decision about attending Gladys's guest supper?"

Rosalind paused, then finished folding the tablecloth. "No, I haven't. You know what she's like. Charles is bad enough, but Gladys . . ." She exchanged a droll look with her mother. Even Ophelia admitted that the wife of her eldest son could be a tiresome snob. "Anyway, I'm weary of the endless questions about the Catbird and Mr. Moreaux." Not to mention the speculative looks and innuendoes.

She plonked the folded cloth in the linen cupboard. "Frankly, I'm sick to death of the whole affair."

"I know." Her mother touched her arm. "Rosalind? You're not keeping something from me, are you? Ever since you visited the Pinkerton's superintendent—Mr. Connelly, wasn't it?—you've been out of sorts."

"I'm sorry, Mamma. The strain of notoriety is a bit wearing. Have you noticed that Alberta still won't speak to me?"

"You shouldn't have asked that . . . that outrageous detective if you could try climbing down the rope." Ophelia Hayes' horror had matched Alberta's.

Rosalind laughed. "I probably wouldn't have if I'd known Alberta had just arrived, dragging along her poor maid to save my tattered reputation."

"Ah, Rosebud . . ." Her mother sighed, and Rosalind's heart twisted at the use of her childhood nickname. "I *never* know what to expect from you. I hoped, you know, after Isaac . . . left—" Abruptly she laid aside a half-folded napkin, looking at Rosalind with anxiety-darkened eyes. "You could have been hurt . . . your brother's betrayal . . . and now your father's condition . . ." She turned away, searching for her handkerchief.

Guilt rolled over Rosalind like clouds consuming the mountains. "Please don't, Mamma. I'm sorry." Sorry she couldn't be the model of demure spinsterhood, or the perfect wife and mother like Alberta. Even the pretentious Gladys enjoyed a level of respectability denied Rosalind.

For some inexplicable reason—doubtless it *was* a flaw in her character—she had never been able to curb the destructive yearnings that propelled her into trouble and caused her mother such heartache. Her guilt intensified with each thoughtless word or impulsive indiscretion, yet she lacked the courage to pack up and leave as Isaac had done. Why did love and loyalty command so high a price?

Rosalind glanced across at her mother. In spite of her perfect posture, she looked tired. An upsurge of love and protectiveness swelled inside Rosalind. She finished folding the last tablecloth and dropped it on top of the others. Then she gave her mother a hug, gently tucking strands of silvery hair back into the chignon Ophelia had worn for over thirty years.

"Why don't you heat some of that sweet cider Tallulah made last night, Mamma? Put your feet up a few moments? You know how much it upsets Papa when the two of us are at odds." She gathered up a load of unpressed linens. "Tell you what. I'll give these to Tallulah to iron and ask her to heat the cider. I need to warn Zeke about the shutters."

"Rosalind?"

"Yes, Mamma?"

"Your Papa . . . I think he knows something is going on. I know I should try to explain, but somehow the words won't come. You know how he leans on me—needs me to be his safe harbor, if you will." She touched the flower brooch she always wore now—a present from her husband, his last before the stroke. "Most of the time I can . . . I'm just returning what he's given to me all these years. But—" Her lips pressed tightly together. Rosalind knew she was uncomfortable sharing such intimacies.

"I'll talk to him, Mamma. Don't fret about it." She gave her mother a last quick hug. "And no, I won't tell him what his wayward daughter has done to disgrace the family name this time."

"Rosalind! Must you *joke* about it?"

Might as well, Rosalind thought as she hurried down the long hall to the back stoop. Privately, at any rate. Somehow she didn't feel as guilty when she tried to laugh off her indiscretions. She hastily tugged on an old jacket and clattered down the porch steps. "Zeke!" she called to the elderly negro servant who, with his wife Tallulah, had remained part of the Hayes family when they left Virginia many years earlier.

"Ma'am?" He dropped the rake and ambled across the yard. "Looks like rain, don't it?"

"Smells like it, too." She regarded his sturdy figure fondly. Tallulah might be a thunderous scold, but Zeke was a rock. For a man he wasn't tall—the same height as Rosalind, in fact. But even encroaching age and a head of kinky gray curls hadn't diminished his strength and stamina.

After Edward Hayes' paralyzing stroke, his eldest son Charles had taken over the family business, along with their finances. The burden was onerous, since he had his own household to run as well. Even then Isaac hadn't bothered to come home, so it had been Zeke who had quietly pitched in alongside Rosalind, assuming responsibility for the household tasks her father could no longer see to.

"Do you have time to check the shutters?" she asked. "I heard at least two flapping pretty hard in the wind. If you need some nails or something, I'll take the streetcar downtown and fetch some from the store." She rolled her eyes. "Assuming, of course, Charles will allow me to set foot inside his door."

Zeke flashed a white-toothed grin. "I'll see to the nails soon as I put the rake away." Wise old eyes surveyed Rosalind's face. "They all still giving you a hard time—'bout seeing the Catbird face-to-face?"

She nodded glumly. "Alberta still won't speak to me." She shivered when a strong gust of wind all but tore her hairpins loose. "The whole family is conspiring to marry me off as quickly as possible. Preferably to a man who lives on the East Coast."

"Uh-huh. So that's why you dug in your heels and won't go to that shindig out at your brother's place. Who they trying to foist off on you this time?"

"Some cousin of the Millers, visiting here from Maine." She tried to make a joke of it. "A Yankee, of all things!"

Zeke scratched his head. "Well now, Miss Rosalind, a good husband would do a lot to ease some of the yearnings I see shining out of your eyes."

Rosalind gave an inelegant sniff. "I yearn for freedom, not a husband. Adventure. Exploring the mountains . . . visiting the mining towns Isaac writes about."

"When's the last time you heard from that rapscallion younger brother of yours?"

Chilly, rain-scented air seeped through the thinning worsted jacket, mirroring the icy uncertainty that troubled her heart. "Not since early summer, and all he talked about was that flim-flam man. The one who tricked Isaac out of all his money. Isaac was on his way to Cripple Creek, still trying to track him down." She bit her lip. "I haven't heard since."

"And naturally you're the only one what knows the truth of it, ain't ya?" Zeke correctly interpreted.

"Well . . . he couldn't very well tell Papa, much less Mamma."

"Your family's had its share of trials, that's for sure. But you're strong, Miss Rosalind, the one keepin' this family to-gether. Lulah and I know it, if nobody else does."

"Tallulah thinks I'm a willful, rebellious troublemaker, even worse than Isaac." She batted her eyelashes. "A lady should know better."

"Mm." His slow smile robbed the underlying agreement of its sting. "But you *do* dress real fine, Miss Rosalind. I expect that's why your family carries on so. You looks more like a real lady than a bevy o' them silly females."

Rosalind grimaced. "I know, I know. It's just that . . ." Her voice trailed off. She absently brushed the fraying jacket sleeves, wishing she'd never opened her mouth.

Deep chocolate eyes studied her face kindly. "You just keep prayin,' Miss Rosalind. The good Lord might have allowed the burden, but He'll always strengthen your back to help carry the load."

She sighed. "Sometimes I'd just as soon have a weaker back and a lighter load."

8

Cripple Creek, Colorado

THE BACKWATER COMMUNITY WHERE crazy Bob Womack stumbled over a gold mine a scant six years earlier had vanished in a floodtide of progress. Instead of a jumbled collection of seedy storefronts and row houses, the mining camp was now an established city, complete with electric streetlights and noisy trolleys.

Adam ducked inside the doors of the new brick depot, his knee-high moccasins making no sound as he crossed the clean-swept floor to the ticket agent's office.

"Howdy, Mr. Moreaux," Sam greeted him with a gap-toothed smile. "Been a spell. You been scalping criminals or preachin' revivals?"

Adam propped his elbows on the counter, leaning down so that he was face-to-face with the wizened old man. "Neither, Sam. More like learning a lesson in humility down in Denver."

Sam slapped his thighs. "So it *is* true! Story's all over town hereabouts, how the Catbird pulled a fast one on Panther."

Adam shook his head, embarrassed but resigned. In the West, respect had to be earned—especially when you were a Pinkerton operative in a town where public sentiment ran ten-to-one in favor of the mining unions. "No sense in trying to hide it," he agreed. "Say, Sam—you seen Booker Rattray lately? Last I heard, he'd set himself up pretty fancy here. Bought himself a house, even . . . what? What's the matter, Sam?"

Sam turned aside, spat into a battered brass spittoon. "Guess you wouldn't have heard, what with all the commotion down in Denver. Rattray lit out of here 'bout two weeks ago now. Bought a ticket to Manitou, I recall."

Adam stood straight, studying the other man. "What else?"

Behind them, the door opened and a couple of drummers entered, arms laden with cases labeled "Dr. Peabody's Magic Elixir." Adam stepped back, enduring the gawking stares and rude comments while they purchased tickets to Chicago. On the heels of the drummers a family of six spilled through the doors, followed by a drunken miner wanting a ticket to the gold mines up in Alaska. It was almost twenty minutes later before the room was quiet enough for Adam to step back up to the window.

"Aw, Panther, don't pester me no more, all right?" Sam avoided eye contact. "You know I do the best I can for you. But things are . . . well, miners don't feel so kindly disposed toward you folks these days, and I—"

"He was too pie-eyed to even notice I was in the room," Adam interrupted. "Took you ten minutes to convince him you could only sell him a ticket as far as San Francisco."

"Mr. Moreaux . . ."

"Is he one of the fellows who entertains thoughts of . . . my untimely demise?"

"Um . . . I couldn't say, Mr. Moreaux."

Adam chewed the inside of his lip, pondering. Sometimes he wished hc had the ability to blend in, work undercover. Like his good friend Simon Kincaid, one of the most elusive and best-kept secrets in the entire Agency until his retirement and subsequent marriage over the summer.

"All right," he finally said. "I'll leave you alone"—the agent's face lit with undisguised relief—"*if* you'll tell me about Booker Rattray." He leaned forward. "He's not even a miner, Sam. He's a conniving trickster who would sell his mother down the river if it would turn him a profit. And I promise—he'll never know where the information came from. You'll be safe, and so will your wife and grandchildren." He hesitated, then reluctantly added, "If you don't help me . . ."

Sam's dismay was almost comical. "You've never threatened me before, Mr. Moreaux."

"I know. And I'd prefer not to start now. But Booker Rattray's my best chance in fifteen years to catch the Catbird." And with an innocent woman's life possibly at stake, Adam was willing to compromise up to the limit of his mostly clean conscience in order to protect her. "Sam—" His voice dropped, altering, and he saw the alarm skitter across the man's face. "What do you know about Rattray?"

"He . . . um . . . something happened 'bout a month ago. Nobody knows what, though it has to do with some greenhorn Booker was looking for. All I know is, when Rattray bought that ticket to Manitou, his hands were trembling, and he was sweating like there was no tomorrow."

"What about the greenhorn?"

"Dunno his name. Just that Booker Rattray was trying to find him. Then Rattray lit out, and he hasn't come back through here since."

Somber, Adam rode down Bennett Street in a grim mood.

According to the Agency's files, Booker Rattray had been the Catbird's middleman for the past fourteen years, though both men were far too cagey to leave proof lying about. One sighting several years earlier of the two men sitting together in a Harvey House in La Junta. The confession of a disgruntled safecracker who claimed he'd once seen some jewels laid out across Booker Rattray's bed that matched pieces the Catbird was rumored to have stolen.

Of course, the crafty fellow might have lied in the hopes of procuring a lighter sentence.

"Hey—Pink! How'd ya like your Injun tail sheared off?"

Adam didn't even turn his head. Keeping Biscuit to a steady walk, he headed down the street toward the Old Homestead, his destination. Booker Rattray was reported to have been pretty cozy with one of the girls at the fancy bawdy house, and he hoped—

"I'm talking to *you*, Pink!" the bowlegged miner yelled

50

again. "Turn around, or I just might use you for target practice here and now!"

Behaving as though he'd just been hailed by a friend, Adam brought Biscuit to a halt, flashing a congenial smile while he noted the size and general tenor of the crowd. Half a dozen surly miners, three uncomfortable matrons, a couple of kids playing on the steps in front of the grocer's. Several other men who might or might not prove to be allies.

He waited for an electric trolley to rattle past. "I know how you feel," he said then, keeping his tone mild, nonthreatening. "In your shoes, I'd not feel too kindly disposed toward me either."

The miner's jaw dropped. "You *funnin'* me?" He ended with an epithet.

"Easy, now." Adam kept his smile in place, but his gaze narrowed. "There are ladies and children present."

A dark red stain colored the man's throat and face, and his hand went to a pistol stuck in his waistband.

"I wouldn't waste a bullet if I were you," Adam advised, steeling his muscles even though he didn't move by even the flicker of an eyelid. "How about if you and I head for your favorite saloon? I'll buy, and you can call me all the names in your arsenal—privately."

The man blinked, swallowing as he stared up at Adam with a look of angry confusion. "You'll buy me a drink?" He glanced around at a couple of other miners, who shuffled their feet in the dirt or stuffed their hands into their pockets. A couple of them walked away, their shoulders hunched.

"One—but no more, unless you join me for grape sarsparillas. They're cheaper," Adam qualified. Also free of intoxicants. He offered a conspiratorial grin. "I'm kind of short on hard cash."

"Huh?" The miner shook his head as though to clear it, then took two steps forward. "What kind of man are you anyway?"

"I'm just a man who's trying to do his job, same as you. And believe it or not, this Pinkerton isn't here to put a stop to the Western Federation of Miners. Just those few who have turned to criminal acts as the way to air their grievances." He waited

51

until the miner met his eye. "And your grievances *are* legitimate," he stated quietly. "But repaying evil for evil is never the answer. . . . By the way, what's your name?"

"Al. Al Crocker."

"Well, nice to meet you, Al." Leaning down, Adam extended his right hand. "Now—shall we be on our way?"

Al stared at the outstretched hand, then at the gaping crowd gathering around. He swung back to Adam again, this time his gaze falling on Adam's left hand, still resting on the sheathed knife. "Can you really throw that faster than a man can draw a gun, like they say?"

"I don't think either of us really wants to find out, do you?"

The miner clenched his hands into fists, then relaxed as his shoulders slumped. "Naw . . . reckon not." He hesitated, glancing around. "About that drink . . . does that go for my friends, too?"

Well, he'd asked for it, hadn't he? "Sure, why not?" Adam swept an all-encompassing gesture toward the other miners. "What do you say, boys? Care to join us?"

Al gave a nervous laugh. Behind him, his cronies let out a roar of approval, while the ladies lifted their parasols and their noses, and the kids scampered down the walk to spread the news.

Adam sent a rueful prayer heavenward and mentally counted the coins he kept stashed in his saddlebags.

9

Denver

ROSALIND WAS SAVORING the rare opportunity of being alone. Zeke had driven her parents to the sanitarium for Edward Hayes' weekly treatments. Tallulah had taken the streetcar downtown. Driven by a compulsion to *do* something, Rosalind had embarked on a bread-baking frenzy, and when the door buzzer sounded, she was up to her elbows in floury dough.

Grumbling, she wiped her hands on a cloth, then hurried down the hall to fling open the door. A skeletal man glared back at her, one hand raised in the act of pounding on the door with his fist. In his other arm he held a large parcel smashed against his side. Dust coated his worn Norfolk jacket and baggy wool trousers.

"May I help you?"

"I'm lookin' fer"—he consulted a dog-eared scrap of paper he pulled from the band of his crumpled hat—"Rose . . . Rosy . . . lyn Hayes."

"I'm Rosalind Hayes," she replied cautiously.

Relief flooded the thin, dirty face. "This here's fer you." He thrust out the parcel, clumsily bound with brown paper and tied with string dangling loose from the corner.

Puzzled, Rosalind accepted the bundle. It was surprisingly heavy. But when she looked up to inquire, the man had already

53

reached to the bottom of the porch steps. "Wait!" she called after him.

The bedraggled man glanced over his shoulder.

"Who asked you to deliver this to me?" Isaac. Please say it was Isaac Hayes.

The man swiped at his mouth with the back of his hand. "Some feller down in Manitou paid me a dollar. I was headed up here anyways." He tugged his hat down farther over his eyes and turned his back.

"But what—" Rosalind pressed her lips together, unwilling to screech after him like a hawker at the county fair.

She stared down at the parcel. Then, decision made, she went back inside, laid it on the seat of the hall tree, whipped off her apron, and snatched a wrap from the stand. She was reaching for the doorknob again when she remembered the bread.

Groaning, Rosalind hurried to the kitchen, threw a damp towel over the dough she'd been kneading, then flew back down the hall and onto the porch.

The man was nowhere in sight.

Rosalind trudged back to the kitchen, scooping up the parcel on the way. She laid it on the scarred worktable in the corner, her heartbeat accelerating as she deftly tugged off string and paper.

Inside was a Bible. A worn, much-used Bible with the warped leather cover cracked and peeling. Utterly flummoxed, Rosalind opened to the frontispiece. "Presented to Pastor Jedidiah Scrivens, Easter Sunday, in the year of our Lord 1853, by a devoted congregation. Lower Queensbury, Gloucestershire." Why, this Bible was over forty years old!

But who was Jedidiah Scrivens, seemingly an English rector? Rosalind traced the ornate script with her fingers. There must be some mistake.

Thoughtfully she eyed the rising bread on the counter, then checked the loaves in the oven. Twenty minutes, at the most. Hugging the Bible, she hurried into the back parlor and sat down at the ladies' escritoire she'd purchased several months after her father's stroke. Shoving aside the week's grocery list, several unpaid bills, and a stack of advertising circulars, she carefully laid the Bible down and began leafing through the crackling pages. Hopefully a note, a letter—even a photograph, would appear, providing a clue to the identity of the sender.

She discovered only marginal notes, mostly illegible, and multiple underlined verses. Some were marked with fading blue ink; one, with a heavy black pen—a more recent marking. But nothing that established either the rector's present where-abouts or his motivation for sending his Bible to a complete stranger.

Rosalind pinched the bridge of her nose. Had to be Isaac. Somehow her brother must be involved, though that possibility made little sense. Isaac had renounced not only his family, but God, that last awful morning before he stormed out of the house.

The back door banged, echoing faintly down the long hall outside the parlor. Tallulah had returned.

Rosalind closed the Bible and tucked it inside the desk drawer. She needed to think before telling anyone else in the household—especially Tallulah. The household had barely re-covered from Rosalind's brush with the Catbird.

"Miss Rosalind! This bread's going to collapse if you don't sashay yourself back into the kitchen. Where'd you take your-self off to?"

"The parlor—I'm coming." Rosalind stood, smoothing her expression before she faced the housekeeper.

Arms folded, Tallulah hadn't even removed her hat and coat. Instead, she stood, looming in the doorway with her infamous "buried hatchet" scowl.

"Goodness, Tallulah, if you're not careful, your face will freeze like that, and nobody will come to the funeral."

"Don't you go sassing me. Don't know what the world's com-ing to these days, when a young girl takes on uppity airs with the hired help."

Rosalind rolled her eyes. When Tallulah referred to herself as "hired help," she was riled. A slight woman, a stiff breeze could have blown her over if she hadn't been anchored by an outsized will as fixed as a hundred-year-old oak tree.

Rosalind tugged the ostrich plume on top of the house-keeper's hat, leaping nimbly aside to avoid a swat.

"One of these days . . ."

"I think I'll check on the bread," Rosalind called over her shoulder. "And Tallulah? At twenty-six, I hardly qualify as a 'young girl.' "

"I calls it as I see it, missy," the housekeeper called back, undaunted.

Several moments later, minus coat and hat, she bustled into the kitchen. "Heard an interesting story at the butcher's," she announced, her hands full of fresh acorn squash, " 'bout that Pinkerton detective you tangled with."

Rosalind tensed. "Oh?"

After a moment Tallulah emitted a sound halfway between a snort and a chuckle—her own distinctive laugh. "Close-mouthed to the end, aren't you, gal? Good. Your sister was always a chatterbox." She began chopping, her leathery black hands quick, capable. "Your detective—"

"He's not *my* detective."

"—is actually famous. Infamous, depending on who you're talking to. Been chasing the Catbird off and on for five years now. Spends most of his time in the mountains, doing who knows what. Way I hear it, mine owners clamor for his services 'cause he's good, but he butts heads a lot 'cause his sympathies lie with the miners."

"I'm surprised he's still alive."

Tallulah snorted. "You saw him—I'd as soon tangle with a wolverine. Did you know he normally wears buckskins, like an Indian?"

Rosalind's mind conjured all too easily a picture of the tall, powerful man, dressed in fringed buckskins, with that wicked knife strapped to his waist. "Why does he, anyway? He's no Indian—not with those eyes."

"Don't know. Next time you see him, ask."

"He's left. I've been talking with Mr. Connelly." Rosalind hoped Tallulah wouldn't notice the tinge of wistfulness in her voice. She glanced at the wall clock. "It's going to be dark in less than an hour."

"Trying to change the subject? Fine by me—all this talking's making my gums sore."

They worked in companionable silence for a while, and Rosalind almost relaxed. She should have known better.

"If you do meet up with Mr. Moreaux again, go easy," Tallulah said. "He's got a reputation for more than them hair and buckskins. Rumor has it he's got the faith of a circuit-riding preacher. But—and this is where you come in, missy—he despises rich folks. Wouldn't spit on a man like Mr. Oliver even if he was on fire. Reckon Mr. Moreaux takes the Lord's words to heart, 'bout money being evil an' all."

Rosalind affected a shrug, ignoring the sensation of plummeting backward off a high cliff. "I may not screech my faith from the street corner, but I *am* a Christian. Besides, it's the *love* of money we're warned about. As for my 'wealth' "—she sliced Tallulah a look—"that's no longer a problem, is it?"

Tallulah dumped the chopped vegetables into a huge pot. "Won't matter. You still look the part, no matter that you work like a darkie from dawn 'til midnight just to keep food on the table. You've more pride than a body ought to, but I'd be disappointed in you if you didn't." She hefted the pot onto the stove with the ease of a blacksmith. "Be that as it may, you're still Alberta Hayes Driscoll's sister—and Mr. Moreaux met you in her house, at the fanciest reception of the season."

"In a Worth gown . . ." Rosalind closed her eyes, remembering the chilly disdain on his face the first time he saw her. Now she understood why.

"So, missy, watch yourself. . . ."

10

Raton, New Mexico Territory

BOOKER RATTRAY! That double-crossing trickster! Oblivious to the other passengers around him, LaRue remained on the platform until the conductor folded up the steps and slammed the door of the last passenger car. Only when the train rolled out of the station did LaRue turn away.

He waited through two seatings at the Harvey House restaurant, dismay escalating to fear, then panic. By the time the last train had come and gone, his mood had mounted to ill-concealed rage.

Under the table, between his feet, sat a battered leather satchel LaRue had planned to exchange for the one Rattray would have brought—one with the Petrovna jewels nestled securely inside. LaRue felt the sweat pooling at the base of his spine congeal to ice. He had to suppress the urge to kick his empty case across the room.

Where was Rattray?

The efficient waitress removed the dinner plates and replaced them with hefty slices of apple pie. LaRue waved his away, shoved back the chair, and hurled his linen napkin to the table. The Harvey girl discreetly stepped aside as he snatched up the satchel, then stalked from the dining room without a backward glance.

He spent a sleepless night, his insides churning. The following morning, his mind made up, he boarded a train back north.

Cripple Creek, Colorado

By the time the train pulled to a halt in front of the depot, LaRue had convinced himself that there must be a reasonable explanation for Rattray's absence. They had been associates for over twelve years, after all, and occasionally life did have a way of tripping up even a careful man.

LaRue waited until the tide of passengers had cleared the aisles before he himself stepped onto the platform. Doubtless he'd find Booker within the hour. By dinnertime, the Catbird would be gazing upon his treasures, savoring the intricate fil-igree, the exquisite workmanship, the superb cut of a perfect emerald—

Someone jarred his elbow, blocking the way. A well-dressed woman, LaRue noted with a spark of interest. Her distressed face was lifted to the conductor.

" . . . and I don't even know the name of a hotel." At LaRue's murmured request to pass, she looked up and their gazes met.

In a single instant he had memorized the quality of her clothing, the fear she was trying to hide in a pair of fine hazel eyes—and the brilliant clarity of the diamonds in the swallow-shaped brooch pinned to the wide lapel of her fur-lined cloak.

"Forgive me." He gave a low bow, adding, "May I be of as-sistance? I don't see the station agent, and you, sir, have a train to run. Since I never like to see a lady in distress . . ."

Plainly relieved, the conductor swiped a hand across his perspiring brow. "The lady's husband isn't here to meet her, and she doesn't know what to do." Irritating, helpless female, the tone implied.

"Ah." LaRue smiled down at the lady, and five minutes later he was helping her inside one of the depot wagons dispatched by the Grand Hotel. He supervised the placement of her trav-eling cases, then escorted her all the way to the lobby.

A lengthy conversation with the manager revealed news of

a large vein of gold discovered in the mine owned by Mrs. Bailey's absent husband. "Doubtless the reason for his delay," LaRue assured her, gently guiding the still distressed woman to a quiet corner. "I'll have a message sent to the mine before I leave, if you like, explaining where you'll be staying. You'll be safe here, never fear." Under any other circumstances, he would have enjoyed the opportunity of relieving her of that swallow brooch.

Then the woman lifted a delicate hand, her throat muscles working as she thanked him. LaRue mentally shrugged. Didn't hurt to spread a little goodwill occasionally, especially among attractive women. "I must be off," he murmured, dropping a gallant kiss to the back of her gloved hand. "I've an appointment of my own."

A pair of jovial drummers provided directions to the most popular saloon in Cripple Creek. They'd even heard of Booker Rattray, though they hadn't seen him about lately.

"Last I heard, he was boasting about some big money heading his way real soon, and how he was investigating a racehorse he'd heard about in Kansas City."

"I thought it was a railroad, out in California."

"Since it's Booker the Snooker, might be both!"

The two men burst into laughter, the one next to LaRue slapping him on the back. "Man's always got his fingers into something. That old feller's a piece of work." He leaned closer. "You a friend of his?"

"Business acquaintance," LaRue corrected.

"Ah." The two salesmen exchanged looks. "Well . . . you know what they say about dining with the devil—best sip with a long spoon!" They guffawed again and LaRue joined in before they tipped their bowlers and hurried off down the street.

Then, tucking away the small wad of bills he'd lifted from the loudmouthed buffoon, he headed in the opposite direction. Helpless women were one thing, braying donkeys, another. With any luck, their train would have pulled out of the station before the loudmouth discovered that his money was gone.

60

LaRue stalked into the gentlemen's parlor of his hotel, his mood vile. According to one of the girls at Cripple Creek's high-stepping sporting palace, Booker Rattray had skipped town three weeks earlier.

"He was upset. Almost sick-upset, if you know what I mean." The blowzy young woman sipped from a lipstick-smudged champagne glass, then smiled up at LaRue. "He's an old dear, isn't he? Even if he would sell a picture book to a blind man."

"Why was he upset?" LaRue ignored the coquettish tilt of her head. "Did he say?"

The girl—he thought her name was Dollie—shrugged. She hadn't known and hadn't cared. LaRue's anger churned inside with the methodical grinding of a gemologist chipping away at a stone. *Why?* He and Rattray had worked together in mutual trust all these years. Rattray liked to brag about his reputation, how conscientious he was about his professional associations—if nothing else.

It had to be the Petrovna jewels. LaRue had been bamboozled—by his own associate!

"You're looking mighty glum, lad." A flushed townsman gestured to the bartender as his gaze wandered over LaRue. "You one of the few poor slobs in town not invited to the bash?"

"I'm just visiting." LaRue hunched his shoulders, discouraging conversation.

"Too bad. They say it's likely to be a crackerjack shindig. Anyone with their pockets lined with gold pieces got invited. Bunch of bigwigs, dressed in all their finery, just to celebrate some old geezer's first million." He took a gulp from the drink the bartender had set in front of him, then wiped the back of his hand over his mouth. "Should've been me. If I just had a little more grubstake . . ."

The voice droned on, but LaRue wasn't listening. *Dressed in their finery, eh?* Abruptly he gestured for the bartender to replenish both his and the stranger's drinks. "Where," he inquired, clinking mugs with the other man, "did you say that party was taking place?"

11

WIND BLEW IN CHILLY PUFFS out of the southeast—not a comforting sign. Adam reined Biscuit back, then lifted a hand to shade his eyes. "Those clouds might just bring the first snowfall," he told his horse. The big gelding flickered one black ear before dropping his head to graze.

Adam chuckled as he reached for his binoculars. The trail he was following had been fairly easy. The pair of hotheaded miners he'd been instructed to bring in knew as little about covering their tracks as they did about explosives. Instead of blowing up mine owner Yancey Dowd, his two employees had blown up the flophouse room where they'd built the bomb.

Dowd had hired Pinkerton's the previous year, when talk of a miner's strike had heated up. On this occasion it had fallen to Adam to pursue justice in behalf of a ruthless, coldhearted man, whose only interest was in making more money. Though Adam accepted the necessity of the role he played, privately he had little taste for this particular task.

Truth to tell, he'd rather be sniffing out proof of Dowd's negligence and corner cutting than the equally reprehensible—albeit understandable—acts of desperate miners. Dowd's silver mine had made him a rich man—but the miners, virtual slaves. "No justice in the world, Lord," Adam muttered. "How long will you listen to the cries before you heed them?"

A strong wind ruffled Biscuit's mane and stung Adam's weather-hardened cheeks. He could almost hear the Voice, whispering through the swirling air currents. Patient . . . but chiding.

"I hear, I hear," Adam said.

He stuffed the binoculars back in the saddlebag. Thanks to the tip from Al Crocker, Adam had been saved days of hard work. By the end of the week, he should be able to resume tracking Booker Rattray and the Catbird, two thorns in his flesh for so long now he wondered what he'd feel when he finally brought the two scoundrels to justice.

Hopefully he'd also have an excuse for another interrogation of Rosalind Hayes. For some reason, the memory of his encounter with the baffling young woman dogged his mind with the same persistence with which Adam was tracking the two miners. And he didn't like it. She was the embodiment of everything in life he despised, but Adam had given up trying to ignore her.

Perhaps it was the incongruity of an expensive gown smudged with dirt, and a pair of stockinged feet peeking from beneath the stiffly formal skirt. Or perhaps it was the amusing descent from icy correctness to blatant curiosity when she spotted the bowie. The dazzling spectrum of moods her face revealed in spite of years of societal indoctrination. Eagerness. Disdain. Fear. Impishness. A zest for life . . .

Rosalind Hayes might be city-raised and reek of wealth and sophistication, but unrestrained *life* radiated about her in an elusive nimbus. And whether he liked it or not, Adam relished the thought of being caught up in that cloud again.

In the interim, however, he had other obligations—and a strong desire to keep Superintendent Connelly from assigning him to guard any more fancy shindigs like the Driscoll affair. One woman like Rosalind Hayes was enough.

Grimacing, he forced himself back to the task of capturing a couple of miners. Gathering the reins, he kneed Biscuit toward the narrow path leading down a needle-thin arroyo. Perfect setup for an ambush. But experience as well as instinct told him that the risk was minimal. The miners were running, casting about for a bolthole, not a likely spot to murder pursuers.

Besides, Kat would have warned him.

Denver

It was late, almost one in the morning. In spite of her grinding fatigue, Rosalind was unable to sleep. The sense of dread was stronger tonight—a heaviness of spirit that had been dragging at her for days. The nights were worse, when she was alone with her thoughts.

The Bible . . . and murky, waiting . . . silence. No more strangers knocking on the door. No explanatory letters delivered by the mailman. Nothing but a silence fraught increasingly with—warning? But of what? And why?

Frustration abruptly boiled over. Rosalind kicked off the covers, turned on the bedside lamp, and yanked on her robe and slippers. The Bible was stashed in the bottom of her wardrobe, and Rosalind tiptoed across the room, avoiding certain planks in the flooring.

After the stroke, with Edward Hayes incapable of climbing stairs, Rosalind had rearranged some of the downstairs rooms into a suite for her parents. Unfortunately, their bedroom was now directly beneath hers, and her father slept so poorly that even a creaking floorboard could destroy any possibility of rest.

Shivering, she carried the Bible back to her bed. For the next hour she searched, a page at a time, until her eyes burned and the print blurred. Even after almost two weeks she'd been unable to discover why the book had come to be in her possession.

Her fingers lingered over one of the verses in the book of Isaiah, underlined in the darker black ink. "Go into the clefts of the rocks, and into the tops of the ragged rocks." What an odd verse for a preacher to mark, Rosalind mused. She leaned back against the pillows and pressed the heels of her hands over her eyes. This didn't make sense—*nothing* in her life made sense any longer. Not the unexpected arrival of the Bible, nor

the notoriety lingering from her unfortunate link to the Catbird.

The furor had subsided only marginally. Several soirees and
a harvest ball had been canceled out of fear of a repeat performance. Irrationally, she thought, she was blamed. Despite
repeated searching through the "Rogues' Gallery" files at the
Pinkerton offices downtown and poring over "Wanted" posters
at the police station, she had not been able to identify any of
the individuals as the Catbird. And everyone behaved as if this
failure were a deliberate act of defiance on her part.

Sighing, she let the Bible fall to her lap. What, she wondered, would Mr. Moreaux think about all this? It would have
been helpful to talk with the fascinating detective—if he hadn't
already left Denver. She hadn't seen him since the night of the
robbery.

"Might not be back for a month or more," Superintendent
Connelly had informed her. "Mr. Moreaux doesn't have much
use for cities."

Rosalind would have queried Mr. Connelly further, but the
superintendent refrained from any more personal tidbits about
the operative known as "Panther." She stared unseeingly at the
verses of Scripture, picturing instead the commanding figure
of Adam Moreaux, wishing with a peculiar stab of yearning
that *she* could roam about the mountains, disdaining the cities
with their noise and choked air, their crowded streets, their
throngs of people. . . .

Her mother's careworn face, once so full of life and dignity,
replaced Adam Moreaux's striking image, followed by that of
Edward Hayes sitting in his wheelchair, his face stiff from the
paralysis on his right side, his dark, intelligent eyes now mirroring the private hell in which he was trapped.

Rosalind focused once again on the Bible lying open in her
lap. " 'Comfort ye my people,' " the prophet had trumpeted in
resounding tones that echoed down the centuries. Bitterly she
struggled against hurling toward heaven her own feelings of
betrayal, disillusionment, and hurt.

Besides, in comparison to most of the world's downtrodden
folk, her own circumstances did not warrant such feelings. She

was neither orphaned, homeless, nor starving. She was sound of mind and body, and if she suffered occasional pangs of rebellion, no doubt it was because she wasn't remembering the unspeakable sufferings Christ had endured in her behalf.

She read the familiar verses once more. A rueful smile touched the corners of her lips as she noted that, at some distant hour in the past, Jedidiah Scrivens had underlined the eighth verse of chapter forty.

And later, for some reason in darker ink—a seemingly insignificant phrase in chapter forty-one.

12

THE PAIN—IT WAS ALWAYS WORSE AT NIGHT. Isaac didn't know why. For the most part, he no longer cared. All that mattered was the goal.

Jed's face swam into view, a smoking kerosene lantern in his hand. "Hurtin' pretty bad again?"

"Oh, I'll be able to travel, come sunrise." He winced again, and Jed leaned closer, his face only inches away. It might have been a homely face, Isaac realized hazily, except for the serenity spilling from the elderly preacher's eyes.

But it wasn't the face he had dreamed of carrying with him to the grave. "If you won't help me leave tomorrow," he insisted hoarsely, "I'll try it on my own."

"If you start out tomorrow, you'll be dead before you make it to Canyon City." Jed gently lifted the tattered blanket covering Isaac. "I don't like the looks of this wound." He bowed his head, closing his eyes. Praying, Isaac knew, for a miracle that wasn't going to happen.

Isaac swallowed hard, tried to lighten his voice. "You think I'm so rock-stupid I don't know what you've been trying not to tell me, Jed? You think that fall took away my sense of smell, too?"

Jed cracked one eye. "Silence, if you please, my boy. I'm talking to the Lord."

Isaac snorted. The old man had been talking to the Lord constantly . . . in fact Isaac's first memory when he regained consciousness was of Jed's unflagging supplications to the Almighty.

Apparently God wasn't in a miracle-granting mood, leastways for a misbegotten sinner such as himself. The gunshot leg had festered in spite of the preacher's competent nursing, and even though Jed had tried to block the view with his considerable bulk, Isaac had glimpsed the red streaks. He was doomed, and he knew it. Booker Rattray's shot hadn't killed him outright—but it was still getting the job done.

Before he left this earth, though, he planned on seeing that Rattray got what he deserved. After that, Isaac would try to make peace with the family he hadn't seen in four years.

He had to make it to Denver. Rosalind was curious as a crow. That old Bible, arriving out of the blue, would be gnawing at her like the pain gnawing his vitals. Be just like his impulsive sister to come looking for answers on her own, in spite of Jed's and his elaborate efforts to keep her safe from the likes of Booker Rattray.

If she accidentally stumbled onto Rattray, there was no telling what the old reprobate might do once he found out Isaac was her brother.

"Jed."

"Shh . . ."

Isaac ground his back teeth and counted knotholes in the rough wood walls until his eyes crossed. "I have to make it to Denver, Jed. Don't make me beg."

Jedidiah opened his eyes. He lifted the blanket again, stared down at the bloodied, mangled mess that used to be a leg, and heaved a sigh. "She should have the Bible by now. And my friend Gustav, down in Manitou, will have the letter I wrote, waiting to deliver to Rosalind when the time—"

He broke off and turned aside to pour water into a cracked earthen bowl and wet a rag to bathe Isaac's brow. "The clues are safe," he murmured, sounding weary, "and so is your sister, since she doesn't know what to look for. Your efforts—"

"Hang it all, Jed! Long as Rattray's loose, nobody's safe." He gasped as a vicious jab of pain stole his breath. "Denver," he whispered, the word a plea. "Have to . . ."

"Easy, son. All right," now the gravelly voice soothed, calmed. "We'll head out at first light. I'll dose you up with the last of the laudanum to help you sleep a little better." He dropped the blanket and lifted his somber gaze to Isaac. "Son . . . I've prayed without ceasing for your recovery, but sometimes God chooses to answer in a manner we humans can't fathom. Since I can't refuse the request of a dying man . . . I'll do my best to see you to Denver." Beneath the beard his mouth twitched. "I'm sorry, boy. If we could have gotten you to the sawbones in Cripple Creek—"

"Don't waste your breath. I should have been dead a week ago." He swallowed hard. It was one thing to blithely accept that one day you'd be pushing up daisies . . . but when that day was breathing down your neck . . . *God, I've been such a prodigal son these past years. If you'll just let me see my family, one last time. . . .*

The callused palm moved to rest against his sweating brow. "Don't fret, son. We'll do what we can, together. Then we'll let the Lord finish it as He sees fit. Don't fret, Isaac Hayes. And don't fear."

"I'm working on it," Isaac muttered. "Uh . . . Jed? Before you dose me up on that witch's brew of yours . . . I want to write a letter of my own . . . to my sister. Will you help?"

13

ADAM DISMOUNTED AT THE ENTRANCE to another narrow canyon, giving his horse a low-voiced command. Biscuit rubbed his head against Adam's chest, then turned, ears pricked. A man couldn't have a better backup than his horse, nor a better scout than Kat. Crouched low, Adam wove his way between clumps of undergrowth and low-branched ponderosas, slowly making his way down the canyon.

Moments later Kat flowed up on his left side. Adam scratched beneath her chin—his wordless signal of praise—and the big cat fell in beside him, obedient as a trained dog. Fifteen paces later he felt her mouth close gently over his wrist, and he stopped.

"Show me," he whispered, then followed Kat down a dry creek bed for another hundred yards.

The odor of smoke drifted into his nostrils, along with the faint but definite sound of voices. Adam knelt, one arm resting along Kat's back as his mouth brushed the tuft of hair springing from her ear. He whispered to the cat, who immediately melted into the brush. Adam waited a moment, then belly crawled until he could see the crackling campfire. Poor hapless souls, he thought. They'd built it with green wood, sending smoke billowing upward. Most of it would dissipate before topping the canyon walls, but twenty years earlier, the two miners would have been ripe pickings for a band of Indian hunters.

He crawled within five yards or so, then waited until both men hunkered down in front of the fire, their backs to Adam. Silent still, he stood and walked toward them until he was only a few feet away.

"Evenin', boys."

They yelped, spinning about, faces beneath their caps distorted into identical expressions of horrified surprise. Only the man on Adam's left carried a gun, which, like Al Crocker's, was tucked inside his belt instead of a holster.

"Don't even think about it," Adam advised when the man fumbled for the weapon. In a whisper of sound, the bowie appeared as though an extension of Adam's hand, blade flashing in the afternoon light. "My name is Moreaux. I'm from Pinkerton's, and you really don't want to kill me any more than I want to injure you."

"There's *two* of us," sputtered the man with the gun. His hand fluttered toward his waist but dropped when his gaze met Adam's. He swallowed convulsively.

"Mm. Well, I have a partner, waiting for my signal." Adam studied the two men. Both of them were gaunt, their hands and faces the sickly white of skin untouched by the sun. Their eyes, he saw with rising pity, were desperate. "How about if you share a cup of that coffee with me before we start back? Wind's rising, and those clouds might scare up a thunderstorm—or even a couple of inches of snow. Never can tell, this time of year."

"They ain't going to do nothin'! The sun's shinin'."

"Shut your trap, Jimmy. Ya sound like a danged idiot." His partner, Hank Steuben according to the marshal in Victor, glanced toward the innocent-looking tufts of gray, then back at Adam. "He don't see daylight much." The flat voice was bitter. "Dowd keeps his workers at it seventeen hours at a stretch. We get to the mine before daybreak—don't leave until pushin' midnight."

"I know," Adam replied, sheathing his knife. "Want to tell me more, over coffee?"

"Tell you more?" Hank echoed. "What for? You're a rat—a

union-busting Pinkerton!" He spat the name like a epithet. "For two cents I'd go for my gun anyway. You're no better than Dowd—keeps you and your missus sleepin' in a feather bed, does he? Chasing down poor suckers like me and Jimmy just for trying to see justice done."

"Give it up, Hank. He don't care." He scrutinized Adam. "You sure don't look like no detective I've ever seen."

Adam took a step closer, letting his hands drop to his sides. "Appearances can fool a body, can't they? Take the pair of you, for instance. On the run from the law, dressed like a couple of tramps—Hank here is even carrying a gun. Nobody would ever take either of you for decent Christian family men, husbands and fathers who only want to provide for your wives and children."

"Well, I am!" Jimmy protested. "Tarnation, we *both* are!" His long, pointed nose turned redder by the second. "Why do ya think we tried to blow up Dowd's carriage? We didn't want to kill him—just force him to listen. We ain't been able to work—"

"Shut up, Jimmy." Hank's eyes narrowed on Adam's face. "You keep blabbing, and Sadie'll be a widow."

"You are wanted by the marshal, and by Pinkerton's," Adam agreed. "So I have to take you both in. But I'm out for justice as well." He paused. "You don't believe me, I know. But if we could share that cup of coffee, you might realize that it's not only my clothing that differs from other detectives." Now he waited until both men subtly relaxed. "As a matter of fact, I don't like Yancey Dowd's treatment of miners any better than you do. If you can think of any way to bring the man down— *legally*—you might want to fill me in. I promise you I'll see what I can do."

"You're just trying to trap us."

Adam studied each man, then unbuckled his belt and laid the knife to the side. "It's my job and my duty to take you fellows to the jail in Victor, since that's where you committed the crime. And make no mistake—I will take you there, and we'll need to leave within the hour."

He spared a sweeping glance upward, deliberately opening himself for attack. From the corner of his eye, he could see the two men studying first him, then the sky. Adam tensed, readying himself, wondering as he always did if he'd made his last error of judgment on earth. Even Kat couldn't protect him if Hank lost control and knew how to use that gun.

"Are you for sure a Pink?"

He shrugged. "Going on fifteen years—since I was barely old enough to shave."

Hank peered at him some more, lips pursed. He raised his right hand, flinching at Adam's response. "Just taking off my hat, mister," he explained hurriedly. "I wasn't goin' for the gun."

He waited a moment, then removed the battered fedora and passed his hand over the tangled mat of filthy, straw-colored hair. Without the hat, he looked young, but the light blue eyes held the cynicism of a feral dog. "You really got a partner out there, backing you up?"

Adam nodded.

"Well . . ." Hank and Jimmy exchanged a last look, the defeated slump of their shoulders more telling than their words. "May as well have that cup of coffee, then. First we've had—stole the beans."

"Couldn't afford it anyways for what old man Dowd charges at his company store," Jimmy muttered.

"I see. I'd be tempted to blow his carriage up, too." While they gauped at him, completely disarmed, Adam strolled over. "If you hand over the gun, I'll see to it that your wives are delivered enough coffee—and any other food items your families need—to keep them through the winter."

Without a word Hank removed the pistol, thrusting it awkwardly toward Adam. He examined the gun—a single-action German model almost twenty years out of date—then emptied the cylinder. "Any more bullets?"

Hank shook his head. "It belonged to my grandfather—he was in the Prussian army. It . . . I don't even know if it would have fired."

"I'll see that it's returned to your wife." Adam turned, whistling.

"That sounded like a real bird," Jimmy said.

"Thanks. It'll fool a human ear—but not a towhee, or my

horse." Adam fetched his bowie knife and buckled it in place just as Biscuit trotted into view. He tucked the gun inside his saddlebag, patted Biscuit's flank, then turned back to the dumbfounded men. "Now . . . coffee?"

"What about your partner?" Hank asked.

"Oh, I think it's best if we leave my partner as lookout." Adam nodded his thanks to Jimmy, who'd handed him a battered tin cup of steaming liquid. "Now, how about telling me everything. . . ."

14

"WELL, THIS IS BY FAR the most irresponsible notion you've entertained in a long time," Charles finished, clasping his hands behind his back and rocking a little on his heels. "What, may I ask, did you plan to accomplish?"

A few days of freedom, Rosalind was tempted to say. "Have I ever asked you and Gladys for anything since Papa's stroke?"

Charles scowled. A tall, fine-figured man with the strong facial features of their father and the ash blond hair of their mother, Rosalind's older brother had always thought a bit too highly of his own comforts. Thanks to a shrewd marriage to the North Carolina textile heiress fifteen years earlier, he was comfortably entrenched as king of a mammoth estate in Capitol Hill, a social lion who knew everybody who was anybody from Kansas City to San Francisco.

He detested having his orderly kingdom disrupted.

"All right—no," he conceded. "You've never asked for anything. Been a dutiful daughter, and the whole family appreciates it." He stalked over to the sideboard and splashed some mineral water into a glass. "It's just . . . this is not a convenient time to bring Father over here for a few days. Gladys is hosting a meeting for the Women's Club day after tomorrow, to discuss their new clubhouse. Vincent's off on some excursion with his schoolmates at Jarvis Hall. And as for the girls, Cassandra is spending a week in Chicago with—"

"So pay for a hired nurse to help while I'm gone." Rosalind glared at her brother. "Leave Papa at home, since you don't want him disrupting your busy lives." Charles flushed, but Rosalind plowed on. "I'm going to Manitou, whatever you say. If you won't pay for a nurse, I'll withdraw the money from my trust fund."

"For pity's sake, sis." He ran a hand around the back of his neck. "Look—I'll arrange for a nurse. And before you twist the knife further, you may recall that Gladys and I have encouraged Mother for the past two years to hire a live-in nurse. You might also remember that it's the two of you who insist on keeping Father at home."

He turned aside, pulling out his pocket watch to check the time. He scowled and snapped the lid shut. "Ah . . . does this burning urge to leave town for a few days have anything to do with that mess at Oliver and Alberta's a couple of weeks ago?"

"No." Let him stew about it, speculate on the whys and wherefores. Rosalind wasn't ready to mention the mysterious Bible. She stood. "I'll bring you back a fresh supply of that bottled 'Ginger Champagne' water you like from Manitou Mineral Water Company, if you'll pay for it in advance."

Charles' clean-shaven face lit up. A dedicated teetotaler, her brother kept varieties of bottled waters from all over the world stocked in his cellar, much as other men hoarded fine wines and whiskeys. "Done. I really liked the one you brought back the last time. That's been, what—a year or two now?"

"Four years this past May. Right before Papa suffered his stroke." Two weeks to the day after Isaac ran away from home . . .

"Oh." Looking awkward all of a sudden, Charles fell back on his role as older brother. "Well . . . I trust Tallulah will be going along to chaperon, and you'll . . . ah . . . conduct yourself with all due propriety?"

"I always try to conduct myself with propriety," Rosalind promised wearily and clamped her mouth shut before she was forced to tell a lie.

Tallulah wasn't making the trip to Manitou.

Georgetown, Colorado

Nerves taut, his fingers stroking a long rope of glistening pearls, LaRue stood at the window of his room at the Hotel de Paris, watching the street below while he waited for the serving girl to deliver the breakfast tray he'd ordered. Behind him, the Prince Albert coat and striped trousers had been laid out on the bed with the fastidious care of a British valet. The new top hat in fashionable dove gray waited on the dresser. All standard attire for a gentleman of means . . . unless one examined the outfit closely.

Inside the coat were numerous hidden pockets, and the waistband of his trousers concealed several of his favorite tools. Last night, when he'd strolled the crowd drinking and gambling at the Mother Lode Palace, his suit had filled rapidly with a tidy fortune in jewelry, including the pearl necklace.

LaRue swiveled on his heel and reached the bed in three long strides, carelessly tossing aside the pearls. He'd as soon throw this whole lot into the dirt street below. Compared to the Petrovna Parure, these few trinkets served only to satisfy a momentary thirst, too easily quenched.

According to the latest information, Rattray had purchased a ticket to Manitou Springs, nestled at the base of Pikes Peak. Advertisements LaRue had read in the local papers touted the place as the "Saratoga of the West," packing in well-heeled tourists by the trainload throughout the spring and summer.

Trouble was, the season had ended two months earlier. So why would Booker Rattray invest his time with the handful of locals and guests indifferent to the approaching brutal Colorado winter?

With any luck, by this time tonight, LaRue would have some answers.

With a little bit more luck . . . by this time tonight, he'd also be able to stand at a hotel window, gazing over the easy marks ambling along the streets below while he caressed the cool weight of his precious darlings.

LaRue still hadn't decided what to do about Rattray's betrayal.

❖

Victor

Adam turned his two chastened but hopeful prisoners over to the sheriff, then spent an afternoon purchasing supplies to be delivered to the men's families. He wrote his report for Superintendent Connelly, curbing with an effort the desire to justify the miners' actions.

As he was leaving the post office, a small sprout with a shock of red hair and a face full of freckles dashed up, tugged the fringe of Adam's buckskins, then thrust a telegram into his hand. Adam flipped the lad a nickel and read the message. So. There had been a raft of jewel thefts over the past two weeks, spreading from Cripple Creek through Georgetown the previous night. Gossip roared up and down the mountains like a north wind, but not a single person could offer a description of the possible culprit. Adam was to return to Denver as soon as possible for a meeting with Connelly, along with Uriah Vangood, the assistant super, some high-ranking official of the American Jewelers' Association, and as many operatives as Connelly could pull in.

Adam hopped aboard a departing trolley but was too late to catch the last train out of Midland Depot. After a perusal of the sky, he shrugged, fetched Biscuit from the livery stable, and followed the train on horseback. Since most of the tourists had left back in September, he figured he could spend the night at Halfway House, then hop a train out of Manitou Springs first thing in the morning.

❖

Heavy frost tipped the mountains in sun-glittered silver. Overhead, a deep blue sky burned off the last blush of dawn as Adam carefully guided Biscuit along the steep trail leading down through Minnehaha Falls, below Halfway House. A quarter of a mile from the hotel, Kat bounded through a thick stand of trees, then leaped with acrobatic skill down a landslide of boulders.

"Good hunting the past few days? I trust you've stayed out of trouble at least." A month ago the cougar had been sighted by a late-season hunting party; a bullet had creased her left flank, turning Adam's blood cold. She was pushing thirteen now, and the thought of not having her around always filled him with raw grief.

Rationally, he knew that considering a wild animal his partner and best friend contributed to his infamous reputation; Adam frankly enjoyed that. On the other hand, he also knew that, while God had given the cougar into Adam's keeping, He had doubtless not intended for him to value a relationship with one of His creatures over *human* relationships.

"One fine day you're going to realize that sharing a bed with a cougar is not near as satisfying as with a loving wife," his friend Simon Kincaid had pointed out just the previous summer.

"I doubt if there's another woman alive like your Elizabeth," Adam had replied. "Your wife's one in a million, my friend. I expect God has decided I can best carry out His will in the manner of a priest—alone."

Adam found himself smiling as he leaned down from the saddle to scratch Kat's ears. His oldest *human* friend—who for many years had claimed a loving God wanted nothing to do with Sim's bloodied soul—had roared with laughter. "I used to think you were the only man on earth who talked to God," he'd mused, still chortling. "Adam . . . don't kid yourself. The Lord just hasn't gotten round to introducing you to the woman who'll be able to tame that wild streak of yours. But He will. He will."

Then he'd punched Adam's shoulder before doubling over again. "A *priest*!" he'd gasped, the green eyes sparking with devilment.

If the sound of his dark friend's joy hadn't filled Adam with delight, he would have engaged in a friendly wrestling match in the front yard of their Montana ranch home. As it was, Adam had ridden off with a rueful grin of his own, hearing the laughter ringing out behind him as he galloped down the lane.

"Well, Kat, it'll be interesting to see which of us is right," he said now. "In the meantime—steer clear of civilization, if you don't mind."

Cougar eyes wide, filled with uncanny intelligence, Kat merely stood next to Biscuit's withers without moving until the horse stamped a hoof. Regretfully, Adam swung down from the saddle, dropped beside Kat, and whispered in her ear. When he stood, the big cat leaped lightly from boulder to boulder, disappearing into the trees at the top of the ledge.

"Let's go," Adam muttered, mounting up and kneeing Biscuit's sides. "I have a train to catch."

15

Manitou Springs, Colorado

IN THE OFF-SEASON, plenty of rooms were available for overnight visitors. On previous trips to the popular springs of Manitou, the Hayes family had stayed at the Barker House, one of the resort town's most prestigious hotels. This time, however, discretion led Rosalind across the street to a smaller hotel. The daily two-dollar rate charged at the Norris House still bit a sizable chunk out of her meager funds, but it was cheaper than the Barker. Torn between exhilaration and trepidation, Rosalind ignored the desk clerk's frosty attitude upon discovering that she was unaccompanied.

Ten minutes of ablutions in the small but clean first-floor room restored her wisping pompadour and rumpled appearance. Spirits high, Rosalind made her way back down Manitou Avenue, enjoying her singular freedom.

To her left, Fountain Creek gurgled merrily, scattering diamond droplets into the bright midday sunshine as the swift-moving water tumbled over rocks and boulders. A bird warbled from the branches of a cottonwood. Other than a lone buggy, a delivery wagon, and a young man riding a bicycle, Rosalind was alone on this early November day.

During the season, she remembered, the broad avenues and tree-lined paths were thick with wealthy tourists showing off their finery and invalids seeking the restorative benefits of

Manitou's mineral waters. Elegantly dressed ladies and gentlemen in straw hats clustered beneath the pavilions over the area springs, sipping soda water from community cups. The air rang with clopping hooves, rumbling wheels, and the jangle of the town's electric trolley. Afternoon concerts entertained strollers in the park, while Pikes Peak, jutting boldly against the sky, lured visitors to scale its barren heights via the Cog Road or a burro train.

Intoxicated by the bright blue sky and crisp air, Rosalind experienced only a fleeting pang when she passed by the Mansions. One memorable night, when she was sixteen and Isaac twelve, the two of them had sneaked out of their bedrooms at the Barker. Isaac, already headstrong, had heard about a hop the Mansions was sponsoring in their Saratoga Room. He'd also wanted to sneak inside a billiards room . . . a gambling hall . . .

With a brisk mental shake, Rosalind shut down the memories. The past was irretrievable, the future uncertain. But for the first time in a long time—possibly since that epoch-making evening with Isaac ten years ago—she was free to pursue the present, unencumbered by the stifling demands of family and circumstances.

Her mission for the afternoon was to track down Pastor Scrivens and learn his motivation for sending his Bible to a perfect stranger. Since the book had been a gift from an English congregation, Rosalind assumed the pastor would shepherd an Episcopal congregation here in America. The church opposite her was a Congregational church, but undeterred, Rosalind crossed the street and confidently mounted the steps. Surely someone here would provide directions, possibly information.

She interrupted a kind-faced minister practicing his sermon. Though pleasant, his replies to her inquiry about Pastor Scrivens undermined her carefully thought-out plan.

"An itinerant preacher . . . who lives in the mountains?" she repeated blankly. "He doesn't pastor a congregation here in Manitou?"

"No, ma'am. Never has." The dignified minister studied her for a moment, his gaze quizzical. "He's tramped the Rockies since, oh, right after the war, preaching the gospel to anyone who will listen. Ministering to anybody in need. Takes in broke prospectors, miners down on their luck, gamblers and drunks. Doesn't matter—old Jedidiah cares about all of them. But nobody knows what happened to him before—he's never talked about his life in England." He glanced at the Bible. " 'Til now, I hadn't known he pastored a congregation at all.' "

Rosalind ran her tongue over dry lips. "Um . . . how can I find him?"

"Find him?" The elderly man scratched his head, looking strangely at a loss. "Well, miss, I don't rightly know." His gaze took in Rosalind's luxurious traveling cloak, with its graceful short capes draped about her neck and shoulders, all the way up to the expensive hat pinned to her head. "How very odd," he murmured. He riffled through the pages of scrawled notes. "I can see that what I've told you is distressing." He paused, adding reluctantly, "If you're in need of pastoral counsel, perhaps I could—"

"No—it's not that. It's just—that is, I'm trying to locate a person I thought Pastor Scrivens might know, actually." Rosalind hesitated, inwardly debating. Her fingers gripped the cloth bag so forcefully, hot needlepoints of pain pricked into her tense shoulders. "My . . . brother."

"I see." He shook his head. "Well . . . like I said, Jedidiah's pretty much a nomad, doesn't spend much time in town. I'm terribly sorry, miss." He paused. "Sometimes, wandering souls do find their own way back home. Why not give your brother a little more time?"

"I would, except some things have changed." She smiled in farewell and turned to make her way back down the dark aisle, her heart heavy.

What if her theory about Pastor Scrivens' connection with Isaac turned out to be nothing but a delusion, fueled by her loneliness? If so, the corollary hypothesis—that her brother might be behind the Bible's appearance—could be equally in error. . . .

"Oh, miss?"

Rosalind glanced over her shoulder. "Yes?"

"There . . . is a man—Gustav Wachtler. I believe he knew Je-didiah Scrivens some years back."

Rosalind turned back to face the minister. "Why didn't you say so earlier?" she asked. "And why are you telling me now?"

"Gustav's something of an eccentric. Downright rude, upon occasion—particularly toward ladies, I'm sorry to say." He watched her a moment, a curious expression of cynicism and compassion shadowing the round face. "I tell you now because you appear bent on a mission. I pray that the experience does not prove disappointing."

Despite the cleric's warnings, some twenty minutes later Rosalind stood in front of Mr. Wachtler's cottage, resisting the impulse to laugh . . . or flee for her life! The tiny house was painted a hideous shade of mud brown, the front porch—what she could see of it—a bilious shade of green. Only a snakelike narrow path led to the front door. The rest of the porch was choked with . . . clocks. Grandfather clocks, cuckoo clocks, reg-ulator wall clocks . . . mantel clocks—

Without warning the front door flew open. "Get off my porch, you gawking female!"

Rosalind's chin lifted. "I'm not on your porch!" she shot back. "But"—she looked from the irate little man to the littered walkway—"I do confess to gawking. I've never seen so many clocks."

"I don't care if you've never seen a clock of any kind. Get out of here."

"Are you Gustav Wachtler?"

"If I am, what's it to you?" A gnome of a man scarcely as tall as Tallulah, the presumed Mr. Wachtler speared her with a pair of deep-set black eyes that sizzled out of a pasty face. His trim, spade-shaped beard liberally streaked with gray covered his chin, jutting forward with belligerence.

"The minister at the Congregational Church directed me here. He said you might be able to help me locate Pastor Je-didiah Scrivens."

The snapping black eyes flared before turning curiously blank. "Never heard of him." He turned, closing the door.

Before he could disappear inside, Rosalind scampered up the steps, her cloak billowing on either side like two gigantic wings. "Wait! Please—" She stumbled to a breathless halt, her foot accidentally striking the dusty case of a forlorn mantel clock whose face was minus its hands.

The door popped open. "Now look what you've done!" he screeched.

"I haven't hurt your clock. It was broken anyway." Rosalind steeled herself, and took one more step forward to catch the door if he tried to slam it shut in her face again. "If you'll look at this Bible and tell me if you know how it came to be sent to me, I'll—"

"Bible?" The word emerged, strangled, but at least she'd caught his attention. "All right. Come inside for two minutes. But don't touch anything!"

Three minutes later Rosalind stood outside on the path again, ears still ringing from the sound of hundreds of clocks chiming the hour, heart thumping against her ribs in hammer-like blows from Mr. Wachtler's words. Time . . . if she measured time right now by the number of her heart throbs, as a poet once suggested, she'd be well into the coming year. Hugging the Bible, she whirled about, marching back toward town. She might not have learned why—but at least she was one step closer to *where*.

Cripple Creek.

She'd have to return to Denver first, somehow persuade Tallulah to accompany her, and her mother to accept nursing help for Papa, at least temporarily. Whether the quest lasted two days or twenty, she planned to find her brother and bring him home to his family, where he belonged.

Forty minutes later she turned away from the depot ticket window. Preoccupied, she was tucking the latest timetable inside her satchel when a hurrying passenger jostled her elbow in his rush to purchase a ticket. Her mind hundreds of miles away, Rosalind stepped aside, nodding automatically at the man's curt apology.

She paused to pin her hat more securely in place, her gaze

roving about the almost empty depot. One of the connector trains to Colorado Springs had just arrived, but few passengers disembarked this late in the off-season day.

Rosalind's hands froze in midair, and a hard knot formed beneath her breastbone.

A man dressed in a dapper Prince Albert coat and striped trousers had entered the depot, then paused inside the doorway to light a cigar. Above thin lips and a hooked nose, the flaring match illuminated a pair of dark eyes that reflected . . . nothing. After he lit his cigar, he resumed walking, passing within a dozen yards of Rosalind on his way through the large porte cochere to the depot.

The last time Rosalind had seen him, he'd been wearing white tie and tails, and just before he disappeared out the third-story window, his eyes had stared through her with that same chilling look.

The Catbird.

She didn't stop to think. Clutching the bag in one hand and the edges of her cloak with the other, Rosalind all but ran across the floor. She reached the doors just in time to glimpse the Catbird climbing into a depot wagon from the Cliff House.

"Are you available for hire?" Rosalind asked a lounging driver, who at her tone straightened to attention. "I just missed the depot wagon. Could you take me to the Cliff House, please?"

16

BY THREE O'CLOCK ROSALIND HAD DECIDED that the Catbird was demented. Either that, or he knew she was following him and had decided to lead her on a torturous tour of Manitou's flashier saloons, gambling halls, and bathhouses. But whether he was demented or devious, she was determined not to lose sight of him.

At one sporting palace, she'd been able to slip inside and huddle at a back corner table, from where she watched the Catbird question the bartender and several patrons. She waited outside the two gambling halls, fearing that he would either decide to play a game or two of faro—or slip out a back door. Less than a minute passed before he exited the first. Five interminable minutes after disappearing into the second, he shoved through the doorway with enough force to slam the door against the wall. The look on his face was murderous.

Fingers not quite steady, Rosalind purchased a newspaper from a freckle-faced boy across the street from a billiards parlor the Catbird had entered. When he emerged from the smoky depths, she was sitting on a park bench, pretending to read.

His next stop was the Silver Dollar Saloon. When the Catbird reappeared this time, he was smiling. Rosalind was so surprised she dropped the paper. Flustered, she leaned to retrieve it, and when she straightened, her quarry was strolling along the walk—toward *her*.

Pulse skittering, Rosalind fumbled open the paper and ducked her head. She could barely hear the scrape of his footsteps over her roaring pulse, and the words might as well have been gibberish. If the Catbird noticed how the paper was trembling, she'd be in a washtub full of trouble.

After several tense moments she lifted her gaze an inch. He had disappeared.

Panic warred with determination, and lost. Rosalind began walking, her gaze darting from one storefront to the next. She must learn the Catbird's destination so she could telegram Mr. Connelly at the Denver Pinkerton office. On the corner, she paused beneath a barber's striped pole, wondering which way to turn. A creeping sensation touched her spine, a shivery feeling that she was being . . . watched. She glanced through the huge plate-glass windows of the barbershop—and straight into the onyx-colored eyes of the Catbird.

One leg crossed over the other, he sat with a cloth draped about his shoulders, while above his head, the barber wielded comb and clippers. For a span of seconds that lingered like a single drop of sorghum, Rosalind and one of the country's most hunted criminals engaged in a visual duel. Fascination and fear lured her as powerfully as a narcotic.

"He's not a killer by nature," Mr. Moreaux had told her, his tone hinting at what Superintendent Connelly later confirmed.

"Two people have died under suspicious circumstances during his robberies in the past four years," the superintendent had reluctantly admitted. "We've no proof but—I think you should know that he's now considered dangerous as well as crafty."

Suddenly the Catbird smiled, a quick flash of white beneath the thin mustache. A shark's smile.

Rosalind willed her heartbeat to slow, then slid her gaze to the man seated in the chair next to the Catbird. She shrugged, made a face, acting as though she'd been looking for someone else. Just as casually she strolled back down the sidewalk, controlling the urge to run as far and as fast as her heavy skirt and petticoats would allow.

When she reached the corner, a depot wagon from the hotel across the street from the Norris House was trundling toward her. Gratefully, Rosalind lifted her arm to hail the driver. Fifteen minutes later, she was frantically scribbling a telegram to send Superintendent Connelly from the hotel's telegraph office.

While she waited for a response—or more accurately, while she hid in her room with the door locked and a chair braced beneath the knob—Rosalind made a list of each place the Catbird had visited.

The prompt reply was terse and startling: "Wait at hotel, in public place. Operative Moreaux will make contact soon. Do not leave premises under any circumstances."

Adam Moreaux? Here? A chagrined smile tickled the corners of her mouth as she grappled with the implications of Superintendent Connelly's response. Well, she *had* secretly yearned to see the famous detective again, though certainly not under these particular circumstances.

Rosalind's smile faded. She shouldn't care two figs about Adam Moreaux's opinion of her. But she did.

17

HE KNOCKED ON THE DOOR a little over two hours later, announcing himself in the unmistakable deep baritone that instantly confirmed his identity. Rosalind dragged the chair away, opened the door, and stared. Instead of an Indian warrior in tie and tails, Adam Moreaux stood in front of her clad in . . . in dust-coated buckskins, scuffed boots, and that horrendous knife sheathed at his waist. He might have stepped off the stage of Buffalo Bill Cody's Wild West Show. Even the ten-gallon hat with a single feather stuck in the band defied all convention.

The hat should have been removed, held politely in his hand.

"Clothes are different, but the man's the same," the detective drawled after a moment. "Not that I'd expect someone like you to understand."

He glanced up and down the hall, then stepped inside the room, forcing Rosalind to give way. "It's not proper, of course, but now at least you can stare as long as you like." A sardonic smile twisted the corners of his mouth. "The telegram waiting for me indicated some urgency, so I didn't take time to clean up." His manner plainly communicated that he wouldn't have bothered anyway.

Well. "Good afternoon to you, too, Mr. Moreaux. So nice to see you again. May I take your . . . hat?"

"Certainly." He doffed it with a mocking bow.

Rosalind all but threw it over a set of hooks inside the entryway, then turned back to Mr. Moreaux. Arms crossed, bewildered as well as annoyed, she searched the taciturn features. "Why don't you like wealthy people?"

Amusement flashed across the detective's face. "Perhaps, Miss Hayes, the problem is with those who think their wealth equals privilege."

Rosalind's jaw dropped. She quickly snapped it shut, but when another lightning stroke of humor flashed through Adam Moreaux's eyes, her wayward tongue galloped headlong into disaster. "I have a problem with people who sneer at manners in order to excuse their own lack of them."

"And how would you define your behavior right now? A little more volume, and you'll be shouting at me."

Rosalind clapped a hand over her mouth. But a sheepish smile crept beneath her splayed fingers, breaking the tension. When she saw that he saw, they both began to laugh.

"My family—"

"Won't ever hear of this from me. Are they out?"

"No." Her spine stiffened. "I'm here alone." Surely a long-haired man in dust-covered buckskins wasn't about to lecture her. . . .

"Good." He gave a decisive nod. "Perhaps the situation isn't irretrievable. Tell me, does that window overlook the street or the park?"

"The . . . street." Bemused, Rosalind watched him stride across the room to the window, keeping his body screened behind the folds of drapery while he peered out. "When I last saw the Catbird, he was in a barbershop at the other end of town."

She shook her head, feeling about like the time she'd fallen off the top rung of a ladder. No social pleasantries for Mr. Moreaux. No queries for information or demands to know what she was doing down here by herself, or why. . . . "I'm sorry—what did you say?" she asked, looking up with a start.

"I asked if he saw you."

"I'm afraid so. That's why I telegraphed Superintendent Connelly as soon as I could."

"Yet you think you managed to give him the slip and return here without his knowledge?"

Even more uncertain, Rosalind tried to decipher Mr. Moreaux's forbidding expression. "I'm certain I did. He couldn't very well leap out of the barber's chair and come chasing after me with a cloth flowing behind him like a sail." She tried a smile. "If he did, it wouldn't have been very subtle. I wondered, after Mr. Connelly's reply to the telegram, if I had inadvertently—" She broke off with a strangled gasp.

Without warning, the knife had appeared in Detective Moreaux's hand. He began tossing it, snatching it out of the air with blinding speed. "The superintendent has talked with you several times about the Catbird, I understand," he said, his gaze never swerving from hers. "So you're aware that when you claim to have given this man the slip, you're not talking about some decrepit burglar with rheumy eyes and creaky knees."

The knife twirled end over end, then disappeared into the scabbard with a whispering sigh. "You're talking about an international jewel thief who has managed to avoid capture by some of the world's best trackers over the past fifteen years."

"You being one of them, I understand." Rosalind eyed the knife, then stalked across the room to her traveling case. She retrieved the piece of Nottingham lacework she'd brought with her, settled in a chair next to the steam radiator, and began working. "Please feel free to fiddle with your knife," she offered, her own fingers flying as she worked the needle in and out of the half-finished pillowcase. "I can understand the need to keep your hands busy. As you see, needlework does that for me."

"How are you at the art of deception?"

Rosalind glanced up. A stillness had come over the detective, the crackling stillness of air just before a lightning bolt splits the heavens wide. The needle slipped, jabbing her thumb. Rosalind jumped, then laid the work aside. "Why would you ask?"

"Because it strains my credulity to believe that a sheltered society girl such as yourself could outfox the Catbird." He padded across to her, the leather fringe of his buckskins stirring with each step. Even in boots, his tread was noiseless. "A more plausible explanation is that the pair of you are in this together, after all." He stood above her, arms folded, looking tough, intimidating—and ready to pounce. "What's your game, Rosalind Hayes? Are you pulling a doublecross on your family? Perhaps . . . your partner?"

"If you knew me at all, you wouldn't waste your breath or your brain on either sordid speculation." She'd crawl on hands and knees back to Denver before admitting the uncomfortable truth that, in his own menacing way, the Catbird was as fascinating as the man standing in front of her.

"If I knew you any less," Mr. Moreaux countered, "I would have been stalking you myself, not wasting time fencing with you." He leaned against the wall and crossed his ankles. "Tell me one thing. Why *are* you here, by yourself?"

"It has nothing to do with the Catbird!" Rosalind flared.

In a swift flurry of skirts she rose, retrieved the traveling case once more, and dragged out the Bible. She turned around, prepared to thrust it in the detective's face. Instead she faced an unsheathed bowie knife, poised in the expert clasp of a man whose stance froze her tongue to the roof of her mouth.

"I . . . what. . . ?" She couldn't swallow, and her fingers had gone numb. The heavy Bible began to slip.

The knife disappeared, and his hand whipped out to lift the book from her faltering grasp. The brush of his fingers shocked Rosalind free of the numbing paralysis. She retreated two steps until the backs of her knees bumped into the bed.

"A Bible?" The deep voice conveyed a paradoxical mix of confusion, regret, and amusement. "You were fetching a Bible."

Rosalind didn't respond.

"Well, Miss Hayes, over the years I've been humbled by a number of circumstances and people." He laid the Bible on the bed. "You're turning out to be the most disconcerting." He held his hand out, palm up. "I'm sorry. You might have been going after a weapon, you see. I can't assume that a well-dressed, articulate young woman isn't as capable of an act of violence as any country bumpkin."

"Th-thank you, I think." For a long moment Rosalind stood

motionless, waiting for her pulse to slow and her muscles to relax. "You scared me out of my wits!" she finally confessed. "Because all I could think, with that wretched knife pointing at me, was that it was a shame the blood would ruin one of my favorite walking costumes."

Hysteria. Had to be hysteria. A fine trembling seemed to have taken possession of her body, and laughter was crowding her throat.

"Wouldn't want blood staining the carpet or counterpane either." He studied her thoughtfully, and Rosalind struggled to bring herself under control.

Suddenly he smiled. "Forgive me for frightening you?"

"Certainly." Rosalind cleared her throat, then began pleating the tail of the ribbon at her waist. "I even understand why you felt it necessary."

"All right, then." He rubbed his palms together. "Now, I need to see if the Catbird's lingering about, or has left town. Will you be all right if I leave you here for another hour or so?"

"Not a chance," she announced baldly. "You don't know what the Catbird looks like. I do. If you leave me here, I'll spend the next hour fuming, and believe me, neither of us wants that."

She marched past Mr. Moreaux to fetch her hat, handing the detective his at the same time. "Far better for us to proceed together. Saves time, and if I spot the Catbird . . . well, you'll be the first to know."

18

Colorado Springs, Colorado

LaRUE SPENT A RESTLESS NIGHT, vacillating between returning to Denver and hunting Rattray down. For many hours he examined pieces from his hits in Leadville and Cripple Creek. A couple of particularly nice stickpins. The delicate lavaliere with a good, fiery Australian opal. A rope of pink-toned Oriental pearls.

Then there was the man's ruby ring he tossed aside in disgust. Dime-store trinket, suitable only for the gutter. Which was where Booker Rattray belonged, possibly stuffed face first in a rain barrel.

LaRue spent several more hours pacing the floor, trying to decide what to do. If he returned to Denver for the woman, Rattray might use the Petrovna jewels to finance a new life, new identity, possibly in Europe. He would disappear, not surface for months. Years, maybe.

LaRue might never find him. Might never hold his darlings again, delight in the perfection of his lifelong dream, celebrate the apex of the Catbird's career. Lose forever the opportunity to prove he was worthy of the name "Napoleon."

He'd purchase a ticket to La Junta first thing in the morning. Yet . . .

The girl had recognized him. The knowledge had been as

clear in those light green eyes as a polished diamond in spite of her attempt to hide it.

That bright-eyed female could send him behind bars for the rest of his life.

LaRue carefully packed all his treasures, then sat down at a small table and scrawled a hurried message to leave with the telegrapher.

Manitou

"Apparently he's chasing Booker Rattray," Adam informed Rosalind Hayes, "who—from what I've been able to learn over the past week—is running as far and as fast as he can." This struck a discordant note to Adam's way of thinking. Booker the Snooker bluffed and conned. He didn't run.

"Who's Booker Rattray and why would the Catbird chase him?"

Adam couldn't help the grin that kicked up the corner of his mouth. The stylish hat and elegantly coiled hair concealed a lively brain. Not to mention a reckless determination that caught him off guard.

Adam would have preferred to stash Rosalind Hayes some-where—a locked room would work nicely, but he had a hunch she'd pick the lock, then chase him down. Over the past two hours she'd matched him stride for stride as he methodically retraced the Catbird's steps. Her cultured voice provided precise directions, all the while pestering him with questions.

He still found it impossible to believe she'd been pursuing the man in the first place. And not just a man, but a highly skilled criminal who had stymied the Agency's best efforts at capture. The little innocent! Adam couldn't decide whether to congratulate her—or send her back to Denver under heavy guard.

"Mr. Moreaux?" she repeated now, tapping her foot. "Who is Booker Rattray?"

Adam mentally hurled his hat toward the moon before he

gave up and answered. "A likable scalawag who's doubtless provoked more heartache, heartburn, and heart attacks than hot
chili peppers."

He wrapped his hand around her arm to gently tug her out
of the way of a pair of small boys chasing a wobbling hoop.
Beneath his fingers the slender arm quivered. Annoyed, Adam
released her while he elaborated. "Our Mr. Rattray's a con artist, confidence man—and a fence for some of the most notorious thieves on three continents. Including the Catbird."

"I see. If the Catbird's chasing him, then it sounds as though
Mr. Rattray might have decided to bite the hand that's been
feeding him, doesn't it?"

"Mmm. Trouble is, it doesn't fit what I've learned about
Booker." He paused, his mind skimming back over the past
months of infrequent but persistent digging. "Remember the
old chestnut about honor among thieves? When a man's a liar
and a cheat, he's got to cultivate a reason for fellow liars and
cheats to trust him, if he's going to make a living as a fence. To
my knowledge, except for his first partner, Rattray's never
pulled a fast one on any of what he considers his business associates."

"Who was the man he betrayed?"

"The father of the wife of a good friend of mine."

Up and down the avenue streetlights began to glow, scattering hazy golden circles through the twilight shadows. Beside
him, Rosalind Hayes' steps flagged, and a sidelong glance revealed the slight droop to her shoulders. About time, Adam
thought, relieved. "I still have some places to go, errands to run.
Your hotel's just down the block. Why don't I leave you there,
give you a chance to rest, have a bite of supper."

"The tickets—"

"I'll purchase tickets for us both and drop yours off at the
front desk if it's too late."

She stopped just beyond the fuzzy yellow circle cast by the
streetlamp. "Yours will be wherever the Catbird's going, and
mine for Denver, I presume?" Her shoulders had straightened
again, and Adam could hear one of her feet busily tapping.

"Something wrong with those arrangements, Miss Hayes?"

"Yes!" she whipped back. "You might have an artist's rendering of the thief's description, but it's not as reliable as my eyes."

"Agreed." He strolled over to prop his hip against a low stone wall flanking the walk. "*I* don't have a problem traveling with an unchaperoned single woman." He crossed his ankles. "Do you?"

Silence descended between them, thick and gloomy.

"I want to say it doesn't matter," Rosalind admitted eventually in a small voice, "but it does. And it's not fair."

Adam saw her throat muscles working, and a curious twinge of pity twisted his heart.

"I didn't mind traveling here alone. But I can't . . . it wouldn't be right . . ." She stopped, then took a deep breath and turned her gaze to Adam. "I know you may not share my views on the . . . the restrictions I choose to abide by. But I have chosen to abide by them," she added as Adam opened his mouth. He closed it, listening to her despite his irritation. "If everyone chose to act as they pleased, dress as they pleased, go wherever they pleased—whenever they pleased—our entire society would suffer."

"Contrary to your insistence, current social mores are not part of the gospel, Miss Hayes."

She swelled like a sage grouse. "I disagree, Mr. Moreaux. Those strictures are specifically designed to prevent behavior God finds offensive. Without standards, without any social etiquette, there is no 'civil' in civilization. Only chaos and savagery."

Adam's jaw clenched. "Is that a slur against the Indian lifestyle?"

"Of course not!"

"Forget it. This is pointless. One's conscience prevents such behavior—not the judgmental dictates of a handful of self-proclaimed Pharisees. Or aren't you familiar with the New Testament?"

She jerked her head back as though he'd spat in her face. "I didn't intend to launch a debate," she announced primly. "But I will point out, Mr. Moreaux, that where there are no standards reinforced by public pressure, civilization crumbles. Look at France during their bloody revolution a hundred years ago. And if everyone decides to live the self-centered life you're advocating, I shudder to think what our country will be like a hundred years from now."

"I do *not* advocate—" Adam caught himself up short. Then, lifting his hands, he smiled at her, impressed in spite of himself. Only his father had ever tried to reason with him in such a straightforward manner. Then he leaned forward until his face was inches from her ear. "But that doesn't mean I agree with you. And it doesn't mean you're right."

They finished the walk to her hotel without speaking again, though the air between them fairly sizzled with unvoiced thoughts.

19

ADAM RETURNED TO THE NORRIS HOTEL later that evening and found a message from Rosalind Hayes waiting for him at the front desk. Somehow he wasn't surprised. "Where's the ladies' parlor?" he asked the sleepy night clerk.

"Room to the right, down the hall."

When he walked through the doorway, Rosalind rose at once from a lounge chair on the far side of the room. "Thank you for coming," she said. Her voice had reverted to its starchily formal tone.

Hmm, Adam thought, studying her pale face and shadowed eyes. "What's the matter? Has something happened?"

Astonishment, quickly veiled, flashed across her countenance, but she didn't answer as she moved to a small library table in the corner. A desk lamp illuminated the Bible she'd pulled out of her traveling bag earlier. "I need to share something with you."

She darted him a look that didn't manage to hide the anxiety darkening the green eyes to a murky gray. "It's the reason I came to Manitou Springs. And it has nothing to do with the Catbird. Seeing him was . . . an unhappy coincidence."

"I don't believe in coincidence, Miss Hayes." Adam gestured toward the Bible. "Not when I happen to believe what the Good Book has to say on the matter."

"Tallulah, our housekeeper, said she heard that you can talk like a circuit-riding preacher. The . . . um . . . words we exchanged earlier, well . . . that's one of the reasons I—" She stopped, her hands fisting, then relaxing at her sides.

"Go ahead," Adam encouraged. "Tell me whatever you need to. I promise—no sermons or debates. At least until you're capable of firing back. All right?"

She wound her fingers together, a nervous mannerism he wouldn't have expected from her. "This matter might require the services of a private detective. I—" She closed her eyes momentarily, then finished in a humiliated rush, "I don't have the funds to pay you very much, but I don't know where else to turn. You need to know that at the outset. It wouldn't be right otherwise."

A sharp stab of real anger jabbed Adam's middle. More than a little disturbed, he grappled with the unwelcome knowledge that this young woman actually had the power to disrupt his legendary even temper. "If money becomes an issue, we'll discuss finances," he eventually managed, ". . . *later*."

Then, because he was feeling defensive and didn't like it, he attacked. "In spite of your low opinion of me, Miss Hayes, I'm not a bounty hunter, nor do I deliberately prey on the misery of other people."

"I never meant—"

Long-buried emotion bubbled too near the surface. "Yes, you did! You have an easy face to read in spite of . . . your pedigree. From the first time we met and you learned what *I* was, you haven't been able to hide your disdain. It was there earlier, when you were dressing me down so self-righteously. Just like the rest of your kind, the stuffed shirts and prim-mouthed matrons, looking down on anyone who isn't just like you."

He swiveled on his heel, all but fleeing to the other side of the room. He was ashamed of himself. The words had been curdling in the back of his mind for days, but his timing couldn't have been worse. *Panther, you're losing it, pal.* "Sorry."

"Don't be." Her voice sounded just as weary as his soul. "*I'm* the one who should apologize. Please believe that I no longer feel . . . disdain." There followed an uncomfortable pause.

Then: "And I agree with you—most of . . . our kind . . . *are* stuffed shirts and prim-mouthed matrons. I've felt the same way about them for years. I just never had the courage to admit it out loud."

Incredulous, Adam turned back around, crossed the ugly cabbage rose-patterned carpet until he stood directly in front of her once more. "Miss Hayes, you're a walking, talking contradiction. It takes a lot to baffle me, but I'll admit you've been more successful than most anybody I've ever met."

Solemnly he held out his right hand. "Since I don't want to be baffled by a stranger, how about if I call you Rosalind, and you call me Adam."

She was shaking her head, yet staring longingly at his outstretched hand. "It isn't—"

"—proper," Adam finished for her. So swiftly she had no time to retreat, he clasped her right hand and held it in his, tightly enough that she couldn't tug it free. "Rosalind . . . I don't care." He laughed suddenly. "Maybe I'll call you Rosie instead."

"I'll smack you into the next county."

"Rosylee?"

"Wyoming." The tension in her wrists and fingers had diminished, so that he was able to hold her hand without pressure.

"Linda? It's Spanish for 'lovely.' " He was enjoying himself now.

"The Canadian provinces. Mr. Moreaux . . . are you *teasing* me?"

"It's Adam. And yes, I suppose I must be." He released her hand and stepped back. "I'm not the complete clod I've been acting like lately." He glanced down at the Bible. "And—you need to trust me, both as a Pinkerton operative—and as a man." He watched the faint color seep under her skin. "Let's sit down, all right? And you can tell me what brought you—all alone—to Manitou, with only a Bible to protect your honor."

20

ALL THE WAY BACK TO DENVER, Rosalind wondered if she'd made the right decision. Every so often she'd touch the traveling bag in her lap. Mr. Moreaux had tried to convince her to entrust Pastor Scrivens' Bible to the Pinkerton's National Detective Agency. He'd lost.

"The preacher's a man of God—none finer in this neck of the woods. While I understand your reluctance to part with the Bible, I also know that I'm the one who can track him down. If I have the evidence, he might be more willing to tell me why he sent it to you."

The rhythmic clacking of the wheels and rocking of the coach seemed to echo the words: *Track* him down, *track* him down. *Sent* the Bible, *sent* the Bible. . .

Closing her eyes, she leaned her head back against the seat and tried to convince herself that she was doing the right thing. She simply couldn't allow Mr. Moreaux to openly investigate a member of her family. Her mother would be devastated, the rest of the family appalled. Papa—she couldn't bear to think about *his* reaction.

Far better to continue searching through the Bible for clues on her own while Mr. Moreaux tracked down the preacher. If in fact there *was* a connection with Isaac, then and only then would she risk talking with her parents.

And it *would* be a risk. The last time her younger brother's name had been voiced aloud, Rosalind had had to send Zeke for Dr. Hawkins. And the physician had bluntly warned them that another emotionally charged scene elevating Edward Hayes' blood pressure might be his last. Well, there must not be another. She'd see to that.

Zeke met her on the platform as she stepped off the train. "Don't mind saying it's a relief to set eyes on you, Miss Rosalind." He picked up her traveling bag and grimaced. "What you totin' in here? Bricks?"

Rosalind ignored the teasing complaint. "Did Mrs. Ingersoll work out all right with Papa?"

"That old dragon does nothing but quarrel with Lulah, bully Mr. Edward, and mutter 'bout the missus when she thinks nobody can hear her."

"I take it you're the 'nobody' who could?" They exchanged a smile. "Mamma must have donned full battle armor. She didn't want me to hire a nurse in the first place, until Charles and I ganged up on her." And Charles had helped convince their mother only because he had refused to have Papa inconvenience their household with his presence.

"Well, your mother did have Tallulah drag out the Haviland china for dinner. Told Miz Ingersoll without batting an eye that she'd be gone all afternoon, making her calls, even though she ain't visited that flock of uppity biddies a single time since Mr. Edward's misfortune. And I ain't worn a livery since we left Virginia—had to borrow it from the Driscolls' head butler."

They exited the station into a blustery, starless night. Rosalind shivered, clutching her coat tighter as Zeke led her to the rows of parked carriages. She tried not to mind the shabby condition of the Hayes family carriage, a once gleaming dark green rockaway with striped moldings. Now the paint was faded and peeling, the striping almost gone from the door Zeke held open for her.

No wonder Mama didn't go calling any longer, she thought bitterly. "I must talk to Mr. Hawkins about a new carriage," she observed, not for the first time. "He'll sell me a curtain rockaway at an affordable price, and it shouldn't be much trouble to add the glass when the weather's unpleasant."

"Mr. Edward needs this one, Miss Rosalind. You know that." He glanced over her shoulder into the darkened shadows of the interior. "I'll try to paint the old gal before the first snow, how's that? Now . . . you just rest your head. I'll have us home in a jack-rabbit minute."

Smiling, Rosalind obeyed, stifling her guilt as Zeke slammed the door and climbed into the driver's seat. She was grateful he hadn't asked about the trip in spite of the questions she'd seen lurking in his eyes. Unlike Tallulah, Zeke, bless his heart, never intruded on a body's privacy.

But instead of napping, Rosalind spent the thirty-minute trip home thinking. Judiciously selecting details from the past two days that would offer less than downright lies—yet none of the truth.

Chaos met them at the front door.

"Your mother's hiding in the butler's pantry," Tallulah informed Rosalind before Zeke even shut the back porch door behind them. "And it's not over that nurse—I sent her packing after she informed me that my meals are harmful to a delicate invalid's digestion."

"Papa?"

"Is fine," Tallulah thumped down a large can of pickled peaches she'd been holding. "For once, try not to jump to conclusions. Not a quarter of an hour after Zeke left to fetch you, some tongue-flapping gent talked his way past your mother's common sense and into the front parlor." Her tone was aggrieved. "If I hadn't been finishing up the supper dishes, none of this would have happened."

"Tell Miss Rosalind what's up, ya contrary female," Zeke growled, plonking Rosalind's case onto the linoleum. "She's wore out and don't need your grumblings."

"I'll grumble about a strange man helping himself to our parlor at nine o'clock in the evening, and you'll be doing the same." Tallulah folded her bony arms over her chest and glared at her husband. "Talks like he's southern as rhubarb pie and just as sweet, and Miz Ophelia refusin' to shoo him out the door.

We've not had after-dinner calling since Mr. Edward's misfortune, yet here's your mother trying to pretend nothing's out of sorts."

"What's his name?" Rosalind hurriedly inserted. "And why did Mother allow him to stay?"

"Calling card says he's 'Nathaniel Beale.' As to the rest, you'll have to ask her yourself. I wouldn't know, only being the *help*. She showed him to the parlor and dismissed me to the kitchen."

Alarmed, Rosalind began tugging off her gloves. "I'll take care of it, Zeke." She paused, thinking hard. "As soon as you tend to the horse, perhaps you'd enjoy an evening snack in the kitchen?"

"I'll leave the door to the hallway ajar," he said, touching his cap before ducking back outside.

Rosalind found her mother composed but pale, though the naked bulb hanging inside the pantry exposed her red-rimmed eyes. She managed a tight smile. "I'm glad you're home." She hugged Rosalind, then took a deep breath. "Tallulah told you about Mr. Beale?"

Rosalind nodded.

"He knows your brother." Throat muscles quivered above the neat bow of her shirtwaist. "It seems . . . oh, Rosalind, he's missing! Isaac's missing, and Mr. Beale is afraid something has happened." Without warning, color stained her cheeks. "I'm afraid *I'm* guilty of a small deception. He asked for your father, and I told him he was out of town. Then I invited him to make himself comfortable while I made some refreshments. I'm ashamed to confess I left it to Tallulah—and I've been hiding in here ever since."

"I'm here now. We can handle Mr. Beale together."

"He's very polite, very nice in a way," Ophelia said slowly. "But he does remind me of Lester Hill, my first beau. Somehow I have the feeling Mr. Beale is telling me what he thinks I want to hear, while all the time carefully withholding the whole truth."

"Sometimes the whole truth depends on who's doing the telling." And on whom you were telling it to, Rosalind added to herself, thinking guiltily of the Bible tucked at the bottom of her traveling bag. "Only one way to find out Mr. Beale's version, Mamma."

Her mother squared her shoulders. "Well, shall we?"

21

A PORTLY MAN WITH A PALLID COMPLEXION and a ruthlessly slicked-down cowlick, Mr. Beale could have been anywhere from fifty to seventy. He rose immediately and sketched a charming bow. "This would be your lovely daughter?"

After the time-wasting rituals of introduction, they all sat down, and Rosalind struggled to clear the cobwebs from her mind. Her mother launched into a polite recital that included the approaching inclement weather and the status of the city's progress in paving the streets, along with carefully spaced inquiries about Mr. Beale's visit to Denver. Rosalind kept a half smile in place and her hands in her lap. She was itching to fire a volley of questions—not engage in mindless chitchat. *One for you, Mr. Moreaux,* she thought.

"Ah . . . I trust you'll understand that I'm not trying to be rude," Mr. Beale finally murmured, clearing his throat, "and on any other occasion I'd enjoy nothing more than a delightful tête-à-tête with you ladies. But I feel a certain urgency . . ." He paused as though searching for words.

"Then, Mr. Beale," Rosalind announced, ignoring her mother's tight-lipped disapproval, "by all means let's dispense with the pleasantries and get right to the point. Where did you say you met my brother?"

"In Leadville, Miss Hayes." He cleared his throat again. "Ah . . . this is difficult, but I'll be frank. The two of us stayed at the same hotel and became friendly. Shared some meals, a game or two of faro." He offered a sheepish smile. "Never for money, however. One evening while I was elsewhere engaged, your brother joined a heated poker game with a table of high-rolling gentlemen, some of them with unsavory reputations."

"My son's . . . proclivities for gambling are not a topic for discussion, Mr. Beale."

A band of scarlet tipped his ears and forehead. "Beg your pardon, ma'am. It's just that I'm afraid there were some allegations made and a good deal of money lost at that game, your son's being some of it. I like to think of myself as a friend, though our acquaintance was short. I wouldn't have intruded otherwise." He hesitated, then drew out his watch and flicked the lid open. "I have another engagement," he began apologetically. "If I may speak very bluntly. . . ?"

Just get on with it! Rosalind wanted to shout, but she waited for Ophelia to incline her head.

"I left Leadville for Cripple Creek without speaking to your son again. Shared my seat with one of the gentlemen at the faro table. He expressed the opinion that your son Isaac had vowed to get even with someone he felt had fleeced him, no matter what he had to do."

"Did you learn his name?" Rosalind asked, leaning forward.

Mr. Beale nodded. "A Mr. Rattray. Apparently suffers a questionable reputation in some quarters. I understand he's a speculator of sorts. Now, I'm certainly not trying to impugn the good name of a man I don't know," he said, "but I feel honor bound to help out a young friend." He glanced down. "I had a son, you see. Always a bit of a rascal, but with a heart of gold. Died when he was only twenty-two." The soft, drawling voice turned husky.

He shook his head, cleared his throat again. "Forgive me. I just wanted you to understand why, when I was coming to Denver anyway, I felt compelled to look you up."

"Please go on," Rosalind prodded.

"My business in Cripple Creek occupied the better part of a

month. Over the course of that time, bits and pieces of ominous gossip about Isaac kept coming my way. Briefly, your son seems to have followed Mr. Rattray for some weeks."

"Mr. Beale, you're being evasive," Ophelia pointed out with a hint of starch. "I find that vexing, to say the least."

"What I have to tell you will distress, perhaps offend you," Mr. Beale admitted, looking even more uncomfortable.

"Bad news revealed is preferable to uncertainty." Her mother held herself very straight, looking her patrician best. "Just tell us, if you please, Mr. Beale."

And hurry it up, Rosalind almost added. She picked up a letter opener, pretending to study the mother-of-pearl inlay.

"According to the sheriff of Cripple Creek, your son Isaac is wanted for robbery. He apparently followed Mr. Rattray, then stole a goodly amount of money from him. Both men have disappeared." He glanced around the room, then looked Ophelia in the eye. "I thought perhaps he panicked . . . he's young, alone. He might . . . ah . . . have returned here, for sanctuary."

Rosalind winced. It had taken no small amount of courage for her mother to sit quietly and listen to this kind stranger air unpleasant truths about the son whose name over the past three years had rarely been spoken aloud.

Isaac, she thought in despair. *What have you done?*

She laid the letter opener down, her mind made up. If Pastor Scrivens' Bible held the answers, Rosalind vowed not to rest until she found both the pastor and her brother. With or without the help of Pinkerton's National Detective Agency.

22

"THIS WOULD UPSET YOUR FATHER DREADFULLY."

"I know." Rosalind stuffed her traveling bag at the back of her wardrobe and shut the door. "So we're not going to say anything. At least not until we hear from Isaac."

Ophelia perched stiffly on the upholstered bench at the foot of Rosalind's bed. "What if he's in jail?" she asked, her voice pained. "I don't know which would be worse. For him to have committed a crime and be too ashamed to let us know, or to be in hiding somewhere, possibly for the rest of his life."

"That's what I'm going to find out, Mother." She sat down on the bench next to Ophelia.

"You're going after him, aren't you?"

"Well . . . I can't very well send Zeke, and can you imagine asking Charles? Or Oliver?"

Her mother sighed. "I see your point. But, Rosalind—you heard Mr. Beale. Those mining towns are full of vice and corruption, totally unsuitable for a young woman of your station. Besides, what on earth would I do without Tallulah?" She lifted her hand in a gesture of apology. "Forgive me, dear. I didn't mean to whine."

Rosalind nudged the rounded shoulders, still gracefully erect in spite of the lateness of the hour. "Mother, I don't think you could whine if you tried."

"Well, I must say the logistics defeat me at the moment. We could probably endure that dreadful Mrs. Ingersoll helping with your father's care, but I'm still not sure I—"

"I'm not taking Tallulah, Mother." She braced herself.

"But we simply can't afford to hire a chaperone."

Rosalind stood and moved to the dresser, keeping her back to her mother. "I know. That's why I'm going by myself."

"What? Rosalind, an overnight excursion to Manitou was questionable enough. But you're talking about a *mining* town, hours over the mountains. We've never been there—know nothing about accommodations. There's no family there, no one to protect you. . . ."

Rosalind waited for her mother to wind down. With each tick of the clock, each earnest objection, tiny needles of doubt pricked her confidence. Which was the greater sin, she wondered—deception or disobedience?

Long after the house had settled down for the night, Rosalind lay sleepless in the dark, listening to the rising wind. A cowardly part of her wished she had just followed Adam Moreaux, sending her mother a telegram to break the news.

But she wasn't Isaac. Trouble was—she wasn't Alberta or Charles, either. Right now, Rosalind didn't know who or what she was. Pummeling her pillow, she waited in vain for sleep and that inner serenity God's reassuring presence always offered. Unfortunately, since she was even now in the very act of rebellion, the Lord might be off somewhere, comforting some more faithful soul.

At first the noise didn't register; on a windy night the house always creaked and moaned. Then Rosalind heard something else—a distinct thump, as if something heavy had fallen. Concerned, she slid her feet over the side of the bed. Her mother might have been fetching something from the kitchen and stumbled in the dark.

Hurriedly tugging on her robe, Rosalind tiptoed out into the hall and listened. Heard nothing but the undulating whistle of wind . . . creaking wood . . . soughing tree branches.

Heard a heavy tread across the squeaky board in the parlor.

Oh, Mamma, Rosalind thought wearily. Both of them deplored their periodic disagreements, though they couldn't seem to find a way to prevent them. Wrapped in guilt, Rosalind turned on the hall light—and pandemonium erupted in the parlor below.

Heavy footsteps thudded across the floor, followed by even more alarming noises—the crash of a falling chair, the sound of breaking glass . . . and a reverberating bang when the front door slammed shut.

Rosalind didn't hesitate. She raced down the stairs to the hall tree, then pawed through the jumble of scarves, gloves, and clutter in its storage seat until her fingers closed around her father's Harrington double-action revolver. It wasn't loaded, but an intruder wouldn't know that.

The door to her parents' bedroom opened and Ophelia peeked out.

"Stay there!" Rosalind hissed.

"I heard a noise—" her mother began, then met Rosalind's eyes and without another word disappeared. The door closed with a reassuring click.

Telephone the police. Charles. Oliver . . . Rosalind silently begged her mother. Though she was fairly certain the intruder had fled, she couldn't afford to risk her parents' safety, or that of Zeke and Tallulah, whose rooms were all the way at the back of the house, beyond the sound of any commotion.

Resolutely she took a step toward the parlor. "I have a gun," she announced, hoping for an authoritative tone. "And my mother has telephoned for help."

Nothing happened. Rosalind gingerly reached for the wall switch next to the hall tree. Reassuring light washed over her, and only then did she feel the tremors shaking her from head to toe.

The parlor was in shambles. The intruder had been busy. Numbly she surveyed the room, which appeared to have been ripped apart by a savage wind.

"Rosalind?"

Her mother's frightened whisper jerked Rosalind back to priorities. "Did you call Charles? The police?"

"They're on the way."

"Papa?"

"He . . . oh, Rosalind—" Her voice broke. "He tried to get up. He—"

Rosalind flew down the hall into her parents' bedroom. She gave her mother a hard hug, then crossed over to the bed where her father lay, tears slipping soundlessly down his cheeks. "Papa . . ." She knelt on the floor beside him and clasped his left hand in both of hers. "Please don't cry, Papa. It's all right. Nobody was injured."

He shook his head, struggling to speak. Ophelia sank onto the bed, next to her husband, and laid a comforting hand on his shoulder. "I understand, dear," she murmured.

Rosalind pressed a kiss to his wet cheek, feeling the roughness of his beard. Her heart lurched as she smoothed disordered wisps of his thinning hair. He'd always been so meticulous about his person.

"I'll come back in a few minutes and tell you what's going on," she promised him. "Mamma will fetch your pad and pencil . . . all right?"

His painful grip on her hand relaxed. He gave her fingers a squeeze—the same firm clasp with which he'd reassured a frightened little girl prone to nightmares. To promise her he was there, that everything was all right.

Rosalind exchanged a single eloquent look with her mother, then rose and left the room. By the time she reached the hall leading to Zeke's and Tallulah's rooms, her own face was wet with tears.

". . . yet you maintain nothing is missing," Sergeant Johnson stated for the third time. Beneath the policeman's cap his stolid face reflected the same doubts Rosalind heard in his voice.

She hung on to her patience and her poise. "That's correct,

which, as I also explained, makes my theory more plausible. He was looking for something."

"Well, he certainly lacked a discerning eye," Charles said. "There's enough money in the objects he ignored to keep an enterprising thief in the lap of luxury for at least a year."

Thoroughly ill-tempered from being dragged across town in the middle of the night, her eldest brother nonetheless had taken care of dealing with the authorities. "I spoke with Oliver. He's agreed for you all to stay there until we get to the bottom of this."

"How thoughtful."

"Don't start, Rosalind." He turned to the sergeant. "Appreciate your coming round so promptly, my good man. I'll see that your superior is notified."

Sergeant Johnson nodded but didn't take the hint to leave. "Ah . . . I wondered, Miss Hayes—if perhaps this was the work of the Catbird?"

Rosalind's heart catapulted to her throat. "I—no. According to Detective Moreaux, he wouldn't behave like this. The Catbird is meticulous, quiet. Undetectable. If he broke into our home, we wouldn't have realized it until we went to fetch a piece of jewelry."

"Do you have to speak as though you knew him personally?" Charles muttered.

"All the same," Sergeant Johnson put in, " 'twould be my advice to alert Pinkerton's. Seems a mite strange for Miss Hayes to have been present for two break-ins in the space of a month, both of them at your family residences."

He took his leave, clomping heavily down the steps and climbing onto his horse. Rosalind scrunched her toes inside her slippers, then reluctantly turned to her brother.

"About the break-in," he announced, peremptory as always. "The policeman didn't catch it because he's a pretty dull sort, but I know your face. There's something you're not sharing, Rosalind."

"I'm about to tell you now, and you're not going to like it." She thought about offering him another mugful of the hot cocoa Tallulah had left on the stove, but decided placating her brother would only delay the inevitable. "I won't be staying with Alberta and Oliver. After Mamma and Papa are settled, as safely and comfortably as I can arrange, I'll be leaving. Something's happened to Isaac, Charles. I'm going to find him. Then I'm going to bring him home, where he belongs."

And while I'm at it, I just might help a panther land a catbird.

23

Victor, Colorado

"JED?"

"Need some help?" the preacher inquired.

"Yeah . . ." He paused, droplets of sweat breaking out across his face. "Can't . . . seem to hold the pen." A ragged, bitter laugh fluttered and died. He heard the slow tread of Jed's footsteps crossing the dark room.

"Ah." Jedidiah matter-of-factly removed the piece of board he'd improvised as a makeshift writing desk, along with the pen and the half-finished letter lying on Isaac's chest. "Here. Take another dose of medicine, then let me help you lie back down. Surviving the ride in the back of that wagon was a miracle of God's grace, but the trip here weakened you a bit."

"How long now?"

His voice was weak, whispery thin, forcing Jedidiah to lean closer in order to hear. Isaac knew the stench from his gangrenous leg was overpowering, but not even a flicker of repugnance crossed the preacher's face. Isaac heard the gentle sound of splashing water, then Jed was smoothing a damp cloth over his face. "Less than a week, probably."

Fear flickered. Drifted away. "Be . . . a relief, I reckon." He managed a feeble smile. "For both of us." A shallow breath rattled in his chest. "Letter. . . . gotta finish . . ."

"I'll finish the letter to your sister," Jed was promising.

117

"Don't worry. Rest now, just for a little while, son. Gather your strength so you'll be able to tell me what you want to say."

As Isaac drifted off again he felt the preacher's hand closing over his wrist, the rough fingers pressing against the pulse.

He woke later from a restless doze. "Jed?"

"I'm here, son. Be at ease."

"Read . . . letter."

"All right." There was silence, then the sound of rustling paper. " 'Dear Rosalind,' " he read, the low rumbling voice washing over Isaac. Calming, reassuring. " 'I never thought I'd be writing this, and I wish, now it's too late, that things had been different at home. Sorry to take advantage of you again, Rosebud . . . you always were too good to me . . . but I need your help, one last time. There's something you need to know. Jed will help—he's a good man. . . . ' " The deep, quiet voice filled the room, and Isaac closed his eyes.

When the preacher finished, he lifted Isaac's hand. "We're placing her life, and the lives of your family, in danger. Is earthly justice worth so much to you, my son?"

"Yes." Stirring, he fixed his wavering vision upon Jed's shadowed face. "Not gonna let Rattray win . . . not fair. Not . . . right."

"Isaac—"

"No . . . listen." Fiery pain savaged his insides. "He'll know. Jed, by now . . . Rattray . . . knows my name." A tortured gasp strangled his breath, but he hung on. "He won't give up, even— after. Gotta protect my family. Tell them, before I—" A groan engulfed the words, and Jedidiah placed a calming hand on his forehead.

"Try to conserve your strength, boy. I . . . I'll think of something. And if your sister Rosalind is as shrewd as she is stubborn, like you told me—she just might figure it out on her own."

PART TWO

RETRIBUTION

24

La Junta, Colorado
Late November

"... AND YOU SAY THIS IS THE MAN who's running a horse Friday afternoon?" Adam asked the Harvey Girl waitress one last time.

"Yes." She ran her fingers over Booker Rattray's grainy likeness on the "Wanted" poster, her smiling eyes solemn. "Too bad. He seemed like such a gentleman, and he left me a lovely tip."

"Being a gentleman doesn't always guarantee a pure heart, much less pure motives, Miss Porter," Adam pointed out, earning a quick sidelong glance. He studied her thoughtfully. "Did you happen to place a small wager on Mr. Rattray's horse?"

"I wanted to. Would have been a sure thing, according to him. Could have had an easy twenty dollars. But Mr. Davis would have sacked me on the spot."

"He might have," Adam agreed mildly. "But he'd also help you find another job. I've known your boss for years, and there are few better men about."

"All the same, I don't see the harm in it."

Neither, Adam thought later as he mounted the horse he'd borrowed, did a host of other rubes who ended up losing more than a job. In his opinion men like Booker Rattray, with their cherubic faces and guileless tongues, were no better than leeches, sucking the life's blood from their unsuspecting victims. *I'm going to nail you one of these days*, he vowed the elderly con artist.

And along with Booker Rattray, perhaps he'd finally bring down the Catbird as well. Hopefully—in between chasing after two of the most elusive criminals in Pinkerton's Rogues' Gallery—he'd find a spare moment or two to help Rosalind Hayes find out what had happened to her irresponsible younger brother.

His motives were murky, ill-defined. What he did know was that Rosalind Hayes needed protection, not only from the Catbird—but more importantly, from herself.

La Junta was located on the western edge of the Great Plains, a dusty desert cow town, its shacks and outbuildings clustered next to the Arkansas River. On the western horizon, the twin mounds of the distant Spanish Peaks offered a hazy, tantalizing glimpse of the mountains. Every time Adam's gaze shifted from the flat desert to these hazy peaks, his insides clenched with longing.

The "racetrack" two miles out of town consisted of a beaten-down oval of dirt surrounded by an unpainted rail, and a ring of horses and buggies. Adam pulled up and dismounted near some men arguing about the merits of the two horses racing that day. A few of the men glanced his way, but when Adam nodded, touched the brim of his hat, and sauntered off, the argument resumed with barely a pause.

He watched most of the proceedings aloof and alone, as the majority of spectators were a blend of town locals and cowhands from area ranches. His appearance for once elicited little more than an occasional shrug.

Over the course of the afternoon, he learned a couple of things. First off, that he didn't have the eye for horseflesh necessary to distinguish a ringer from a winner. More significantly, that if Booker Rattray did show up with one of his schemes, exposure might lead to a swift, quite final lynching. These men took their horse racing seriously indeed, no matter that the animals were local steeds bred, from the look of it, mostly to chase steers and provide transportation.

That evening Adam sent two telegrams—one to Maxwell Connelly, the other to Simon Kincaid, who wasn't likely to thank him for it. At least Connelly's terse message provided some leverage. "Kincaid best judge of horseflesh west of the Mississippi. Probably east. Best of luck luring out of retirement. Name of miscreant should help. Compensation minimal. Letter follows."

The following morning a bellboy delivered both the superintendent's promised letter and a telegram from Sim. Adam glanced at the letter but ripped open the telegram first. "On the way" was all it said. Adam smiled, not realizing until then how tense he had been about his friend's response. Simon and Elizabeth had been married less than six months, and Adam knew the couple wouldn't relish the separation.

He'd been right to dread Connelly's letter.

Rosalind Hayes, the hardheaded woman, was on her way to La Junta, with the intention of helping Adam capture Booker Rattray.

". . . and when I persuaded her (an accomplishment in itself) to describe the 'good Samaritan' who stopped by with news of her brother, the description—surprisingly lucid—matched to a chilling degree our Rogues' file description of Booker Rattray. When I showed her his likeness, she admitted he was the same man, using the moniker Nathaniel Beale. I am of the strong opinion that you should cooperate with Miss Hayes in securing evidence against Rattray, but recommend that you send her back to Denver as soon as possible thereafter."

Translated, in three days Miss Hayes would arrive on the afternoon train from Denver, doubtless with blood in her eye. Adam stroked his chin, very real amusement vying with his frustration. Trying to control Rosalind Hayes would be akin to riding herd on a roomful of hungry cats. On the whole, he tended to feel almost sorry for Booker the Snooker.

25

"MY SUPERINTENDENT IS STILL NURSING the emotional bruises you inflicted," Adam greeted Rosalind when he handed her down from the train late Friday afternoon. He took her worn leather case from the porter. "Tired? You look—" *Dead on your feet*, he'd started to say, then checked himself.

"I'm sure I look like every other weary traveler, Mr. Moreaux." She straightened her coat and checked the pins holding her hat in place. "Insults, however, won't prompt me to go back to Denver."

"Too bad," Adam returned. "And I'd readied a whole arsenal of them, just for you."

"Nothing you say or do will prompt me to return to Denver," she repeated.

Adam shifted his grip to her elbow and steered her around a clutch of noisy cowboys.

Rosalind pointed to her trunk, and he hefted it down from a flatbed piled high with freight, nodding to the relieved baggageman. "Did you pack every feminine frippery you own, along with your personal maid? This trunk weighs as much as my horse."

"How often do you carry your horse, Mr. Moreaux?"

Grinning, Adam desisted. At least she no longer looked as though she might pass out at his feet. "Is the Bible in your hand case or the trunk?" he asked after he and the baggageman had loaded her luggage into the rental buggy.

"Hand case. I didn't want it out of my sight."

"Good." He handed her up, climbed in after her, and picked up the reins. "Do you know how to handle a buggy?" When she nodded, looking puzzled, Adam plucked the carrying case off her lap, then transferred the lines to her hands. "You drive. We're going to the racetrack, by the way. It's two miles outside town, down this road. Don't worry, Buddy here's a dependable sort as long as you treat his mouth gently."

"Mr. Connelly told me you're staying at the Harvey Hotel here, and that you reserved a room for me."

Adam nodded, his mind on the Bible. He retrieved it from the case and opened it to the first page Rosalind had marked. Second chapter of Genesis. *"Toward the east?"* Hardly inspirational at first glance, yet there *were* spiritual applications. . . .

"Is that the hotel?" She gestured across the street.

He glanced up absently, nodded again. "You're lucky all the meals won't consist of cold beans and stale tortillas—here now! The track's the other way."

"I need to freshen up first."

Adam closed the cover of the Bible. "The racing," he pointed out with what he thought was commendable mildness, "starts in an hour."

"I'll be ready in thirty minutes. We'll have plenty of time."

She expertly maneuvered them across the crowded street, pulled up in front of the hotel, and then just as expertly squeezed between a loaded buckboard and a pair of dozing cow ponies. "Stay here and study Pastor Scrivens' Bible, if you like. I've started a list of those underlined verses on a piece of paper, folded once." She sent him a mischievous smile. "Tucked in the book of Revelation. I thought that might help."

Adam smiled in spite of his annoyance. But regardless of Rosalind Hayes' nimble mind and adventurous spirit, he wasn't prepared to allow her to run the show. "If you're not back in twenty minutes, I'll leave without you."

"But I need—" She clamped her lips together. "All right. Twenty minutes, Mr. Moreaux."

"Call me Adam, or I'll leave in fifteen." He kept the smile in place, but this time he wasn't teasing. Rosalind searched his face for a long moment, and Adam saw the knowledge creep into her eyes.

"Why are you being so contrary about this? Just because it isn't proper—or to irritate me?"

"Mostly because it riles you." He paused. "There is another reason . . . Rosalind. You're an unusual woman in many respects, full of grit and intelligence. But you're in over your head here—and not only with Booker Rattray." He stroked the scarred leather cover of the Bible as he spoke, his gaze never leaving hers. "You're not here because you bullied Superintendent Connelly, or because you've decided Rattray's your best hope of finding your brother."

"I didn't bully—"

"You're here because the Catbird is chasing Booker Rattray. And since you're still the only living person who can identify either of them on sight, the *real* reason you're not being herded back on the next northbound train . . . is because you're Pinkerton's best hope."

"I've already promised to help in any way I can."

She held her head high and back, while beneath the hem of a fine merino gown her foot began tapping the floorboard. So he'd pushed her a bit too far, had he? All the better. Adam had realized early on that an off-balance Rosalind Hayes was far more malleable.

Unfortunately, she wasn't off-balance enough.

"I'll help, *after* you help me find my brother Isaac." With majestic hauteur she turned to get out of the buggy.

Adam reached swiftly across, closing his hand around her wrist. "I think not." Through butter-soft leather gloves he felt her pulse accelerate. "Listen . . . this isn't a battle between you and Pinkerton's."

He released her wrist, grappling with the need to elaborate, wary of Rosalind's response. The need for her to understand won. "In my mind, it's more a battle between good and evil. Doesn't matter that the evil is packaged inside a congenial old man or an attractive thief—no, don't shake your head at me.

126

I've watched you from the beginning, remember. Intellectually you know that the Catbird's a criminal—but you're also fascinated by him."

He expected her to deny, argue, and was already composing his reply when her low-voiced confession exploded the last of his preconceptions about Rosalind Hayes.

"I . . . you're right. And I'm ashamed of it." Her gaze slid away. "Perhaps that's one of the reasons I've been consumed with finding Isaac. It seemed—safer."

In spite of his amazement at her candor, Adam kept his response neutral to spare further embarrassment—even the tip of Rosalind's nose was flaming a deep rose color. "I'm glad you can at least admit it. The Catbird's that breed of man who deceives women into trusting him. Apparently with little effort."

"I didn't—!"

"Easy now. I've realized you're astute enough not to trust him. What I'm not sure of is whether I can convince you to trust *me*. So . . . call me Adam."

"That's absurd. Trust has nothing to do with being on a first-name basis."

"Ah . . . but it does engender a sense of familiarity." Deliberately he lifted a hand to brush his fingers against her cheek.

Automatically she jerked her head aside.

With a pang of regret he hadn't anticipated, Adam sat back. "This isn't a drawing room, Rosalind, or Miss Fanny's School of Manners for Young Ladies. Either abide by my rules, or I'll stuff you on the next train to Denver so fast you'll be ten miles out of town before your breath catches up."

"Why?" she demanded. "I don't understand you, Mr. Mor—Adam, then! If I really behaved the way you're implying, I'd never have gone to Manitou Springs alone, never seen—much less followed—the Catbird. And I certainly wouldn't be here in this dirty little town, trying to help capture him."

Adam studied her frustrated face. Indignation had disguised the pallor of fatigue, darkening the green eyes and rouging her cheeks. Beneath the perky velveteen hat, a single tendril of mink brown hair had slipped free of pins, unfurling down the side of her neck. In spite of the errant hair, she was still one of the most carefully groomed, perfectly decked-out society belles he'd ever had the misfortune of wrangling with.

Yet with a force that almost tumbled him out of his seat, Adam realized how much he wanted to sift that silky-looking hair between his fingers. Rip the stylish hat from her head and tickle her chin with the long pheasant feather. Make her lose that infernal starchiness, the ladylike perfection that irritated him like woolen long johns.

If he were smart, he'd run as fast and as far as he could from Rosalind Hayes.

On the other hand, he'd never been able to resist a challenge. And he did need her help. "You're right." He waited a beat before adding, "But you still have to call me Adam." He lifted a hand, stilling her response. "I'll spell it out for you. This is a test of sorts. A measure of how much you're willing to trust me, trust my judgment."

Her gaze rested on the Bible in his lap, and all at once she looked lost, and vulnerable.

Deliberately, he hardened his voice. "And lack of trust— Rosalind—could cost both of us our lives."

26

Perkins, Colorado

MR. FENWICK CLOSED the jewelry store promptly at five every evening. Moments later, a light would appear through the windows over the store where the store owner lived in a couple of rooms. LaRue knew this, because he had searched the upstairs rooms earlier in the day, when Fenwick had been helping a dithering matron select a pair of gold cuff links.

It was a little past ten now, and the street was quiet, deserted. Predictable provincial mentality, LaRue thought. He flexed his hands as he slipped from shadow to shadow, silently working his way down the street to the jeweler's. Why people lived in a backwater place like Perkins he'd never understood, but for tonight it made his task easier. Rattray must have figured he would be safe, unloading some of LaRue's darlings on a half-blind, unsuspecting mark who wouldn't know a quality gem from a piece of hard candy.

The two-timing Judas might have gotten away with it, too, if he hadn't stolen the Petrovna Parure. LaRue would search every one-horse town from ocean to ocean to recover the prize of a lifetime. He'd prowl every hole-in-the-wall saloon, every house of ill repute, and every gambling palace until he caught up with his business partner. Make that his *former* business partner.

He still couldn't understand why, after all these years, Rattray would pull such a stunt. LaRue would have been eaten up with rage if the sense of betrayal hadn't gnawed his insides with pain instead.

It was time. He listened, waiting until the desert wind accelerated into restless gusts. If he accidentally stepped on a squeaking board, the noise would blend in with the other night sounds.

Moments later he slipped inside the jewelry store, quietly shutting the door. Fenwick kept the safe in a small back room. Easy pickings. After stuffing a strip of dark cloth beneath the door, LaRue switched on a lamp.

Within seconds he had opened the safe. His gaze fell on the neat trays of jewelry. Not much here, he realized with a prick of annoyance. Quickly he scanned and discarded a couple of inexpensive lockets, all the jet pins and ear bobs, and a dozen gemstone brooches. None of the quality worthy of the Catbird, though it was probably just as well.

By now reports of his Colorado forays would have reached the ears of the Pinks. The last thing LaRue needed was a trail blatant enough for a blind man, much less that big fellow who dressed like an Indian scout. The botched Denver job had almost turned into an out-and-out disaster, courtesy of the Catbird's silent nemesis.

One day, LaRue promised himself, he was going to have to do something about the detective known as Panther.

A small velvet sack in the back corner quickened his breathing. Without touching the other pieces, LaRue deftly lifted the pouch, then dumped the contents into his palm.

So. The old fox really had betrayed him. Regret tasted bitter on his tongue. He held the Egyptian motif cornelian bracelet up so the light fell across the translucent red gemstones, allowing the memory to soothe the bitterness.

Ten months ago . . . a boisterous thunderstorm. The owner of the bracelet, LaRue recalled with a smile as he caressed the delicate links, had jumped at every thunderclap. He'd watched her for a long time, amused by the clawlike fingers clutching her escort. The irritated gentleman finally removed them himself. When he abandoned her on the flimsy pretext of fetching refreshments, all LaRue had had to do was offer a consoling smile and his arm. By the time the next drumroll of thunder faded, the bracelet was in his pocket.

Booker Rattray had almost deprived him of the exquisite piece.

The man would pay for his perfidy.

Thirty minutes later, foot propped on the saloon counter's brass boot rest, LaRue ordered a well-earned drink. The loquacious barkeep remembered Rattray—had served him two days earlier. Now they were discussing the weather. "Yes," LaRue agreed congenially, "I do believe you're right. The wind feels as though it might be blowing in a storm. Hope my train's not delayed."

"Where you headed? Santa Fe, was it?"

"That's right," LaRue lied. "This is a nice little town. Sure am sorry I can't stay longer."

The barkeep shrugged. "Most folks don't. Fact is, we don't have too many strangers in these parts. That's why I knew right off 'bout your friend. Funny thing about it, now that I study on it—he said the same thing you did. Thought this was a real nice town. Said he was sorry he'd arranged to meet some friends up in La Junta. Something about a horse race?"

27

La Junta

IF MR. BEALE—RATTRAY, Rosalind corrected herself—was in La Junta, it was beginning to look as though it wasn't to fix a horse race or two. For over an hour she and Mr. Moreaux had mingled with the good-natured, oftimes boisterous crowd, strolling about, always with an eye on the track.

She craned her neck now, trying to see around the burly man who'd moved in front of her. Rosalind's fingers itched to remove his derby. She was about to tap his shoulder when Adam's arm snaked past her, the fringe of his buckskins tickling her face.

His hand dropped onto the burly man's shoulder. "I'm afraid you're enjoying the view at this lady's expense, friend. How about if you step aside and let her in front of you?"

The man glanced around, flushing. "Beg pardon, ma'am." He immediately shifted.

Rosalind sweetly thanked him, scanning the other side of the track, where two horses were being led to the starting line. A lusty cheer heralded their arrival, and the riders grinned, waving at the crowd. One of the horses, a bay, tossed its head, then tried to lunge forward.

"Keep him steady, Fred!" a cultured masculine voice called in friendly warning. "Got a bundle riding on this one. . . ."

Rosalind inhaled, her head swiveling sharply.

"What is it?" Adam asked. Then, more urgently, "Where?"

"By the gate. Next to the cowboy with the ten-gallon hat and red kerchief."

She was grateful her voice didn't betray her alarm. Between the shock of actually seeing the man who had called himself Nathaniel Beale, and being pressed by the crowd much too close to Adam Moreaux, Rosalind was surprised that her tongue could shape a coherent syllable. "He's wearing a striped suit, black derby, and . . . boots! He's wearing a pair of boots."

"Good girl," Adam murmured in her ear.

She tried to step away, but there was nowhere to go except through the fence. She took a deep breath and ignored the strange, not unpleasant sensations prickling her skin. "I wouldn't have recognized him if he hadn't called out to the rider. He hasn't completely disguised his southern drawl."

"Wait until the gun goes off and the attention is focused on the race. We'll work our way to the back of the crowd and come up behind him."

Two minutes later, ears still ringing from the pistol's loud report, Rosalind found herself herded through a crush of cheering, waving spectators, both male and female. She tried to picture one of her mother's friends screaming at the top of her lungs, but the image defeated her. With a start Rosalind realized how much she herself longed to join the enthusiastic crowd. "I had hoped to watch the race," she commented when she could speak without yelling.

Adam, the insensitive oaf, laughed. "Perhaps another time," he promised. His expression sobered. "Do you remember what I told you in the buggy?"

"Let him see me. Act surprised. Be quiet and listen to his response. Let you set the tone. I understand. Stop looking like a nervous schoolmaster waiting to see what the troublemaking pupil does during the performance of a school play."

Almost laughing at his expression, Rosalind felt the brief attack of jitters fade. She actually found herself looking forward to the pending confrontation. It was exhilarating, this business of chasing criminals. Of helping to see that justice was done. Booker Rattray deserved to spend the rest of his life behind bars, and hang it all, she relished having a part in placing him there.

Adam's hand closed over her wrist. "I think he's about to spot you."

There wasn't time to prepare. The small group of cowhands and townspeople surrounding Booker Rattray had dwindled. He nodded to acknowledge some remark as he smoothed the crumpled bills filling his hands with a skill and speed that should have sent decent folk running. Tucking the money inside his coat, he half turned, a congenial smile blossoming across the flushed round face.

"Mr. Beale!" Rosalind exclaimed, stepping forward. "What a surprise! Imagine meeting you here like this."

"Miss . . . Hayes?" A barely perceptible flicker of his eyelids was the only reaction Mr. Rattray betrayed. "What an unexpected delight. Um . . . I wouldn't have thought . . . I mean—are you here for pleasure? Have you learned news of your brother?"

His questions were perfectly plausible, Rosalind realized. Nonplussed, she went blank. She had expected dismay, blustering, stammering—anything but this urbane performance that had thrown *her* into a state of confusion instead.

"Your escort?" Rattray nodded to Adam. In spite of the western-style boots, the old man, complete with derby and walking cane, looked like nothing more than a distinguished gentleman out to enjoy an afternoon at the races.

"I . . . yes. Yes, it is." Rosalind performed the introductions, then turned to Adam with a fierce smile. "Mr. Beale's the gentleman who wants to help find Isaac."

Calmer now, she watched Rattray loop the cane over his left wrist so the two men could shake hands. "Mr. Moreaux's an operative with Pinkerton's Detective Agency." For effect, she added a guileless smile. "We've secured their services to help us—why, Mr. Beale, what's the matter?"

"You look ill." Adam stepped close. "Need a hand? Where's your buggy?" He made as though to put a helping arm around the older man's shoulders.

"Thank you, but no." Rattray tugged out a large handkerchief and mopped his perspiring brow. "I have these spells, unfortunately." He tucked the snowy white square away, and smiled. "They're a nuisance, but then I'm not getting any younger, so—"

"Hey, you!" an angry voice shouted. "I *thought* it was you— you conniving cheat!" A red-faced man shoved his way through the crowd. "I swore if I ever saw you again, you'd regret it." He tore off his jacket, slung it and his derby to the ground, and rolled up his shirt sleeves.

"Perhaps we'd better—" Adam's hand closed over her arm. Rosalind pressed her lips together and waited, every nerve leaping.

"Calm yourself, my good man." Rattray took a nervous step backward. "I'm not sure who you think I am—"

"You're the four-flushing, smooth-talking cheat who sold me ten thousand dollars' worth of shares not six months ago in a mine that played out four *years* ago!" the man yelled. "And now I'm going to give you what's coming to you. . . ."

"I think not," Adam said—and bedlam erupted.

28

SNARLING, THE ENRAGED MAN drew back his fist and landed a bruising blow on Adam's cheekbone. A nearby cowhand made a grab for the attacker's arm, but with another lurid oath, the man lashed out again, knocking the cowboy against Adam. Rosalind felt someone grabbing her, thrusting her out of harm's way as a half dozen whooping cowhands entered the melee.

Screams and shouts filled the air. Heart racing, Rosalind finally managed to turn her head to thank her rescuer—Booker Rattray! Instead of releasing her, he began to pull her toward a nearby line of buggies.

"Let go!" she ordered.

Mr. Rattray ignored her.

Rosalind twisted against the restraining hands, knowing that Adam was smack in the middle of the flailing arms and flying fists, unable to help her. "Let *go* of me!" she demanded again.

"Not on your life, girlie." The cultured tone had disappeared, along with the congenial expression. "You're coming with me."

Furious, Rosalind dug her heels into the hard-packed earth. She might as well have tried to stop a stampede. Mr. Rattray was at least sixty years or more, with a banker's portly girth,

136

but he still possessed the strength of a bull. Rosalind changed tactics, jerking her arm at the same time she kicked out at his shin with her hard-soled half boot.

"Feisty piece, aren't you?" He panted, grimacing, but not relaxing his punishing hold on her upper arm.

"Let me go, *Booker Rattray*!" She yelled the name, all of Adam's careful instructions forgotten.

The shock reflected in the pudgy face reverberated all the way through his body, causing him to loosen his grip. Rosalind instantly pulled free. She had taken only two steps when his walking cane whipped across her middle. Gasping, she doubled over, the unexpected pain almost bringing her to her knees.

"Come quietly, or the next time you'll end up in the dirt, Miss Hayes. I don't want to harm you, but I'll do what I have to."

Outraged, wanting nothing so much as to hit *him*, Rosalind instead allowed the man to march her a half dozen steps. Where was Adam? He should have extricated himself from that wretched scuffle by now.

Rattray seemed to be maneuvering them toward a closed phaeton parked under a cottonwood tree. Rosalind walked another few steps without protest, then dug in her heels again.

"What have you done to my brother?" She hurled the question, hoping to catch him off guard a second time.

Rattray turned on her, the one-handed grip shifting so that he held both her upper arms in an unbreakable vise. "Your brother ruined my life!" He shook her. "Because of him, I'll never be safe again!"

"It's because of the Catbird that you'll never be safe." Rosalind braced her palms against his shirtfront and pushed. "Tell me what you've done to my brother!"

"What do you know?" His grip tightened, and she fought not to cry out. His face had turned from the shade of a ripe plum to a sickly gray. He shook her again, harder. "*What do you know?* It's impossible—he fell over a cliff. . . ."

A roaring buzz filled her head, drowning out the surrounding noise. Rosalind quit fighting. She could barely shape the words. "Who fell? Mr. Rattray . . . who fell over a cliff?"

All trace of Rattray's former self-confidence was gone. His expression now reminded her of a hunted animal. "He stole the Petrovna Parure," he said, his voice hoarse. "He stole it . . . and I have to find it." His eyes focused on Rosalind. "It's not just my life anymore—you'll find out."

Rosalind paid scant attention to the incoherent ramblings. Only one issue mattered—Isaac. "My brother," she repeated. "Where's my brother, Mr. Rattray?"

"Your brother's . . . dead."

Her gaze fixed on Rattray's sweat-slick face. "I don't believe you."

But the old man was looking over her head now, his fingers digging into her shoulders. "The little sneak's dead," he muttered. "He deserves to be dead. And you'll be next. The Catbird will hunt you down, same as he is me. He'll do anything to get it back. Anything . . ."

He shoved her away. Caught off-balance, Rosalind fell, crashing gracelessly into the dirt. She rolled to her knees in time to glimpse Rattray scrambling into the phaeton.

He yanked down the curtain and cracked the whip, urging the horse to a reckless gallop across the open desert.

29

ADAM REACHED HER SIDE just as Rosalind managed to regain her feet. "I'm . . . all right. Rattray's in that buggy. If you hurry—"

"Don't be foolish." He steadied her, frowning when she winced. "Can you walk?"

"Of course. Just turned my ankle, I think." Impatiently she took a step, all her attention riveted on the fleeing Booker Rattray. "Oh! Oh, dear . . . that smarts a bit." She would have collapsed if Adam hadn't wrapped his arm around her waist.

"A bit, hmm?" He helped her limp across to the cottonwood tree. "Here. Sit down, and let me see your ankle."

"Adam, Booker Rattray's escaping. If you don't hurry, you'll lose him." She sat, unable to resist the pressure of his hands, though she'd die before admitting he was right.

Adam shaded his eyes with one hand. "He's headed for town, probably the next train out. Can't be helped."

"Can't be helped?" Rosalind echoed in disbelief. "What's the matter with you? How can you just let him get away like that? Where's your gumption? Your . . . honor?"

With casual grace he dropped down beside her. "Take it easy." His voice was surprisingly gentle. "Here." He dug into a small leather pouch fastened to his belt and pulled out a piece of peppermint candy. "Suck on this. Sit quietly, then you can tell me what happened while I was escaping from a dozen rowdy men looking for any excuse to enjoy a good dust-up."

Rosalind took the candy, ashamed of her trembling fingers, grateful when Adam didn't comment on them. The sticky sweet did help. After a few moments she leaned back against the rough bark of the tree trunk. "Sorry. I'm glad you're still in one piece, though I'm not surprised. I'm . . . only a bit shaken, truly—more by what Rattray said than by his manhandling."

"What did he say?"

Rosalind swallowed hard, staring at her dirt-smeared gloves. Her best and last pair of good gloves, and now they were likely ruined. . . . She couldn't think about her cloak or the skirt she had made from a bolt of prime English superfine just this past spring. Most of all, she couldn't think about . . . Isaac.

"Rosalind?" All of a sudden his hand was cupping her chin, lifting her face. "I know you've had a shock, but you must tell me everything he said. Take your time, but tell me."

Shocked by the tenderness of his tone, Rosalind blinked. "He told me . . . my brother Isaac is dead."

Adam stilled, then his breath gusted out in a sigh. "I see. That explains a lot. He's a liar, Rosalind. Probably trying to jar you into revealing something."

Chagrin flooded her. "I'm afraid I did—reveal something, that is. I called him Booker Rattray."

"Ah. And how did the unflappable 'Mr. Beale' respond?"

Rosalind searched his veiled expression. All the way from town he'd reminded her over and over not to slip up and let Rattray suspect she knew his true identity. She'd ruin an ongoing investigation of some months by tipping the Agency's hand . . . possibly spoil their chances for finding the Catbird— perhaps even her brother. . . . "Why aren't you angry?" she asked.

A flicker of something like sheepishness glinted, disappeared. He shifted, leaning back against the tree himself, and removed his fierce-looking knife. "When I was in Denver, I asked about you and your family," he replied obliquely, testing the knife blade with his thumb. "I learned about your father's stroke. About how your older brother lives in his Capitol Hill

mansion, and your sister and her husband in theirs—leaving
all the burden of your father's care to you."

"I was still living at home, unmarried," Rosalind mumbled.
"There was no reason to move my father out of familiar surroundings—what am I saying?" She scooted away, ignoring the
dust collecting on her favorite cloak. "Stop changing the subject—*diverting* me, or whatever it is you're doing. If you're
angry, just say so. I'm not going to collapse in a sniveling bundle. I'm certainly not going to give you more fodder with which
to demean my character like everyone else tries to do."

"Who else tries to demean you?" he probed softly. "Your . . .
family? Friends?"

She stared at a scuff mark on her boot. "What difference
does it make? All you need to know is that it only makes me
more . . . determined." She refused to admit to any other emotion, especially to the unsettling, intuitive man beside her.

"Now *that* I believe. It strikes me, Rosalind, that you could
out-stubborn a fence post. Ahh. Calm down—I'm actually paying you a compliment of sorts."

"Then I'd hate to hear a criticism," she sputtered.

"Don't worry." He tilted his head, studying her for a long,
uncomfortable moment. "You've a strong sense of family loyalty and far more pride than is wise. I'm trying to decide
whether it's the loyalty—or the pride—that compelled you to
flout all your precious social conventions in order to find out
what happened to your brother. I'm trying to decide, Rosalind,
how much *I* can trust *you*."

"I see." She stared at her hands, for the first time facing the
risk she had posed—not only to herself, but to Adam. And was
ashamed, because she had actually considered herself as capable as this highly trained Pinkerton operative. A man revered
by peers and grudgingly respected by foes. A man whose reputation stretched from San Francisco to Boston.

In the past four years, Rosalind had grown accustomed to
being in charge. Competency was never an issue: if she couldn't
do something, she worked until she mastered whatever task
had arisen. She felt compelled to atone not only for her brother's lack of responsibility—but also for that secret part of her-

self that yearned to follow his selfish example.

Somehow Adam Moreaux had sensed her divided heart almost from the very beginning.

Absently she began a feeble attempt to brush the dust from her gloves. "Um . . . if I confess to the sin of willfulness, will you tell me why you're not pursuing Booker Rattray?"

"Ah. Are you? Committing the 'sin of willfulness,' that is."

She was only making the stain worse and pressed her palms together. "Not deliberately."

Another uncomfortably long pause ensued.

Sighing, Rosalind lifted her gaze to the horizon, where a fiery glow burned the western sky and the darkened bulk of the mountains seemed to swell as they swallowed the dying sun. "I just knew I had to come, even if I wasn't sure what I was getting myself into," she finally admitted. "But I do know I can help, if you'll give me another chance."

"What would you do," Adam asked, "if I said no?"

Rosalind felt as though she'd been immersed inside an airless box, her only view Adam's alert, patient eyes. "I'd feel, well, a fair amount of shame. Some guilt. But I wouldn't quit searching for answers on my own. My family disowned Isaac. I think they're wrong. He might be reckless and irresponsible—but he's not evil. Not like Booker Rattray and the Catbird." She dropped her gaze, confused by Adam Moreaux's expression. "Do you have any family, Adam? Parents? Brothers or sisters? If one of them was the victim of Booker Rattray, would you turn your back, leave them to suffer the consequences alone?"

"Probably not." He paused. "As for family, I don't have any I can claim. I . . . never knew my mother. My father died when I was twenty. But he was the godliest man I've ever known." A wistful smile lifted the corners of his mouth. "When I'm alone up in the mountains, sometimes I catch myself talking to him instead of to God. Wondering if he approves of what I'm doing, what he'd advise if he were still around—"

His expression hardened. "It's hard to admit, but I would probably have hunted down anyone who harmed my father—regardless of the consequences."

"Then why—"

142

"But first I would have taken the precaution to learn how to go about it, so I wouldn't send the guilty party bolting down the road, out of reach."

The matter-of-fact censure stung, even delivered gently. "Then teach me what I need to know, so that next time I'll do better." Rosalind waited, her heart hammering. "There *will* be a next time?"

Adam stood, then lifted Rosalind to her feet as well, balancing her until she was steady. "Yes," he said. "There will definitely be a next time, Rosalind Hayes. I've always admired a woman with . . . spunk." The long fingers flexed, holding her a little too close before he released her.

Relief flooded Rosalind, coupled with a strange lightness that sent her heart soaring. "I've always admired a man who admired a woman with spunk," she retorted loftily.

Adam smiled. "Fair enough. Then let's be off. There's a lot to do."

Rosalind's smile faded. "I know. Now we have to find Booker Rattray all over again."

"Not," returned Adam, "with Simon Kincaid shadowing him."

"Simon Kincaid?"

"Superintendent Connelly sent him along on the same train as you. Most likely he even secured a seat in the same coach. You wouldn't have noticed—Sim's moniker when he was still an operative was 'Smoke.' He's been following us all afternoon, with orders to watch Rattray once the quarry put in an appearance. Probably would have broken his cover to rescue you, if I hadn't been able to."

"In that case, I'm glad he didn't have to."

He put a hand beneath her elbow to help her across an uneven patch of earth. "And friend Rattray would have more chance of losing his own shadow than he would of losing my old friend Simon Kincaid."

30

THEY REACHED THE OUTSKIRTS OF TOWN as the sun slid behind the mountains in a burnt orange puddle. "Pretty sunset," Rosalind said.

"Mm . . ."

"Turns cold in a hurry here, doesn't it?" Oh, that was even better. Next, she'd be making some equally trivial comment about night sounds. Obviously Adam preferred his own thoughts. She fiddled with the seam on her gloves and tried to keep from squirming on the seat.

"Rosalind?"

"Yes?" she prompted when he didn't continue. It was almost dark now, but a passing streetlight briefly reflected an almost saturnine cast to his face. Cold shivers roughed her skin. "Adam? What is it?"

Two horses loped by, their riders touching their hats in greeting. Adam nodded back but didn't speak until they'd pulled up in front of the sheriff's office.

After securing the reins and setting the brake, he half turned in the seat. "Are you going to be able to handle it if Booker Rattray was telling the truth about Isaac?"

"I don't have any choice, do I?" Rosalind set about tidying her person, smoothing wrinkles, shaking dust out of her cloak—anything to achieve a semblance of control. "I've waited every day for the past four years, wondering if the postman would deliver a letter with the news. If a telegram would arrive . . . or even a telephone call. I used to think Mr. Bell's invention was the miracle of our generation—but, of course, I never expected to hear an impersonal, disembodied voice telling me my brother was dead."

Absently she began to count the number of bars covering the windows on either side of the sheriff's office. "It's impossible to prepare for that kind of news, of course. But if you're asking whether or not I'd collapse into hysterical tears, the answer is . . . no. At least, I hope not."

"Let's leave it with the firm 'no.' " Adam leaped lightly to the ground, then strode around to help Rosalind. "I think we've delayed about as long as we should. Ready now?"

Was that what he was doing? Stalling? Allowing her a chance to . . . gather her resources? She gathered the hem of her skirt and climbed the steps to the sidewalk. "Thank you, but the delay wasn't necessary. I'm quite capable of taking care of myself."

She started when his hand pressed against the small of her back, offering both support and guidance. "Possibly," he said. "But I couldn't seem to help myself. You're full of contrasts, Rosalind Hayes. Being around you is a bit like"—he reached around her to open the door—"like handling my friend Kat. She's a very independent-minded gal herself. But every so often, she comes to me for a little comfort and companionship, even when she doesn't quite understand her need."

"Kat?" Rosalind whispered. What would it be like, she wondered longingly, to have someone like Adam Moreaux speak to her with a seductive blend of respect and affection?

"Kat," Adam stepped aside to allow her to precede him. "She's my partner when I'm working in the mountains between Denver and Pikes Peak. Unlike you, she won't go near a town, much less a city."

A *woman* partner?

Mystified, Rosalind stepped into the office, a large square room with few amenities. The sheriff, a barrel-chested man with a badge pinned crookedly to his vest, hip propped against the desk, was talking to another man, probably the operative Adam had told her about. Whipcord lean, the second man turned to face them now, and Rosalind found herself under yet another thorough scrutiny.

31

"ONLY FOR YOU WOULD I BE EATING dust and dirtying my hands with riffraff," the man announced, his affection for Adam obvious. He crossed the room and the two men exchanged unselfconscious bear hugs. "Good to see you, Panther. Especially in one piece, even if you look—"

"Never mind how I look, Sim." Adam lifted his hand, wincing when he touched the bruised skin. "This is nothing but a misdirected blow, aimed, by the way, at friend Rattray."

"Sorry, pal. I thought about intervening when I saw you go down. But by then he'd grabbed Miss Hayes." He turned to Rosalind. "Since Adam's not long on social convention, I'll introduce myself. Simon Kincaid, Deer Creek, Montana."

She offered her hand. "Rosalind Hayes. I'm relieved to meet you, Mr. Kincaid. I'm afraid I wasn't very polite myself when Mr. Moreaux refused to chase Booker Rattray down. You *did* apprehend him, didn't you?"

"Yes, ma'am, that he did," the sheriff supplied, strolling over to join them. "And the culprit's resting nicely in my best cell. Sort of peculiar, actually. Almost seemed like he was pleased to be in custody." He scratched his whiskered chin. "Next breath, he's oozing like a cussed snake-oil salesman, trying to convince me the two of you are the ones who ought to be behind bars."

"Doesn't surprise me a bit." Adam exchanged a look with

Simon that Rosalind couldn't interpret.

"I trust you turned a deaf ear to his 'oozing,'" she said to the sheriff.

"Might not have myself, but Mr. Kincaid here's not one I'd care to trifle with." Chuckling, he returned to the desk, riffled through a stack of "Wanted" posters and pulled one out. "This flyer added weight, you might say. Also Mr. Kincaid told me about your attempted abduction, ma'am. We don't take too kindly to such, hereabouts."

Rosalind glanced at the poster. "May I speak to Mr. Rattray?"

The sheriff shot a questioning look at Adam, then shrugged and shuffled over to retrieve a ring of keys. "Be my guest, but it won't do much good. Man speaks out of both sides of his mouth. Don't expect you'll get any kind of confession out of that one."

"Miss Hayes has reason to believe Rattray's withholding information about her brother," Adam explained, following Rosalind across the room. He glanced at Simon Kincaid. "We're at the Harvey House. My room's twelve. Meet me there in a couple of hours?"

The other operative inclined his head. Then he vanished, as silently and swiftly as—a puff of smoke.

While she waited for the sheriff to unlock the door, Rosalind concentrated on controlling her breathing. She offered Adam a fleeting smile. "I trust you didn't let him keep his walking cane," she tried to joke. "It would make an effective weapon."

The jangle of keys assaulted her ears. The barred windows and the sheriff's holstered pistol unnerved her. What was she doing in this alien, violent world?

Suddenly a warm hand closed over her elbow, and the smell of leather filled her nostrils. "I'm here," Adam murmured softly. "Regardless of what he claims, I promise to uncover the truth."

The sheriff opened the door and stood back to allow them to enter the dark hallway. When the door closed with a heavy thunk, Rosalind froze on the spot, as though her shoes were nailed to the plank flooring.

"I never finished telling you about Kat," Adam said.

"What?" Out of the corner of her eye, Rosalind glimpsed the stirring of a shadowed figure in the cell at the end of the short corridor. "Stop trying to distract me. It won't work—"

"She's a mountain lion. Cougar, my dad always used to say. Makes a dandy trail companion, and she's unmatched for stalking." Eerily cougarlike eyes gazed down at her with something like compassion.

"Kat's a . . . a *cat*?" Rosalind wanted to press her fingers against her throbbing temples. "Not a woman?"

Down the way, Booker Rattray moved across his cell to the bars. "Well, well, well, what a surprise. Fancy seeing you here, Miss Hayes," he called. "How nice of you to drop by."

"Kat's really a cat," Adam's voice whispered in her ear, forcing her to listen to him instead of Rattray's taunts. "But while she may not be a woman, she's definitely female. Bit of sweetness, claws I stay clear of . . . temperamental, too, like most ladies."

Bristling, Rosalind suppressed the urge to jab him with her elbow. "Don't you bait me, Adam Moreaux."

"Wouldn't dream of it, Rosalind Hayes." His fingers folded around her elbow and gently squeezed. "Ready to dig those claws into Booker Rattray now?"

"If I don't dig them into you first," she muttered, but the sick uncertainty had faded.

"The two of you sure are cozy," Rattray said. "Tell you what. Think perhaps we can come to some sort of agreement, just the three of us?"

Rosalind marched down the aisle until she stood directly in front of the cell. "Mr. Rattray, I'd as soon make an agreement with a . . . a . . ."

"Snake?" Adam suggested. "Scorpion?"

"Slug," Rosalind snapped, the last of her queasiness swept away by a healthy dollop of outrage. She leveled her haughtiest stare upon the red-faced Booker Rattray. "Tell me about my brother Isaac," she ordered for the third time, a glorious burst of temper cascading through her. "And tell me the truth, if you can remember how."

"The truth, Miss Hayes?" For a long moment the old man

stared back, then emitted a short laugh. "The truth of the matter is that I don't know where your brother is . . ." He paused. "Though not for want of trying. He fell over a cliff, and that interfering preacher found him."

"Jedidiah Scrivens?" Rosalind whispered. The flimsy facade of temper collapsed.

Rattray shrugged. "Doesn't matter. Nothing matters. Whether he's dead or alive . . . whether you find him or his grave. Won't matter. You'll never be safe again, and it's all courtesy of your stupid brother."

"That's enough, Rattray." Adam stepped forward.

"It's the truth. Isn't that what you want?" The aging man studied Rosalind, a twisted smile gradually spreading across his fleshy cheeks. "Here's another one for you. Right now, I'm a lot better off than you are chasing a ghost. At least I'm safe behind these bars. Thanks to Pinkerton's National Detective Agency,"—he swept Adam a mocking bow—"I might see another sunrise or two. But you, Miss Hayes . . . you'll never know. The Catbird knows by now that your brother's the one who stole his lifelong dream—"

"Those jewels do not belong to the Catbird," Rosalind pointed out. "He has no right—"

"What you and your watchdog here think is right don't matter a Confederate dollar to the Catbird. Not when it's the Petrovna Parure that's at stake." Rattray stepped back, stuffing his hands inside his waistband and rocking on his heels. "Now that I'm out of the picture, your brother's his last link to them. Frankly, I'd just as soon keep it that way. When the Catbird discovers that Isaac Hayes left behind a nosy sister, he'll be coming after you, Miss Hayes."

"*If* he finds out," Rosalind countered, "he'll be in for a disappointment, because I don't know anything that will help." *The Bible*, she thought. The Bible . . .

The mocking smile widened. "Of course not. Give him my regards, if you have the chance." His gaze slid to Adam. "How long do you think you can protect your innocent lamb? It won't matter that she's a woman, much less that the Catbird's not fond of murder."

"Booker, you're beginning to annoy me," Adam said, but Rosalind caught a glimpse of his expression. She wasn't surprised when Rattray backed away from the bars.

"He knows all about you, *Panther*," he jibed from a safer distance. "You'll never catch him, because he'll do anything to recover the Petrovna Parure—including murder."

"Then we're even." Goose bumps sprang up on Rosalind's skin at Adam's lethally soft tone. "I'm not fond of killing either. But if he harms Miss Hayes, or anyone else—including you, Booker Rattray—the Catbird will pay the price."

32

SPURS JANGLING, LaRUE sauntered down the dirt street. A Mexican sombrero covered his head and most of his face. The filthy duster he'd lifted from the back of a range hand's saddle completed his disguise. LaRue despised such slovenly attire but—like Booker Rattray—he'd learned to do whatever was necessary to avoid detection and capture.

Unfortunately, Rattray had missed the mark this time.

The whole town of La Junta was full of the story—how some smooth-talking gent from Kansas City had come to town with a horse he'd claimed nobody could beat. How he'd been accused of salting a mine, or selling worthless shares—they weren't sure which. All they cared about was the ensuing fight. "More entertaining than a whole passel of horse races," one old geezer had observed.

LaRue also got an earful of accounts about the tall buckskinned stranger with Injun hair who had flattened six men in as many seconds. Some accounts claimed he'd tossed aside a dozen as though they were pesky flies.

Panther. Had to be, though whether the Pink was looking for LaRue, Rattray, or both, was impossible to determine. Didn't matter. Booker Rattray had been arrested in his hotel room, and was now cooling his heels in the town jail.

LaRue turned on his heel and headed back for the hotel. It

was dark, almost seven. His stomach was growling. No wonder; he hadn't eaten since he'd left Perkins on a dawn express train. Any further information could wait for a change of clothes and a good Harvey House meal.

A woman draped in a full-length cloak was just leaving the jail as LaRue passed by on the opposite side of the street. He paused, struck by the stylish flare of the cloak. The woman was followed by a tall man with long hair—

A quick stab of elation galvanized LaRue. It was her! The woman from the foiled Driscoll job in Denver. Escorted by none other than Panther. LaRue slowed his pace, then edged closer to the buildings to blend in with the night shadows. When the couple was a block ahead, he leaned down and removed his spurs. Then, silent as a drifting cloud, he followed.

They passed the hotel and turned toward the depot. LaRue's step quickened. He slipped inside the entrance seconds later, ducking behind a stack of steamer trunks.

"It's closed," the young woman said, her dismay plain to see.

"As I tried to warn you, this isn't Denver," Panther returned. "Try not to worry. We'll have plenty of time to purchase your ticket in the morning."

"It's just that I don't like waiting until the last moment."

"I know. Come along now. You're still limping, and you're exhausted. What you need is a hot meal and a good night's sleep."

"What I need is to find out about my brother."

"We'll find him." Amazingly, the detective's voice sounded as gentle as though he were soothing a hurt child.

They retraced their steps, walking within a few yards of LaRue. So—that's the way it was. The big Pink was hovering over the girl like a protective swain. Good. Lovesick men grew careless, didn't notice much beyond the perfume. If the man they called Panther was nitwit enough to be distracted by a woman, so much the better.

LaRue waited until the sound of their footsteps faded away before slipping back outside. As he followed the couple he sorted through the nuggets of information he'd overheard. The girl was looking for her brother. And she just happened to be in the same town as Booker Rattray, who for the past month had been searching for some unknown greenhorn. The missing brother, perhaps?

It appeared as though he might be taking another trip to Denver, if Booker Rattray died before he could be persuaded to talk. LaRue's smile faded. Miss Hayes might be an intriguing piece, with a neck made for jewelry, but she'd suffer the same fate as Rattray if she stood between him and the Petrovna Parure.

The mountains, near Cripple Creek

A torrential rainstorm beat down on Jedidiah Scrivens' unprotected head, plastering his hair to his skull and running down his beard in cold rivulets. Every so often he paused in his labor long enough to swipe his face and catch his breath. This morning, he felt every one of his seventy-two years.

Of course, digging a grave was a daunting task no matter what a man's age, particularly when one wasn't sure where the departed soul would be spending eternity.

Grimly the preacher planted his mud-caked boot on the shovel again. Shouldn't be long now—his nose was level with a clump of yucca. The task had taken two days, even in the rain-soaked soil. Usually he asked for help with the burial of the poor souls he'd cared for, but—as on many other occasions over the years—this was one of those times when discretion was essential.

When the hole was finally deep enough, he heaved his aching body out. Head lowered against the lashing rain, he trudged back to the cabin to fetch Sheba, on whom would fall the sad burden of carrying the remains of Isaac Hayes to his final resting place.

Jed's footsteps slowed, his shoulders slumped with weariness of spirit as well as body. The boy had suffered mightily these past days. Over the years Jed had nursed many an injured, oftimes dying soul, but none of them had touched him as much as this troubled young man. Even with the finality of eternity staring him in the face, Isaac clung to his irrational litany that justice be done, his family protected.

"Lord . . . be merciful to this tormented sinner," Jed whispered, uncertain at that moment who needed divine grace more. Isaac Hayes—or the shepherd who had failed to rescue a lost sheep.

An hour later, unabashed tears mingling with sweat and rain, Jed began the thankless task of filling the grave he had dug. For his own safety, Sheba remained the sole witness—both to the fact of Isaac's death as well as the location of his grave. Almost completely spent now, every so often Jed rested from his shoveling, leaning against the warm, soggy hide of his faithful companion.

"Wish he'd listened," Jed mused to the donkey. "But he was stubborn—just like you, old girl. Nothing mattered but his harebrained notion of justice."

The downpour dwindled to mist, but the wind picked up, sighing through the rain-wet spruce that would stand sentinel over the grave. Shivering, Jed lifted his head to scan the sullen sky. Fresh snow capped the mountains to the north and west, warning of the fast-approaching winter. Bleak and black, the thick stand of timber crowding the lower slopes waited stoically to endure another season of death.

Numb with cold now, he fumbled for his personal Bible, tucked into the oiled leather knapsack lashed to Sheba's withers. He knelt stiffly, heedless of the wet ground. "Lord," he began, "as you have shown mercy to your sorrowful servant, I now ask for mercy in behalf of Isaac Hayes. . . ."

Two days later the preacher shut the cabin door behind him and set his face for Manitou Springs. He had a letter to reclaim from his good friend Gustav Wachtler. After leaving Sheba with two miners in Victor, he caught a train into Cripple Creek.

"Afternoon, Sam," he greeted the station agent, who was

halfheartedly sweeping the floor.

"Preacher!" Sam wiped his hand on his sleeve and thrust it out. "Well, where in tarnation have you *been*? It's been weeks since I seen your homely face. Got a telegram gathering dust behind the counter there somewhere—" He propped the broom against the wall and ducked behind the ticket window. "I was about ready to send out a search party but figured it wouldn't do no good, you being prone to wander. Say, didn't I hear you were nursemaiding some feller again?"

Absently Jed nodded, his gaze on the telegram Sam handed him. A warning chill ghosted down his spine when he saw that it was actually a cablegram. From England.

"Well? Who's it from? What does it say?" Sam hurried back around the counter, curiosity overcoming respect for Jed's privacy. "Hey . . . you all right? Is it bad news?"

For once, words failed Jed. He stared down at the lines of type, feeling as though he'd been sucked into the maw of Jonah's whale.

"Preacher? You havin' a heart spasm or something? Maybe I should fetch the doc."

"No—I'm . . . all right, Sam." His voice sounded rusty. He couldn't think. "I have to go back to England—as soon as possible."

"*England?*" Sam snatched the cablegram from Jed's nerveless fingers and read hurriedly. "Say, what's this mean? 'Your daughter is dying. Please come immediately.' I never knew you had a daughter, Preacher."

Jed stared unseeingly through the window. *Blessed is he whose transgression is forgiven . . . whose sin is covered. . . .*

"Neither did I, Sam," he said. "Neither did I."

33

La Junta, Colorado

AT A LITTLE PAST EIGHT O'CLOCK on a windy, starless night, a slightly built man entered the sheriff's office. The sheriff—Gillman was his name—glanced up from his desk, struggling to look alert.

"Evenin'," said Napoleon LaRue and touched the brim of his Stetson. "I'm Marshal Fawkes." He hooked his thumbs over his lapels, drawing attention to the badge he had stolen. "According to the law down in Perkins, you're holding a man for me—Booker Rattray?"

Gillman stood. LaRue decided he resembled a large, dumb ox.

"I wasn't expecting you 'til morning."

"Caught a northbound freight."

Tense, LaRue waited with outward indifference for the sheriff to decide whether or not to pursue the matter. He relaxed when Gillman grunted assent and bent to retrieve a set of keys from a hook under his desk.

"Say—you hear any more about that Catbird feller?" the sheriff asked. "The Pinkerton detectives I've been working with claim old Rattray's been his middleman for years."

"Naw . . . but I'll admit mention of him's made me more cautious 'bout fetching your prisoner here. I don't trust anyone as slippery as the Catbird. Fact is,"—LaRue pushed the brim of

his Stetson higher and fixed a rueful eye upon the gullible sheriff—"I'm not too pleased to be in charge of Rattray. It's going
to be a headache, keeping him safely locked away if the Catbird
really is looking for him. Nope, I'd sure rather leave the whole
mess in your hands."

The sheriff stood, walking around the desk. "I see what you
mean." He clapped LaRue's shoulder on the way to the door.
"Tell you what." He dropped the set of keys on top of a stack of
papers. "How about if I fetch us a pot of coffee and some sweet
buns from the cafe? Sort of sweeten the task?"

"Sounds real nice. Thank you kindly." He watched through
the window until the sheriff was halfway across the street.

Idiot, LaRue thought. Then, his movements swift, he strode
over to the door leading to the cells, on the way snagging the
keys, along with a pair of handcuffs lying on a table beneath
the gun cabinet.

Rattray had been lying on a cot. He swung his legs to the
floor, rubbing his hands over his face. Looking rumpled and
sleepy, he grumbled, "What do you want? Who are you, anyway—where's Sheriff Gillman?"

LaRue casually removed the hat and dropped it on the floor.
"Hello, Booker," he greeted him. "It's been a long time. Too
long, wouldn't you say?"

"*LaRue . . .*" The older man lumbered to his feet, then stood
swaying, hands trembling at his sides. "It wasn't my fault! You
have to believe me—I didn't steal anything! It was that kid—
that greenhorn. He stole them, LaRue. Not me. It wasn't me."

LaRue began swinging the handcuffs, his gaze never leaving
the flaccid, sweating face. "You expect me to believe a fresh-
faced yokel managed to steal my babies from you, Booker?
Don't waste my time. Not when I've had to chase you all over
the mountains, wondering if I'd ever hold them again. Pinks
breathing down my neck so close I could smell their rancid
breath . . ."

With difficulty he swallowed the festering rage. "All right,"
he continued in a more rational tone, "let's just say I'm willing
to buy your story. Tell me about this greenhorn. What's his
name?"

"Isaac Hayes. His name is Isaac Hayes. He followed me to my stash, LaRue. Somehow he followed. He must have stayed there all night, because he . . . he transferred everything but one bag. I caught him, but it was too late. He fell over a cliff—I shot him in the leg . . . I didn't want to kill him—" He backed away, blubbering incoherent pleas as LaRue's hand shot through the bars and twisted in the folds of Rattray's wrinkled shirt.

"You wouldn't lie to me, would you, Booker? We've been associates—*trusted* associates—for a long time."

All the hurt and anger eating at him for weeks welled up again as LaRue searched the frightened, watery eyes inches from his own. Abruptly the rage exploded. He reached through the bars, jerking Rattray forward until the fleshy face was pressed against the cold metal. "Be very sure that you're telling me nothing but the truth."

Booker Rattray had dissolved into a blubbering mass of lard. He was terrified—of Napoleon LaRue. The sense of power throbbing alongside the rage was almost as satisfying as fondling a magnificent Persian emerald.

"I swear it's the truth." Rattray swallowed, almost gagging. "I would have gone after the boy myself, but he fell. Some old preacher got to him first, LaRue. I was—" He closed his eyes. "I was afraid, so I ran. I knew—the Petrovna jewels . . . ."

With a contemptuous shove, LaRue released Booker. "I want them back," he said, lifting the keys. "And you're going to help me."

"I don't know anything!" Booker protested. "It was Isaac Hayes! He . . . he has a sister! She's here in town, LaRue. Maybe she knows something. You don't need me—you need her. Rosalind Hayes."

"I know all about Rosalind Hayes." LaRue turned the key in the lock and the cell door opened with a quiet snick. "And you're right. I do need her. But I need you too, Booker." He met his former associate's gaze as he fastened Rattray's hands together with the cuffs. "And if you don't do exactly as I say, I might decide that what I need you to be is—dead."

34

"GIVE ME ONE GOOD REASON WHY I shouldn't haul his scheming carcass down to Georgia—see that my wife's family is finally vindicated."

Adam suppressed the urge to pound his head—already throbbing—against the wall. His old friend might be spoiling for a fight, but having already survived one bloody battle moments earlier, Adam was in no mood for another.

Deliberately, he removed his buckskin shirt and tossed it on the bed. "I can give you several, but I'll stick to the most pertinent. The war's been over for thirty years, Simon. Trying to prove Rattray stole that Yankee gold instead of Elizabeth's father is a waste of your time, and you know it." He sat down to tug off his boots. "Elizabeth's put it behind her. You do the same. 'Let the dead bury their dead,' as they say."

"Booker Rattray isn't dead."

"Yet." Adam ran a hand around the back of his neck. "Did Elizabeth ask you to turn this trip into a private crusade?"

Silence. Adam finished pulling off the second boot and glanced up at the man he considered his closest friend. "Thought not." He watched the scowl deepen on Simon's face, lending it a seemingly hard, even dangerous cast. But Adam knew his friend's heart. "Let it go, Sim," he repeated. "Help me nail him on the current charges, and let it go. Don't get caught in the revenge trap."

"This is justice, not revenge."

Adam didn't back down. "It's taken you fifteen years to accept God's loving presence in your life again. He restored your faith, gave you a loving wife as well. You trying to throw those away?"

"I wouldn't—" Simon stopped, his face finally relaxing in the semblance of a smile. "All right. I can accept that decision if I must. I won't like it, mind you. But—you're right. What Elizabeth and I share is too . . ." He hesitated, looking mildly uncomfortable, then shrugged. " 'Precious' is how Elizabeth puts it."

Adam chuckled, finally feeling the tension draining from his weary muscles.

"While we're on the subject of motivations," Simon added casually, "you may have been tracking Rattray since Elizabeth and I married, but the reason has changed, not to mention your objectivity. Bit of the pot calling the kettle black, wouldn't you say?"

Adam thought about arguing, but he was too tired. Might as well give in with grace. "Touché."

He stretched, then stood and moved to the washstand in the corner of his room. "In my defense, once I discovered Rattray's connection to the Catbird, that became my sole motivation for tracking the old fellow."

Even to his own ears the justification sounded feeble. Muttering beneath his breath, Adam poured a pitcher of water into the bowl, then wet a cloth to wipe over his face and sweaty torso.

"Your 'sole motivation,' eh?" Simon studied the ceiling, the curve of his mouth producing a queasy sensation in Adam's gut. "Miss Hayes is an . . . interesting woman. Not your sort at all."

Adam hurled the soggy cloth into the basin and swiveled around. "No. She's not." Groaning, he stretched out on the bed and leaned back against the headboard. "Rosalind's a problem. But not for the reason you think."

"Talk to me, Adam. Get it off your chest."

Trapped, Adam pulled out the bowie, running his thumb over the blade. Maybe if he did verbalize his feelings about Rosalind, he could change them into something more comfortable. Safer.

He inhaled deeply. "She's the only woman I've ever met who dresses like a member of the Social Register, yet refuses to behave like one. The little wildcat is fighting me tooth and claw about going back to Denver where she belongs. She wants to *help*. Before I left her earlier, we . . . exchanged words." He gave a rueful smile and gingerly touched his cheek. "Wouldn't be surprised if she hadn't left these bruises, not some fellow at the racetrack."

"Ah. Connelly hinted at something, but you know what he's like. Fastidious—and devious. All I learned about Miss Hayes was her connection to Rattray and the Catbird. I was to follow her down from Denver. Guard her on the train, see if anyone approached her. Make sure she wasn't molested."

"Well, as to that . . ." Adam smiled involuntarily now, at the memory of her juniper green eyes spitting fire when he refused to chase Rattray. "Underneath those fancy clothes beats the heart of a rebel. A frustrated rebel with a conscience the size of Pikes Peak. Did you know she's virtually supported her mother, invalid father, and the two family servants for almost four years? Her brother and sister live in their respective mansions, throwing money and 'advice' her way. But it's Rosalind who wears the ball and chain."

"She sounds a lot like Elizabeth."

Adam's eyes slitted. "I don't like your tone of voice. You sound . . . smug."

Simon laughed. "Do I?"

Adam pinched the bridge of his nose. "Probably. Maybe not. I don't know—Sim, every instinct I have warns me that she won't stay in Denver."

The words burst forth and, once started, spilled out like a river at flood stage. "She's determined to find out about her brother Isaac, refuses to believe he's dead. Doesn't matter what I tell her—the danger, the risk—I even threw the issue of propriety at her. She doesn't believe me." Even now the memory of their argument tied his stomach in knots. "No matter what I say, even if she appears to be listening, I can tell she doesn't believe me."

"I understand." Simon walked across and dragged a chair up next to the bed. He clapped a sympathetic hand on Adam's shoulder, then straddled the chair and propped his forearms across the back. "I think I have a solution of sorts for your dilemma here in La Junta."

"Sim . . ."

"I can only give you a couple of weeks though. I promised Elizabeth I'd be home before Christmas and I won't break that promise. Not even for you."

"I would never ask that," Adam said, and meant it.

"I know. Now—here's my plan." Simon leaned closer and began to share his idea.

Five minutes later Adam was feeling a mountain of relief.

Then someone knocked on the door.

35

AFTER BREAKFAST the following morning, Adam ushered Rosalind into the hotel manager's private parlor. Years of practice enabled him to hide his tension and turmoil. He even managed to tease Rosalind about her perfect appearance. "Not a hair out of place. Not a wrinkle in sight. Sure you didn't bring along a personal maid in that trunk?"

"No. I brought an iron. Adam . . . is something wrong?"

So much for his famous "inscrutable countenance." He turned away from the window, where he'd been scanning the street, the people—even the rooftops. "Why do you ask?"

She laid the Bible on a large table covered with magazines. Her hands began to straighten the untidy collection, and Adam watched color stain the still oval of her face.

"You're . . . distant. Preoccupied. I know you're angry with me. I know I more or less blackmailed you, refusing to let you keep the Bible if you didn't help me find Isaac."

"Rosalind,"—he kept his voice gentle because he didn't want to frighten her—"if I wanted the Bible, you couldn't stop me from taking it."

Her head reared back, her eyes cutting to his with the flash of a drawn sword. Adam held up a hand. "Don't worry—you keep the Bible until I can fetch it—and you—in Denver." He held her gaze. "And you promise to stay there until I do."

164

"I know what I promised."

Adam almost smiled at the grudging tone. Almost. "And . . . I wasn't angry with you last night. Anger's a waste of time. I was frustrated as much with the circumstances as with you, all right? Frustrated, and—" He stopped, wanting to kick himself. He was scared out of his buckskins, but if he confessed that unsettling truth he wasn't sure how Rosalind would react. "—concerned," he finished. "But that's over, all right? There's something I have to tell you now, before we search the Bible, and before I put you on the train."

"I appreciate your concern." Her voice carried the same chill as the frost-coated morning. "But I don't need any more lectures on what is wise, prudent, or safe. I've promised to return to Denver—"

"Booker Rattray escaped last night. A man impersonating a U.S. marshal talked his way past Sheriff Gillman. Simon and I are afraid that man was the Catbird."

She stood as if turned to marble, her eyes wide, unblinking.

"Gillman said the man never removed his hat, though he does remember that he had a thick handlebar mustache. I know—a pretty useless detail. But try not to worry. Simon is tracking them." He tried to sound reassuring. "There's nobody better."

"Except you."

"I prefer working with Kat. Simon doesn't need any help." He studied the dilated eyes, waiting patiently for her to recover, knowing it was important for her to feel competent, in control. He wanted to hold her. Instead, he took her hand, ignoring her instinctive start. "I haven't had a chance to tell you about Kat, have I? I found her mother, oh, about fourteen years ago. She'd been mauled by a bear, was pretty torn up. I saved her life, and she stayed with me over two years. Kat's the runt of her last litter, and the two of us developed a relationship from the very first."

"What happened to the mother?"

"She died. I buried her in a grove of aspens on a bright June afternoon. Kat was about three months old at the time. We've been together ever since." Rosalind's fingers flexed inside his, and Adam realized he'd been stroking the back of her hand in much the same way he would absentmindedly soothe Kat by stroking her ears.

"I'd like to meet her. Would she let me touch her?"

Adam hadn't felt like smiling since a shamefaced Sheriff Gillman knocked on his door the previous night. But a picture of Rosalind in her prim skirt and starched pinstriped shirt-waist, petting a half-wild mountain lion, startled him into a grin. "Depends on her mood. She's not much for socializing."

"No wonder the two of you stick together," Rosalind grumped.

Relieved, Adam noted the bit of color returning to her cheeks. "Neither of us has much use for cities or city life," he agreed. "On the other hand, you've adapted to my world better than I would have expected."

"Except for these clothes, I'm no different from a woman living in a sod hut on the prairie or a cabin in the high country." She stepped back, challenging him. "How long were you going to wait to tell me Booker Rattray had escaped?"

He shrugged. "I've told you now. What we plan to do with the news is what matters." He'd seriously considered asking Simon to bundle Rosalind off to Montana and stash her with Elizabeth for a couple of months.

"Do you need for me to be the tethered goat?"

"The . . . *what*?"

"I could stroll about town while you and Simon follow, out of sight but within reach. If the Catbird—"

"If you take more than three steps without—" Adam snapped his jaw together. Then, because he didn't trust himself, he backed away, pointing to one of the chairs stationed around the cluttered library table. "Sit. Don't move, or we'll both regret it." He strode across to the door. "I'll be back."

He left, slamming the parlor door behind him with such force, a lady reading in the lobby dropped her book. Adam never broke stride, shoving through the front doors and into the chilly morning air. He stood on the porch, hands clamped over the waist-high railing, breathing hard and waiting for the emotional landslide to settle.

166

Not since he was seventeen years old and his father suggested one more stab at a reconciliation with his mother, had Adam erupted in such volcanic anger. He'd as soon face down a roomful of riot-minded miners as to be overtaken by such destructive emotions again. The pompous words he'd spoken to Rosalind not five minutes earlier rang in his head like a clanging cymbal.

Closing his eyes, head bowed, Adam struggled against a shame almost as powerful as the burst of anger. God help him, he didn't know what he would have done if he'd stayed in the room with Rosalind. Hurling a chair through the nearest window had been tempting. . . .

Of all the harebrained, idiotic notions! Did the woman possess even a half ounce of common sense? Self-preservation? Did she have any idea—*any idea*—what it did to his insides when she looked up at him with that intent, earnest expression and calmly volunteered to risk getting herself abducted? Murdered?

The way he'd behaved, likely she did. He'd be fortunate if she allowed him in the same room, after he'd all but terrorized her himself. If it would have helped, Adam would have banged his head against the corner post. He deserved the pain. He deserved to be horsewhipped, dropped to the bottom of a mine shaft—

"Adam?"

He stiffened, then forced his muscles to relax. "Don't you ever do what you're told?" he said to the post.

Rosalind ignored the resigned question. "I wanted to tell you I was sorry." Her tone was stilted, and the last of Adam's temper evaporated. "It was a silly idea, and I'd only mess everything up again."

"It was a brilliant idea, and would probably work if either Rattray or the Catbird are still in the vicinity." Or if he'd been willing to allow it. Adam turned to face her, and his heart clenched at her expression. "Rosalind . . . don't be afraid of me. Please. I would never hurt you—could never hurt you, or anyone smaller, weaker. I'm sorry—"

"You think it's a brilliant idea?" she interrupted, staring at him, and Adam belatedly realized that she wasn't frightened at all. She was . . . stunned. "Then—why did it make you angry?"

Stunned, but naive—about men, anyway. Adam scrubbed his hands over his face and tried to discipline his riotous thoughts. "Where's the Bible?"

"I . . . um . . . I left it at the front desk."

He gave up the battle with his conscience. "Will you come back to the parlor with me?" He cupped her chin, causing her eyes to widen in startled confusion. The baffling woman had blown all his pride and preconceptions to dust, yet possessed not a shred of awareness of her power. "I promise not to lose my temper again. Or—" he amended wryly, "that is, I promise if you don't offer to sacrifice yourself in the pursuit of justice again."

"Um . . . I . . . ah . . . Adam, your hand. I mean, you shouldn't . . ." Her own hands fluttered like disoriented pigeons.

Adam badly wanted to kiss her. But Rosalind would be mortified by the public display of intimacy, and he cared enough now not to dismiss her sensibilities in spite of her charming fluster. "I know I shouldn't," he whispered, caressing the firm little chin. "But the temptation is great."

For a long moment she gazed somberly up into his face. "Yes . . . I know."

Head reeling, Adam followed her back inside, down the hall, and into the parlor. For the first time since becoming a Pinkerton operative, he had no idea of his surroundings.

36

"... AND MAKE SURE you don't harm her," Booker finished, with a meaningful look directed at the two hulking men LaRue had hired.

LaRue had insisted that Booker go along with this implausible scheme, and since he was in no position to argue, he had reluctantly followed the Catbird's ludicrous instructions. Take these two ruffians, for instance. Wouldn't be wise to turn one's back on either of them, to Booker's way of thinking.

He cleared his throat and tried to sound authoritative. "You can threaten, frighten—no more. If she can't tell us how to find the cache, you won't be paid."

"Do not worry," the half-breed Carlos promised. "La señorita will sing like a meadowlark for you."

Carlos's partner, a beefy ex-prizefighter named Briggs, only smiled, revealing a mouth full of rotting teeth.

Rattray badly wanted to mop the perspiration from his face. "Just keep her alive," he muttered. "And your mouths shut. If that Pinkerton operative—"

Briggs spat. "Leave Panther to us. He may know how to flatten some pie-eyed cowhands in a brawl, but he ain't met me an' Carlos."

Five minutes after the two minions had disappeared in a

169

cloud of dust, LaRue rode up from the opposite direction, on the far side of the outcropping. He pulled up next to Booker and dismounted. "All set?"

"Yes," Booker answered miserably. "They'll meet us in Pueblo. But I still don't understand how they plan to lure her off the train."

"Don't worry about it—I've taken care of everything."

"Yeah . . . well . . ." Booker removed his bowler, pulled out a large handkerchief, and mopped his forehead. "I warned them not to hurt her, but I don't trust them."

"Wise of you." A large Stetson concealing his face, LaRue silently contemplated his dust-coated boots.

When the silence began to grate on his nerves, Booker cleared his throat. "We need to be going if we're going to catch the evening train. I need to clean up a bit. . . ." His voice trailed away when LaRue finally lifted his head.

"You're right," he said, pushing his hat back to search the tumbled boulders behind Rattray. "Don't know how you've lived out here all these years, Booker. Nothing but dirt and sky, with a few weeds here and there."

"I've pretty much stayed farther west, in gold mine country, LaRue." Booker glanced around, for some reason feeling his stomach muscles contract. "Little bit too . . . deserted around here, for my taste." He laughed, and the false jocularity was snatched away in the bitter November wind. "Say . . . I meant to tell you the mustache is a nice touch. Hardly recognize you myself."

"Thank you." LaRue stroked the silky strands brushing either side of his mouth. "Looks like the real thing, doesn't it?" He dropped his hand. "With Briggs and Carlos gone, looks like there's not another soul around for miles. Maybe you should have buried my precious possessions out here, instead of— where was it you told me? Below Cripple Creek somewhere?"

"In a deserted mine shaft," Booker mumbled. "If that cursed Hayes boy hadn't found it, everything would still be there." He tried to sound hopeful. "LaRue, the Hayes boy wouldn't have had enough time to move the sacks very far away. Now that his sister's in the picture, I'm sure we'll find him soon—couple of days at the most. He must have told her what he'd done, else she wouldn't be trying so hard to find him."

"I always knew you were a smart fellow, Booker." LaRue reached inside the pocket of his black duster. "And you've been a trustworthy associate. I'd even go so far as to say 'friend.'"

He was regarding Booker with a peculiar blend of sorrow and regret. For some reason, Booker felt as though a loaded pistol had just been pressed against his spine. His pulse rate accelerated, making him light-headed, and he wished he hadn't left his cane in the rental buggy. "I've been . . . a friend?" he repeated numbly. "You talk like things are going to change. I thought you believed me, LaRue. I didn't steal anything—I'd never do that to you. To any of my clients." He tried to swallow. "I've a reputation of my own, remember."

"It was the Petrovna jewels that did it, wasn't it? You just couldn't resist them. I, of all people, shouldn't blame you for that, Booker." LaRue shook his head. "But I do." Beneath the false mustache, his mouth had thinned to a grim slash above the coal black eyes. "Those jewels are everything to me—I planned for three years to possess them. I took all the risks, Booker—and I held them for mere days before I entrusted them to you. Only days . . . because I trusted you."

"You can still trust me. . . ." The declaration died in his throat. With pitiless clarity exploding in his mind, he realized why LaRue had insisted they meet in this deserted spot.

"I wish that were so."

Booker was still staring at him in disbelief when LaRue lifted the gun and pointed it at his heart. A spasm of grief flickered through the dark eyes, but LaRue didn't hesitate. "If only it hadn't been the Petrovna jewelry," he whispered, and fired.

37

ADAM GLANCED UP from the piece of paper he'd been studying for the past hour and watched Rosalind instead. At the moment she was absently chewing on a lock of hair she had tugged free of the pins, and her face wore an endearing scowl of rapt concentration. Through the curtained window at her back, arid desert stretched toward the cloud-draped mountains.

With each tick of the regulator wall clock, the beckoning peaks loomed higher, calling to Adam with a power he had yet to resist. How, he wondered, did people survive in flatlands, or cities whose only canyons consisted of crowd-choked streets bound by soulless brick buildings?

His attention returned to Rosalind. She'd finally relaxed enough to remove the jacket of her traveling dress, a ridiculous costume with enormous billowing sleeves and a wide collar trimmed in rows of braid. The deep pink blouse underneath wasn't a whole lot more practical, since another set of equally voluminous sleeves draped her shoulders all the way to her elbows. Cascades of ruffles frothed down the front. In Adam's admittedly uncharitable opinion, women's fashions bordered on the realm of absurdity. Yet somehow Rosalind always looked feminine and refined. Adam might tease her, but he couldn't deny that she presented a pleasing picture.

Abruptly he gave himself a mental shake. Next thing he knew, he'd be balancing a derby on his head or stuffing himself back into a monkey suit in a pathetic attempt to match her stylish sophistication.

"Found another verse in the Psalms, one that I missed earlier," Rosalind exclaimed, managing to sound both elated and weary. "Like the others, it makes no sense at all from an inspirational context."

"Let's see." Adam tweaked the Bible around. "Hmm. '. . . rock into standing water,' then 'into fountain of waters . . .'" he quoted. He looked up at Rosalind. Her expression sent a tingle of anticipation through his sluggish veins. "What? What are you thinking?"

"Let me see the paper." He handed it to her, watching her lips silently form the words of the four verses she'd neatly inscribed. "Adam, every one of the underlined verses—they're all . . . directions, or descriptions of scenery!" She pointed, her voice rising as she read aloud. "See? 'Toward the east,' in Genesis. 'And so northward,' in Joshua. 'Go into the clefts of the rocks—'"

"I think you're right." Adam snatched the paper back, scanning the verses again. "We figured this one in Joshua had to refer to whatever your brother found. 'Hid in the earth in the midst of my tent' is fairly specific, insofar as it goes."

Flushed with the thrill of discovery, Rosalind searched his face. "I could still go to Manitou Springs instead, try to find Pastor Scrivens while you—"

"Don't, Rosalind. Please."

She pressed her lips together and didn't speak again.

"It could take weeks to find your brother and Jedidiah Scrivens. Months. I wish you'd take my advice, go visit your relatives in Virginia for a while. Stop fretting over your brother."

"I wish you'd quit bringing it up. Believe me, I fully appreciate the fact that you're far better suited to tracking people down and traipsing about the mountains. But it's not *your* brother who's in trouble."

In spite of his irritation over her single-mindedness, Adam grinned. "You remind me of Kat on a stalk. Actually, compared to you, Kat's a docile kitten. Most of the time, all I have to do is whisper directions in her ear, and she obeys." He watched a becoming blush the color of her frilly shirtwaist stain the bridge of her nose.

"How many times has Kat clawed you when you tease?" Rosalind muttered.

"Not very many. I know how far to take it." He stood abruptly, planted his palms on the table, and leaned down. "What makes you think I was teasing?"

Her eyes widened. "Because you're always teasing me," she responded faintly. "Adam?"

She looked fetching and fresh. And uncertain. A man could stand only so much. And yet . . .

"Yeah. That's all it was," he managed. "Teasing."

They stood there, the table between them, while the air seemed to crackle. He wanted to reach for her, stroke the off-center nose with its irregular bump in the middle—courtesy, she'd explained, of a fight with Isaac when they were children. He wanted—

With a half-stifled exclamation, he turned and stalked over to the window. Bracing his hands on the sill, he leaned his forehead against the cold glass and closed his eyes.

"I . . . if you'll excuse me," she said, "I think I'll go freshen up. M-make sure my trunk is ready. It's almost noon and we need to leave the hotel by one, I believe you told me. And—"

"It's all right, Rosalind." He turned, though he remained by the window. "Appearances to the contrary, I'm not going to throw you over my shoulder and carry you off"—he inwardly smiled at the way her head snapped back and her eyes darkened—"even though I'd like nothing better," he finished, enjoying the way her hands fluttered as though she didn't know what to do with them.

Then she spoke, her unsettling candor once again rocking him to his toes. "Me too," she admitted. "Adam? What do people do when they feel like this?"

He had to laugh. "Depends on the people," he answered, equally frank. It was a novel experience, this freedom to speak to a woman without having to screen every word. "Some, no

doubt, give in to their feelings. Others might barricade themselves behind the nearest door and scream for help."

"No one I know would ever find themselves in these circumstances in the first place," Rosalind pointed out.

"Ah." Adam inclined his head. "You're right, of course." He
took a step, relieved when she stood her ground instead of re-
treating. "So . . . we have all the saints and sinners covered.
Where would you and I fall, hmm?" He advanced another step.

"Tortured sinner and tempted saint?"

She was staring at him with an expression of longing—and
deep uncertainty. Adam's resolve began to crumble. Slowly, giving her time to evade or reject him, he drew her into his arms.
"Perhaps," he whispered, "we can find a middle ground?"

He cupped her face in both hands, noting with faint irony
that his fingers were trembling. *God*, he whispered in his heart,
please don't let me fail this woman—or you. "How many kisses
can I steal before your conscience troubles you?"

"How many—?" she sputtered. Suddenly she grabbed two
fistfuls of Adam's shirt and shook him. "What kind of question
is that, Adam Moreaux?" she practically yelled. "I don't know,
you impossible man! And my conscience is *always* troubling
me."

"Rosalind, I—"

Abruptly she threw her arms around his neck, stretched on
tiptoe, and planted a clumsy kiss squarely on Adam's lips. Then
she wrenched herself free and retreated behind a parlor chair.
"One," she gasped. "One is all . . . even if I'd like more." Her
hand lifted, almost in supplication—and dropped to her side.

Then she gathered her skirts and fled, the sound of her confession still ringing in the quiet hotel parlor.

38

AT A LITTLE PAST THREE the train pulled into the Pueblo depot in a cloud of steam and a succession of clanging jolts. Even after it came to a complete halt, Rosalind remained hidden inside the stateroom boudoir of a luxurious private car, where Adam had stashed her back in La Junta.

The car was a rental, on its way to Denver. Naturally Adam had known the train conductor, who naturally agreed (with a twinkle in his eye) that Miss Hayes should avail herself of its privacy and comfort. For her safety, of course. Naturally . . .

With her index finger, Rosalind traced the intricate pineapple design decorating the velvet seat. Rationally, she knew that she was safe. Adam could charm the stripes off a skunk, and he was almost as masterful at planning as Rosalind herself. Not only had he concealed her in this private car, but the brakeman had agreed to patrol the vestibule at odd moments along the way.

Besides, on the seat beside her lay a silver meat server she'd found in the private car's dining room. If anyone other than the conductor or the brakeman appeared in the boudoir, Rosalind was prepared to attack.

Regrettably, she was ill equipped to defend herself against an aggressor for very long. Even if she had possession of a gun, she wasn't sure she could fire it. Twenty years of lessons in deportment, dress, and drawing-room dialogue had not included instructions on how to fend off a potential murderer.

She *had*, however, been taught the appropriate way to discourage unwanted or improper advances.

With nothing to do but sit and wait, Rosalind's thoughts returned to the scene in the hotel parlor as she tried once more to analyze her attitude toward Adam Moreaux. As always, the exercise proved to be as depressing as it was confusing, because his advances, though improper, were not unwanted. In fact, it was a moot point as to which of them had been making "improper advances."

Weeks earlier, Rosalind had admitted to herself that she was attracted to him. Fascinated by him. Infuriated, intimidated, intrigued. Her nimble brain could devise plenty of adjectives, but the exercise merely provided a diversion to avoid the truth. Which was, that she was thoroughly smitten with Adam Moreaux.

And they had exchanged a kiss.

With a groan Rosalind leaned her head against the seat back and closed her eyes. Had she committed an unpardonable sin? Or merely broadened the boundaries of acceptable social behavior? *"Try not to confuse the two,"* Adam had counseled her on the buggy ride to the depot when she had bravely tackled him with the thorny question.

He professed—and lived—a deep faith in God. A faith demanding an even higher honor, Rosalind knew, than her respect for family. So . . . was the predicament spiritual—or social?

In a surfeit of vexation she pounded her fists against the seat. Then, sheepish over the outburst, she redirected her thoughts altogether by focusing on the scene outside her window.

A small boy wearing a peaked cap wrestled with a dog tugging against its leash. Farther down, a mother, her face lined with fatigue, perched on a narrow wooden bench, holding a baby. Sober-suited businessmen brushed shoulders with cowhands in their broad-rimmed Stetsons and spurred boots. Arriving and departing passengers gathered between steamer trunks, suitcases, and a flatbed cart piled high with mailbags.

Rosalind's heart skipped a beat when she spied two police-men weaving a determined path through the crowd.

What was going on? Had Adam telegraphed ahead with some new information, perhaps with a request that she be escorted the rest of the way to Denver? She watched the serge uniforms' resolute progress along the station platform, noticing that they seemed to be searching the train windows as well as the crowd.

Questions battered her mind, but just as Rosalind had convinced herself to go make inquiries, a cowboy stopped directly in front of her window. He was swathed neck to ankle in a full-length duster, a large Stetson pulled low over his forehead. Rosalind stiffened, startled by the impression of proximity in spite of the glass separating them.

Then the cowboy turned, pushed the brim of the hat back, and stared up through the window at her.

Rosalind recoiled, slamming back against the seat. Rational thought deserted her along with her breath, and she pressed a fist against her breastbone, where her heart seemed to be bursting through her ribs.

Nonchalantly, the Catbird glanced toward the two police-men before taking a step nearer the window. She could not escape the bold black sweep of his eyes, the knowing smile. He tilted his head, watching her, *beckoning* her without words. It was as though he had reached inside her mind, sifting through the fear and abhorrence to enflame the shameful attraction she could not deny. *Come on. I dare you*, he seemed to be saying.

Rosalind stood slowly—and accidentally kicked the traveling case with the Bible inside. The brief jab of discomfort brought her up short, lending her the impetus to back away from the window. She was separated from the country's most sought after criminal by a thin pane of glass and less than three yards. Yet he might as well have been on the other side of the mountains. Even if she screamed and waved, nobody would hear, much less come to her aid, thinking only that she was trying to catch someone's attention.

But if she lost sight of him in an effort to secure help, he'd escape again.

A wagonload of luggage trundled past, at last forcing the Catbird to move. He lifted his hand, pulling the brim of his hat back down, then sauntered toward the depot. In an agony of indecision, Rosalind stood, impotence burning her insides in a white-hot fury.

The Catbird turned—and smiled again.

It was the smile that pushed Rosalind over the edge. He was baiting her deliberately. Goading her. He thought she was help-less, trapped inside a golden cage—as safe to taunt as a chained circus bear—

How had he known she was here?

At that moment Rosalind neither knew nor particularly cared. Anger and determination catapulted her across the small room, set her hands to scrabbling at the door. She ran down the narrow aisle and burst through the door.

"Hurry! I saw the Catbird!" she yelled to Hank, the brake-man Adam had asked to guard her.

"Miss Hayes—?"

"There are two policemen at the other end of the platform!" She gathered up her skirt and leaped from the vestibule down the metal steps. "Tell them I saw the Catbird—he's inside the depot now—wearing a long black duster, tan western hat with a turquoise beaded band."

"Ma'am, wait. You're supposed to stay in the car!"

"I can't lose sight of him!" Rosalind called over her shoulder. "Just hurry!" Then she plunged into the crowd, darted around a stack of barrels, straining to locate the tan Stetson.

By the time she burst through the doors on the opposite side of the depot, she was almost weeping with frustration. A sea of wagons and buggies stretched before her, waiting for passen-gers. She would never find—

All at once hands closed over her arms, hauling her back-ward. A bulky man with arms as thick as tree trunks crowded in front of her, blocking her ability to free herself from the sec-ond set of arms yanking her toward a nearby delivery wagon.

Its dark interior gaped wide, like the maw of a hungry beast ready to swallow her whole.

Rosalind opened her mouth to scream, and something hard slammed against her head, right above her ear. Lights exploded in a dazzling sunburst before she fell headlong into blackness.

39

ROSALIND SURFACED FROM SLEEP, groggy and confused. What, she wondered vaguely, had disturbed her? "Tallulah?" She tried without success to lift her hand to her head, which throbbed with a dull pain. "What—?"

"Carlos. Hey, Carlos! She's finally comin' round!" a rough male voice announced nearby.

Rosalind's eyes fluttered open. It was dark and cold. She was lying on uneven, unforgiving ground instead of a soft mattress—oh. Must have had trouble sleeping again . . . gone outside to watch the stars and drifted off. Someone talking too loud—one of the neighbors?—had disturbed her.

Above her aching head, naked tree branches clattered in the wind. An involuntary shudder of cold alerted Rosalind to a host of equally aching body parts. The faint odor of smoke stung her nostrils.

It was the smoke that finally stirred Rosalind's dulled senses to unpleasant reality. With a leap of horror she remembered: she had been knocked senseless, then apparently hauled off somewhere.

Disoriented and panicked, she tried to stand, thinking only that she had to escape. Her limbs refused to obey. Flailing about on the ground, she was unable to put up even a token resistance when two huge ruffians loomed up out of the darkness.

"Hey, there, missy. 'Bout time you come to." It was the owner of the coarse, bottom-of-the-barrel voice. He squatted beside her, reaching a dirty, rawboned hand to brush strands of hair from Rosalind's face. "You sure got yourself a fine head of hair. Let's have a look-see."

"Touch me and you'll regret it," Rosalind mumbled, jerking her head back. A bolt of pain stabbed, violent and throbbing.

"La señorita does not care for your type, amigo," the other man—Carlos?—observed, dropping to his haunches as well. "Myself, I do not blame her."

"Both of you . . . stay away from me." Rosalind tried to focus on the smaller man. Mexican, she decided. Clean-shaven . . . but sinister. Like the Catbird. "Where is he? He did this, didn't he? . . . The coward."

Somehow she rolled to her side, braced her hand in the dirt, and tried to lever herself to a sitting position. Nausea swam thickly in her throat. "Water," she gasped, closing her eyes. "Please. . . ."

"Here," instructed a cultured, smooth voice. "Drink this." Something cold and metallic was pressed against her tightly pressed lips. A firm hand held her head steady.

The voice belonged to none other than the elusive, darkly attractive Catbird. She was wrapped in the arms of the Catbird! Didn't matter that his face was now fully bearded and his balding head covered by thick, unruly hair. Oh, it was a wig. He'd donned a disguise, of course.

But not the eyes. He couldn't disguise those eyes.

Water suddenly filled her throat and she choked, unable to swallow quickly enough. The Catbird waited until she quit coughing, then returned the canteen to her lips.

"This time, more slowly." A thread of impatience ribboned through the words. After a moment he set the canteen aside. "You've been unconscious longer than I anticipated. We don't have a lot of time."

"Serves you right," Rosalind managed, even though she didn't understand. Time . . . for what? "Complain to the hired help, not me." A groan escaped before she could throttle the sound. "Your disguise didn't work. I recognized you anyway." She wished the Catbird weren't so . . . close. Someone had built a small fire, and the flickering light illuminated his high forehead and winged eyebrows, the shadowed mystery of his eyes. How could such an attractive man possess such a mutilated soul?

"Miss Hayes, you've proven to be a lot of trouble. I'm beginning to think your name should have been Kate." He sat down in front of her, studying her with an intensity that caused Rosalind to stir uneasily. "I trust you won't torment me as much as Kate provoked Petruchio."

"You . . . you've read *The Taming of the Shrew?*" Rosalind gaped. An international jewel thief who quoted Shakespeare?

Annoyance tightened the thin lips. "I am not some brain-deficient nobody, Miss Hayes." He laced his hands around an upraised knee. "It's a shame, perhaps, that I don't have more time for us to get to know each other better."

"You could tell me your real name."

Even in the fitful light she could see his expression alter, sense a surge of malevolence so powerful her mouth went dry. Then he blinked, and the moment passed as though it had never occurred.

"No," he said. "Nobody . . . alive . . . knows my name. I'm trying to think of a way to avoid killing you, you see. If I told you, your demise would become inevitable."

He spoke as though he were regretfully turning down a dinner invitation. Rosalind swallowed hard, wishing her head didn't throb like a locomotive. Somehow she had to convince him to keep her alive until an opportunity to escape presented itself. One would, she had to believe. One would—*Adam.*

Adam would learn of her abduction. He'd search for her. He was nothing like the Catbird. Adam was a good man, an honorable man. He'd find her, Rosalind promised herself.

Until then, she'd have to depend on her own wits and rely on her link to the Petrovna Parure to keep the Catbird from carrying out his threat. "You won't kill me," she began, trying to sound confident. "You've had other opportunities, and you didn't take advantage of any of them. You're no murderer. You might be a thief—but you're not a murderer."

"Not," he responded with a matter-of-factness that set Rosalind's teeth to chattering, "unless I have no other choice."

So much for logic and calm persuasion. "Why do you do it?" she blurted. "Steal, I mean. You're intelligent, agile . . . a-attractive. . . ." She stopped, shame burning like live coals.

"You find me attractive, Miss Hayes? How very flattering." He leaned back against a tree trunk, his gloveless hands looking ghostly against his dark clothing. "As to why I steal—why shouldn't I? It's the only way to procure my priceless treasures." For a moment he studied her, lips pursed, head tilted sideways. "I've an openwork Egyptian necklace that could have been made for your neck. Gold, with emeralds and aquamarines. Pearls as translucent as your fair skin."

"Why shouldn't you steal?" Rosalind repeated incredulously, ignoring his remark. "It's wrong! Illegal, not to mention sinful."

"According to whom? I live by my own code." Abruptly he leaned forward, the dark eyes trapping her with their intensity. "As for sinful—I find nothing sinful in surrounding myself with items of priceless beauty. Living a life of enjoyment, challenge, and satisfaction. Tell me how that's . . . *sinful*, Miss Hayes."

He sounded so assured, without any of the doubt-riddled introspections plaguing Rosalind for most of her life. She herself had yearned to live like that. "You're depriving the rightful owners of their enjoyment—their satisfaction."

"I wonder," the Catbird whispered in her ear, "how you would like a new life, Miss Hayes? One free of obligations and financial worries. You and your brother can keep the rest of Booker Rattray's stash—he told me it was worth over a million dollars. Give me my treasures, and I'll give you—and your brother—a life beyond your wildest dreams. Think of it . . . all the money you'll ever need, and then some. You'll be able to do anything you please. Go anywhere your heart desires . . ."

A million dollars. *A million dollars*. Rosalind couldn't wrap her mind around so vast a sum. But in those dark surreal moments, with the Catbird's mellow voice curling around her,

painting such an alluring picture, it was difficult to resist considering the possibilities.

Complete financial freedom for the rest of her life. For her
parents' lives. She could ensure better treatment for her father—even take him back East. They would no longer be de-
pendent on the largess of Charles or Oliver. Rosalind herself
could finally travel. Explore the wonders of the world she'd only
been able to read about in books.

A million dollars—or thirty pieces of silver?

40

THE SILENT QUESTION intruded out of nowhere, slicing into Rosalind's heart in a stream of sun-shot silver. The darkness seemed to shrink, then dissolve as the light spread through Rosalind in a cleansing, powerful stream. She closed her eyes in repentance—and relief.

"Tell me what you know," the Catbird cajoled. "Trust me. . . ."

Rosalind opened her eyes. Warmth and strength continued to flood her being. No longer was she distracted by pain, or cold, or the debilitating helplessness of being alone. No longer did a seductive voice and mesmerizing eyes hold her in thrall, tempting her beyond her power to resist.

"Why should you needlessly suffer for your brother? It was his own selfish actions that put you in harm's way. I'm offering you more choice than your own flesh and blood, Miss Hayes." He paused, then continued softly. "I can hurt you. We both know that, don't we? I don't want to, but at my word, those two ruffians can have you begging for help. You'll promise to tell me anything I want to hear."

"I know you can make me tell you anything," Rosalind agreed steadily. The metallic taste of fear was gaining strength. Her heart was racing. But there was no longer any doubt what her course must be. "But I—" she faltered, then finished simply, "I still won't tell you."

"Brave words." He stood, pulled on gloves, then hauled Rosalind to her feet. "Perhaps it won't be necessary to kill you after all. I'll just turn you over to Carlos and Briggs, who can thereafter dump you in one of the bawdy houses in Cripple Creek. You won't last long there."

Nobody had ever spoken crudely to Rosalind, but in another flash of illumination, she recalled some painted ladies she had seen once with her mother, when they were carrying baskets to an orphanage in an unsavory section of Denver. Rosalind also remembered how smugly grateful she had felt that she *was* respectable, above reproach. Clothed in . . . self-righteousness.

"You can frighten me—and you have. But I will never give in willingly." The words emerged more feebly than she wished, because she was light-headed, stiff with cold. But at least she'd flung them in his face. "Any shame will be yours—not mine."

"Principles offer small comfort when you're abandoned by everyone you know, everyone who matters to you."

"Not . . . by everyone." She stood straighter, squaring her shoulders.

"Your snaffled detective can't find the nose on his own face. He's been chasing after me for years. Even if he does eventually stumble over Rosalind Hayes, it will be too late. By then, he likely won't recognize you."

"I wasn't talking about Detective Moreaux." Rosalind's lips curved in a real smile for the first time in hours.

"Ah." His answering smile mocked her. "You delude yourself if you think *God* cares what happens to you. If He did, you wouldn't be in this position now, would you?"

Rosalind shrugged. "You are the one responsible for my being in this position. God had nothing to do with it." Except to allow it . . . which made it bearable. Just. Swallowing hard, she stood before him, swaying yet resolute in her heart, and praying that God would live up to all those divine promises He'd made in His Book.

"Have it your way." The Catbird stepped back, lifting his voice. "Briggs! Carlos! Miss Hayes needs some more inducement." He gave Rosalind a parting look that shook her badly, because it was an uncomfortable blend of anger, determination—and regret.

Then Briggs appeared at her side, an anticipatory grin on his face. The Mexican's eyes devoured her, while his hands lifted a strip of cloth. "No need to fill the air with your screams," he told her.

"She'll have to be able to talk, remember," the Catbird's voice floated back through the darkness.

They dragged her away from the fire, deep into a stand of cottonwoods. Gagged and overpowered, Rosalind nonetheless refused to go quietly. Squirming, she chewed on the cloth covering her mouth, tossed her head, and was attempting to stomp Briggs' foot when a figure erupted out of the darkness.

The massive arms pinning Rosalind dropped away. With her limbs the consistency of water, she sank to the earth, transfixed by the utterly calm ruthlessness of an avenging angel with blazing eyes and long hair.

In a blur of furious motion, Briggs was laid out on the ground, unconscious. With the same lethal speed Adam turned to Carlos, who was crouched to attack with an upraised dagger. Adam didn't even pause. One moccasined foot kicked the dagger from the Mexican's hands, and seconds later Carlos was flat on his back with the point of a knife pressed against his throat.

"You have one choice." Adam spoke in a stranger's voice Rosalind prayed she would never hear again. "Jail in Pueblo—or a grave."

"Jail," Carlos whispered.

The bowie disappeared. Adam rose, waiting. Carlos slowly dragged himself up, then bolted. Adam caught him in three steps. Rosalind heard another series of thuds and choked grunts—and the Mexican went crashing to the ground. This time, he didn't move.

Silent, watchful, Adam crossed over to Rosalind. He stared down at Briggs' sprawled form, then turned to her. For a lightning-brief second Rosalind met the remote intensity of his eyes. Then he knelt, hooked his hands under Briggs' shoulders, and unceremoniously dragged the dead weight across the ground. After dropping him next to Carlos, Adam melted into the blackness.

Rosalind had time only to draw one shaky breath before he returned carrying a coiled rope, which he used to bind the two men together. Then he was kneeling beside her. "You're safe now. They can't hurt you anymore."

He removed the gag with gentle hands. "Nobody will hurt you like that again, I promise."

"Where—?" She struggled for composure, determined not to dissolve like wet sugar. "How—?"

He lightly stroked her cheek with his thumb, brushing damp strands of hair aside. But the faint glow of the campfire reflected the expression in his eyes, burning with a violence hotter than the wood. Like his touch, his voice was preternaturally calm. "I was on board the train. The Catbird staged a robbery—timed so that we'd be delayed in Pueblo. I was talking to the sheriff and a couple of policemen when Hank found me, told me what you'd done."

Reaction set in, and Rosalind could no longer subdue the tremors. "Tricked me, too." Humiliation burned her throat, the words cutting like ground glass. "S-sorry."

"Shh. It's all right . . . you're safe. That's all that matters." He held out his hand, but didn't touch her.

All she could do was shake her head. Her mouth opened, but the only sound that came out was the broken sound of his name as she let herself fall forward.

Adam lifted her into his arms and held her while she finally wept.

41

AFTER ROSALIND QUIETED, Adam picked her up and carried her over by the fire. Under any other circumstances, he would have savored the feel of her in his arms. But not right now. Not when she was shivering from cold and shock, with a shattered expression in her tear-swollen eyes that would haunt him for a long time.

Why hadn't she stayed on the train?

Carefully he laid her on an unrolled blanket next to the fire and started to turn away. Cold, dirt-smeared fingers grabbed fistfuls of his shirt and clung.

"Shh. It's all right." He stripped off his gloves and chafed the cold fingers with his bare hands. "Let me fetch your waistcoat and your cloak, stoke the fire. You need to get warm."

Almost violently she shook her head, winced, then bit her lip. Adam gathered her close again. After a moment he began stroking the tangled mess of her unbound hair, carefully avoiding the swollen lump behind her ear. His mind seething, he entertained a number of shamefully repugnant thoughts about the Catbird and his despicable lieutenants. The latter were trussed, still unconscious—doubtless the safest circumstances for them. Considering what they'd planned for Rosalind, they were fortunate to be alive.

He heard her whisper something into the folds of his shirt.

"Hmm? I didn't catch that." Adam gathered a thick swath of hair at the base of her neck and gently moved it aside so that he could hear. "What are you trying to say?"

"C-Catbird. . . ?" The single word was barely audible. Another shudder rippled through her body.

"Escaped." Adam ruthlessly tamped down the frustration. "I didn't see him—just heard the sound of his horse. But I will catch him . . . even if it won't be today." He hesitated, then plunged ahead, needing to know. "I want you to answer one question for me. You mustn't feel shame, or . . . or . . ."

"They—nobody . . . harmed me."

That shattered expression in her eyes still worried Adam, but the nightmarish images he had fought and feared for the past six hours began to fade. "Thank God." The anger at Rosalind for her monumental recklessness was gone as well, swept away by his consuming need to comfort her.

He hugged her. "Don't you think you could at least have grabbed your coat on your way to catch a thief?"

"I . . . didn't think." Her breath hitched, the throat muscles working. "I saw the Catbird through the window . . . didn't want to lose him. It was foolish, I know."

"Easy now. No need to panic. In a sense, your impulsiveness was what saved you. A woman back at the station noticed your bold pink shirtwaist. Wondered why you weren't wearing your coat or hat. She was still staring when those two brigands manhandled you into the back of the wagon."

Rosalind stirred, lifting her head. "Oh . . ." At last some of the light seeped back into her face, her voice. "Even then, God was taking care of me . . . and you came." A faint smile appeared. "You came. . . ."

Adam felt as though a gigantic boulder had rolled off his rib cage. Very carefully, so as not to frighten her, he gathered her in his arms. When her hands crept up to close over his shoulders, his breath wedged in his lungs.

"Adam," she whispered.

As their lips met in a tender kiss, the last of his panic drifted up into the trees like dissipating smoke. God had granted his fervent prayer. His arms tightened, holding her as if she were the most precious treasure in the universe.

42

ADAM LOADED BRIGGS AND CARLOS, still trussed together like a pair of Christmas turkeys, into the back of the delivery wagon. Cowed, the two men didn't argue even when he tied their ankles together as well.

"I'm glad I wasn't conscious when they dumped me back here," Rosalind observed, watching while she held Biscuit's reins. "This wagon stinks."

Adam winced, then—because he knew she needed it—gave a short laugh. "Next time you're abducted, make sure your host offers more suitable accommodations." He shut and latched the wagon doors, then secured Biscuit with a lead line.

"I can't believe we're joking about it."

"Nothing wrong with embracing life," Adam said. "Especially after a brush with death. My father always used to say that humor's one of the Lord's most effective healing agents."

Smiling, he fingered one of the thick wool caplets adorning the top of her cape. Once he would have sneered at the affectation. Now he was grateful that the extra fabric provided added warmth for Rosalind.

Moments later they were headed back toward Pueblo, this time with Rosalind sitting warm and snug at his side.

"Adam?"

"Hmm?"

"I've decided to go back East, to my great-aunt in Virginia, until you find Pastor Scrivens and Isaac."

"Because of what happened?"

Her shoulders lifted in a restless shrug. "Not . . . exactly."

"Rosalind, trust me. Nothing you tell me is going to shock me, all right?"

"Well, it shocked me," she muttered with a flash of her old spirit. "He tried to . . . to make a deal with me! And . . . I was tempted. He said if I helped him, Isaac and I could have all of Booker Rattray's stash, except for the Petrovna jewels. He didn't care about the money—a million dollars or so. A million dollars!"

Adam slid her a swift sidelong look. She was facing straight ahead, but even in the dark he could discern the rigid line of jaw, the stiffly held body.

"It doesn't matter that I was hurt, afraid. That anybody else might have responded the same way. I knew better—but I was tempted."

"Did you give in?"

"No . . . but I was still tempted."

The relief made him light-headed. "Temptation is a part of life," he reminded her. "It's giving in to it that's the sin. Be easy with yourself, Rosalind—"

"But I'm still planning to leave. Run away. Doesn't that make me a coward? I'm afraid of what I may do . . . if the Catbird corners me again."

"What it makes you is *smart*. You've learned a lesson."

He could still hear the tear-thickened voice, sharing her ordeal while she sat by the fire, sipping bitter coffee the Catbird had left boiling over the flames. Even now Adam grappled with the shock of how close Rosalind had come to dying. "Paying with your life is too high a ransom just to capture a thief."

The words emerged more as a growl, and he immediately softened his tone, not wanting to disrupt Rosalind's barely restored poise. "Why don't you try to sleep? Here—" He wrapped his arm around her shoulders and tugged her over. "Lay your head on my shoulder. Stop worrying about the Catbird. That's my job—not yours." And this time, he planned to ensure that it remained that way.

"I've never rested my head on a man's shoulder."

Adam's grip tightened. He felt her rub her face against the thick sheep's wool of his shearling jacket.

"I don't know why, but when I'm with you, I'm not afraid of anything or anyone." Beneath his supporting arm, a deep sigh unraveled tight muscles. "I wish . . ."

Swallowing hard, Adam waited for her to finish, but the only sound stirring in the vast emptiness of the night was the steady clop of horses' hooves and the rattling creak of the delivery wagon. Rosalind had fallen asleep.

The trust humbled him; her innate honesty elated him. Tenderness and desire flowed unabated through his veins. Adam no longer fought the battle with himself—in truth, he'd lost it weeks ago. He was in love with Rosalind Hayes, and there was nothing left to do but thank God for it.

And make arrangements to keep her safe until the Lord told him what to do with his unexpected gift.

43

SIMON KINCAID WAS WAITING FOR THEM when Adam finally pulled the droopy-headed horses to a halt in front of the jail, at a little past two in the morning. Stuporous with sleep, Rosalind barely raised her head from Adam's shoulder, her eyes fluttering open only long enough to recognize Mr. Kincaid.

"Am I glad to see you," Adam said, the muscles beneath Rosalind's cheek flexing as he stretched.

"Thought you might stop by." Mr. Kincaid sounded as relieved as Adam. "I see our prayers were answered. How is she?"

"A little bruised, with a nasty bump on her head. Otherwise, unharmed. But the Catbird escaped. Two men he hired to kidnap Rosalind are tied up in the back, however."

"I'll find someone to help unload them. Adam . . ."

"What is it, Sim?"

"Why don't you bring Miss Hayes inside?" Simon returned, sounding evasive. "It's, ah, warmer in there. We can probably scare up a cot or something where she can lie down while we talk."

Silence descended. Adam's coiled stillness was so ominous Rosalind sat up in a clumsy rush. "Something's wrong." Her gaze darted from Adam to Simon Kincaid. "Isaac? You found Isaac. What's happened?"

"Whoa, now, Rosalind. Don't put words in the man's

196

mouth." In a single swift motion he leaped from the wagon seat to the ground, then turned and lifted her down. "Let's go inside, all right?"

Simon led them down a narrow hall, into a small room devoid of furniture except for a cluster of straight-backed chairs shoved against several dilapidated filing cabinets. Adam seated her in one of the chairs while Mr. Kincaid closed the door and turned, his face grim.

"May as well get it over with, Sim," Adam prompted. "Let's have it."

After a moment's hesitation, the other man complied. "I found Booker Rattray. Dead. Single shot, point-blank to the heart."

After the bald pronouncement, nobody moved or spoke. Rosalind was numb. Her mind as incapable of thought as her emotions seemed incapable of feeling.

"Where?" Adam finally asked, looking weary beyond measure.

"In some rocks about two miles out of La Junta. Tracks indicate the presence of at least three men on horseback, one of them arriving from a different direction than the other two. Rattray had driven a buggy—horse returned to the livery stable on its own. Easy enough to backtrack. I found Rattray buried under a pile of stones."

He glanced at Rosalind. "Miss Hayes, you don't need to hear this," he suggested, his voice gentle.

The numbness was fading fast. "Isaac?"

Mr. Kincaid shook his head. "No sign of anyone else, Miss Hayes."

She was shocked to hear about the blustering con artist, but she couldn't grieve for him. Not when Isaac's fate remained unknown, more uncertain with each passing day. Now, with Booker Rattray dead and the Catbird free, all she could do was pray that her brother was still alive. He had to be—

"Rosalind," Adam began, "let me—"

"I'm all right!" She erupted out of the chair, dashing limp strands of hair from her eyes. "Perfectly all right. I survived a kidnapping without hysterics, didn't I?" Angrily she swiped at more hair. "I need some hairpins! Couldn't they have had the decency to leave me my hairpins?"

Adam forced her to sit back down, then he knelt in front of her, resting his wrists on the back of the chair. His face was lined with weariness and grime, darkened by beard stubble, yet an expression of kindness burned in his eyes. "I'll find you some hairpins," he promised. "As many as you need. It's all right," he soothed. "Now, relax. No matter how difficult the news about Isaac—we'll face it together." His hand enclosed hers in a comforting grip. "Finish it, Sim."

Kincaid lifted a brow, then shrugged. "That's pretty much it. Soon as I turned Rattray's body over to Sheriff Gillman, I caught a freight over here."

"And? It's plain you're reluctant to provide details," Adam stirred, betraying the first hint of impatience Rosalind had seen. "Dragging it out only makes it worse. Spill it and get it over with, Sim. Rosalind can handle it."

"I promise, no more displays," she added, coloring a little.

"Very well, then. There's something odd about this whole thing with Rattray," Kincaid muttered uncomfortably. "His body had been—arranged. Laid out, not just tossed in the rocks and covered. Derby and cane neatly placed across his chest, hands folded. It was almost as if . . ."

"As if the murderer regretted the act, though not enough to be sorry he'd committed it," Rosalind finished for him. Her voice sounded strange to her ears, almost detached. "It was the Catbird, wasn't it?"

"What makes you think so?" Adam asked.

"Something about the way he was looking at me, right before he turned me over to Carlos and Briggs."

This time the silence reverberated with murderous intent around the barren little room. When Adam finally spoke, goose bumps sprang up on Rosalind's skin, lifting the hair at the back of her neck.

"Simon, Jedidiah Scrivens' Bible is locked in the depot safe. On your way back to Montana, I'd like you to transport it to Superintendent Connelly for me. I'm going to escort Miss Hayes to her great-aunt, in Virginia. When I return, I'll go after the Catbird." He paused. "And I won't stop until I've . . . caught him."

"Adam, no!" Rosalind protested. "I don't want you to escort me anywhere." She rose again, tugging her hand free. "Think! The longer you wait to pick up his trail, the less chance you have of finding him before he finds Isaac."

"She's right," Simon interjected. "Not only that, you'd be too noticeable, my friend. Might as well leave behind a trail of gold dust."

"I'll figure something out." His face was savage. "I don't want that monster within two miles of her, ever again."

"Adam—" Simon laid a calming hand on his friend's shoulder. "You're not thinking clearly." He hesitated, exchanged a single look with Rosalind, and expelled his breath. "Listen—*I'll* escort Miss Hayes wherever she needs to go."

"Don't be absurd. What about your ranch? Elizabeth?"

"The hands can look after the horses for a couple of weeks."

"You mustn't even consider it, Mr. Kincaid," Rosalind objected. "I would never impose—"

"It will be an honor, not an imposition." Simon smiled then, and the change in the hard-looking face was remarkable. "That's what friends are for. Isn't that so, Adam?"

Rosalind watched in amazement as acceptance, and finally peace, gradually smoothed Adam's taut features. "Yes," he said, his arm coming around Rosalind to haul her against his side, "that's what friends are for."

PART THREE

RANSOM

44

Mountains near Cripple Creek, Colorado
December 1896

POWDERY SNOWFLAKES dusted Adam's shoulders as he ducked inside the Midland Depot at Cripple Creek at a little past two in the afternoon. A snow squall had boiled up over the mountains an hour earlier, suffusing the air with an eerie glow and shrouding the earth in a white pall.

Adam glanced around the deserted station, absently swiping melting flakes off his coat. "Sam?" he called, his voice echoing in the empty room.

After a moment the agent poked his head around a doorway. "Panther! Been a spell." He coughed, looking both relieved and—edgy? "I . . . ah . . . I was beginning to wonder if one of them hotheaded miners had blown your head off, after all."

"Now why would you think that?" Adam asked, folding his arms across his chest while he pondered the fidgety man.

Sam scowled at his boots. "Been some talk," he finally muttered under his breath. "You know what it's been like hereabouts, ever since the strike in June. And you being on the side of the mine owners—no offense," he hastened to add. "Most folks know you're straight as they come, Panther. Even if you are a Pink. I mean, a Pinkerton agent."

"Thanks, Sam. I prefer to think I'm on the side of right, though I realize that what's right is not always what's legal." He stopped, pulling a deep breath. "Listen, I'm not chasing miners right now, so relax. All I need is the latest on Jedidiah Scrivens."

"You *have* been occupied elsewhere, ain't ya?" Sam puffed out fleshy cheeks as he patted his pockets for a plug of tobacco. "The old boy's a sly one, for all he's a man of the cloth, so to speak." He laughed, shaking his head. "The preacher's gone back to England, Panther. But I'm the only one who knows why."

Gone back to England? Adam walked with a deliberate tread across the room until he'd all but crowded Sam against the doorjamb to which he was now clinging. "I'm about to become the second who knows why."

"I'm not sure—"

"Sam, don't. Not today. It wouldn't be . . . wise."

Sam gawked, his mouth working. "I catch your drift, Panther. Yessir, I do." He coughed again, and spat a stream of tobacco into a filthy spittoon. "Old Jed, ah, he got a telegram. Gathered dust in my office for close to two weeks. 'Tweren't good news for him, I can tell you. Appears he fathered a kid, back in England—a daughter. Can you believe it? Telegram said she was dying. Pastor turned the color of rock salt and took the next train out. Haven't heard since. And that's gospel, Panther."

One by one Adam unclenched his fingers. The unexpected development was a major blow, yes, but Rosalind was in Virginia. Safely tucked away and out of the Catbird's clutches. So relax, pal, before you cause Sam apoplexy.

He managed a smile. "How long ago since Jed picked up the telegram?"

Visibly relaxing, Sam scratched his beard, shuffled over to lean through the ticket window to check a large wall calendar. "Back the second week of November, I think it was. Right after the election? Sorry day that was—still can't believe they elected that ol' windbag McKinley. Him and his silver . . ."

"I see." Without Jed's help to interpret the Bible verses, there was little hope of finding Booker Rattray's treasure and the Petrovna Parure. Or Isaac Hayes.

Adam scrubbed a hand over his face, feeling the beginnings of a headache. "Anybody else asking after the preacher?" he asked. "Other than townsfolk, that is."

Sam shrugged. "Not that I recollect. He doesn't spend much time in town, you know. Sorry, Panther—no, wait a minute!" He grabbed Adam's arm. "There *was* this feller, just last week, up from Manitou Springs. I remember 'cause he was a pretty peculiar cuss."

"What did he look like? What did he say?"

"C'mon, Panther. You're asking a lot, now. You know how busy this place is when a train pulls in."

Adam leaned closer. "Try."

"Aw, fer—" Brow furrowed, Sam thought for a few seconds, hitching up his suspenders. "As I recall, it was the same day the fumble-fingered nincompoop I hired as a janitor near burned the station down. Only reason I remember the feller asking after Jed is because he was so dadblamed rude. Not my fault the preacher bolted across the Atlantic, is it?"

"Of course not, Sam." Adam clenched his jaw and offered a coaxing smile. "And the only reason I ask a lot of you is because you're reliable. You've a good eye and ear, Sam. I appreciate it."

"Well, now . . ." Chest swelling with pride, the agent beamed at Adam. "That's a right nice thing to say. Like I told you, you're a good man, for a detective."

"So this rude person . . . was it what he said, or how he said it, that made him stick in your memory."

Sam chuckled. "Both, I reckon. Pushed his face right through the window, he did. Had a beard—gray, spade shaped." The pudgy face lit with excitement, and he turned eagerly to Adam. "He was short, barely the height of a rain barrel, but skinny. Reminded me of a monkey, he did, Panther."

So. It wasn't the Catbird. Adam hid his disappointment. "Fine, Sam. What did he tell you?"

"Well . . . he called me an upstart old lamebrain, for one." He spat another stream of tobacco juice. "Then he said the next time I saw old Scrivens, to tell him not to bother using him as a post office again, since he'd never bothered to pick up his blamed letter!" Sam beamed triumphantly. "And he didn't even leave the station. Took the train right back down the mountain to Manitou."

"Good job, Sam!" They shared satisfied grins. "Tell you

what. I'm going to ask my superintendent to send you a personal letter of commendation. You've been a big help."

"Now, don't be doing nothing like that." Sam's grin disappeared. "Not that I don't appreciate it, mind you. It's just that . . . well, if folks in town thought I was cozying up too much to the Panther, I might go home and find it burned to the ground. Understand?"

"I do." Adam dropped a hand on the older man's shoulder. Right now, he'd never felt the isolation of his chosen vocation more keenly. "Don't worry. I understand." He walked across to the hat stand and lifted his hat, then turned around, stroking the damp feather. "Sam . . . if anybody else asks about the preacher, will you let me know? Telegraph the agency in Denver—after hours, if you like, when nobody else is around."

"Well . . ."

"You won't be betraying miners or any of your friends. This case has nothing to do with the miners' strike."

"Since it's you, Panther, reckon I can do that."

Adam set his hat firmly in place. "Thanks. I'll be in touch."

He stepped outside, where the drifting snowflakes now swirled lazily in descending spirals from a rapidly lightening sky. The snowstorm, he realized gratefully, was dissipating. Stride brisk, he headed down the street toward the livery stable, where he'd left Biscuit enjoying a warm stall and a bucketful of oats. *Sorry, fella*, Adam apologized to his absent horse. Two inches of snow couldn't constitute a deterrent this afternoon.

With a bit more of God's grace, they'd make it as far as Halfway House by nightfall, and by the following morning Adam would be scouring Manitou Springs for a short, irritable man with a gray, spade-shaped beard. And hopefully a letter from Jedidiah Scrivens.

45

ROSALIND HALFHEARTEDLY PACKED AWAY a collection of colorful German nutcrackers, the last of her great-aunt's Christmas decorations. Her thoughts were miles away. Over a thousand, actually.

"I agree," Wilhemina Stratton observed from her rocking chair. "A dismal month, combined with a depressing task, makes a body melancholy."

"Hmm? What was that?" Rosalind glanced across the room.

"You were sighing again. If I didn't know better, I'd suggest you were pining for a sweetheart." She set the big old rocker in motion, nodding her head with the gentle rhythm.

Rosalind fastened the lid of the wooden crate and straightened. "If only it were that simple," she whispered, the ever-present uncertainty chilling her heart.

The cloudy afternoon reflected her gloom. Icicles draped from eaves, and the snow-crusted lawn resembled a bleak tundra. On such a day, one would be foolish to venture outside, Rosalind knew. But even as her mind rebelled, her imagination conjured up images of the even colder, more inhospitable Colorado climate.

Adam shivering inside his jacket, somewhere up a snow-covered peak, where every breath was a knife blade slashing across his lungs. . . .

Isaac hiding inside a rickety cabin, waiting for spring, or—far worse—buried somewhere in an unmarked grave. . . .

As for the Catbird—no, she ordered her unruly thoughts. No.

"Come sit with me for a while, child." Wilhemina gestured to the comfortable horsehair sofa next to the rocker, her brisk tone reminding Rosalind of Tallulah. "You've been working like a dervish for weeks now. Ever since you received that mysterious letter from someplace in the New Mexico Territory, specifically."

She adjusted her shawl closer about her shoulders. "Why don't you try talking about it for a change? I'm old, but I haven't forgotten how painful love can be."

Rosalind sat, knowing her aunt was right . . . about the talking, anyway. Adam's last letter had been short, impersonal. Almost curt. Gustav Wachtler, the eccentric little man she had met that long-ago day, had been another blind alley. His house—clocks and all—had been locked up tight, deserted; the old man's whereabouts unknown. Superintendent Connelly had reassigned Adam to another case down in the New Mexico Territory.

Before he'd left Manitou Springs, Adam had written a letter to Pastor Scrivens, who was still in England. Rosalind hadn't heard from him since. She must school herself to patience.

Her mending bag was on the floor next to the sofa. She picked out a torn lace collar, settled into the cushion, and took a deep breath. "Aunt Minna, what I feel for Adam is too . . . complicated to be classified as love."

"Balderdash! You think about him all the time. You worry about him all the time—don't shake your head at me, miss. I may be old, but I'm no simpleton. You might try to hide behind that sweet smile and efficient manner, but those woeful eyes tell me I'm right. Probably dream about him at night, too, don't you?"

"I don't know," Rosalind almost snapped. "For your information, I also spend a lot of my time worrying about Isaac, not to mention Mamma and Papa."

"The great-grandson of a friend of my neighbor's housekeeper is suffering from consumption. Perhaps you'd like to add him to your list of worries."

The rejoinder brought Rosalind's head up; after a moment the tension knotting her fingers and insides began to unravel. "Papa used to warn me about you," she observed wryly. "Very well, Aunt. I surrender. You're right—I do tend to take on others' burdens more than I should."

"If I recall my Scriptures correctly, I believe that's the Lord's job, not ours." Wilhemina tilted her head. "Put that down and come closer, child. I want to share something with you."

Rosalind obediently laid aside the collar, knelt beside the elderly woman's chair, and waited.

"Believe it or not, I was once very young—and to a woman of eighty-four, 'very young' includes someone of your years, my dear. Don't ever let your silly sister shame you into thinking that women are on the shelf if they're not married by the time they're twenty."

"Alberta gave that up when I passed twenty-three."

They smiled at each other, then her great-aunt rested her head against the back of the rocker and closed her eyes. "My parents sent me to England on a husband-hunting trip, back in forty-four, it was. I'd just passed my twenty-first birthday, and they were desperate to secure me a suitable husband. Wealth—or a title, if not both."

"Is that where you met Great-Uncle Malcolm?"

"No, child. Malcolm was much later."

A faint smile touched with sadness shadowed the lined face. Rosalind studied her in mounting concern. Lately Minna's lips seemed blue tinged at odd moments, and beneath the finely wrinkled skin and aristocratic bones, a grayness had begun to blur the image of indomitable vigor. But light and life shone undimmed from her brown eyes, so reminiscent of Rosalind's father before his stroke that sometimes her heart clenched in a spasm of homesickness.

"I met a young man in Scotland," Minna announced. "He was dashing and gallant. Impossibly wild—and hopelessly unsuitable. So of course I fell in love with him."

"It's not like that with Adam and me," Rosalind put in uncomfortably.

Wilhemina opened her eyes and silenced her with a look. "*If you would allow me to finish the tale, you may be surprised, Rosalind.*" She shook her head, looking more like an offended queen than an engaging elderly aunt. "Impulsive. Your father always fretted over both your and your younger brother's impulsiveness."

"You're absolutely right. I apologize."

"I detest it when you're too agreeable as well." She sat up to sip from a lukewarm cup of tea. "It reminds me of myself." She set the cup down with a rattle. "I eloped with Ian MacKenna. Ha! That will teach you to leap to conclusions, won't it?"

Rosalind opened her mouth, swallowed her first comment. "Yes, ma'am."

"Marriage lasted less than a year—but long enough for me to learn that the devil truly does relish the opportunity to blind impressionable young girls with good looks and charm."

"Adam doesn't try to impress me," Rosalind blurted. Quite the contrary. He'd gone out of the way to keep her at arm's length. That day in Pueblo when he'd put her on the train with Simon, they'd barely spoken at all.

Minna snorted. "Did I suggest he did? From the bit I've gleaned, the two of you invested more energy in fighting your attraction than acknowledging it. As for Ian and myself . . ." Her voice trailed away, and the haunted shadows deepened. Then her chin lifted. "I am not going to share the sordid details. The lesson I offer you, my child, is one of discernment." She took a sip of tea, then waited expectantly.

"I'm listening," Rosalind promised. "And—no protests or arguments until you're finished."

"Impulsive but wise." Briefly, one fragile hand rested against Rosalind's cheek. "The Almighty does not require you to bear responsibility for others' actions, child—only for your own. You—and you alone—are responsible for cultivating that relationship. It is also my firm conviction that the Lord will then provide counsel and direction in matters of the heart."

"Aunt Minna," Rosalind's voice was hesitant, "I'm afraid I'm not following you. . . . It never crossed my mind that Adam and I could—would consider a serious relationship." *You're lying to her and to yourself, Rosalind.* "I mean, we're from different worlds. He actively despises mine, and I—"

"What you're doing is dithering—and deceiving yourself. Just like I did with Ian MacKenna. I saw emotionally, not spiritually. But God in His mercy allowed a second chance, and taught me the difference by bringing Malcolm into my life."

"Fine, but how did you *know*?" Rosalind stormed to her feet, waving her arm. "How do you know if God even *wants* you to marry, much less to whom? Does He tell the man as well? Am I supposed to wear my hair in braids down my back, give away my gowns for homespun and calico? Follow Adam around the mountains like a . . . a squaw?"

"I'm not the one you should be asking." Wilhemina stood as well, her spine straight as a darning needle. She picked up her cup and saucer. "I think I'll go see what Sadie's making for supper tonight."

Foot tapping, Rosalind watched with crossed arms until Wilhemina reached the fringed portieres framing the doorway. "Aunt Minna," she called, unable to stem her curiosity, "what happened to Ian MacKenna?"

Wilhemina turned, her expression remote, closed. Then, as though listening to some internal voice Rosalind couldn't hear, the imperial gaze softened. "My parents secured a certificate of divorce and brought me back to Virginia."

The ugly word screamed like a banshee in the quiet room. "That's right, child. A divorce. Believe as you please, but it is not an unforgivable sin. Yet for over a decade I lived in shame, in secret—despised and rejected by those who learned of it. The object of pity in our family."

Rosalind could barely form the word. "Uncle M-Malcolm? How—?"

"Ah. He was new in town—the young physician helping old Dr. Porter ease into retirement. Took him two years, after meeting me, to convince me he didn't care about my past. Nor did he give two hoots about public opinion. God forgave me, he said, and that was enough for him."

She waited, the aged, aristocratic face serene. "We were, as you know, married for forty-eight years before the Lord chose to take him home before me. Listen to God first, child—then listen to your heart. You'll know. Trust me, you'll know the path to follow, and whom to walk beside."

46

IT WAS ALWAYS A CHALLENGE, carrying out a job during a full moon. But instead of embracing the opportunity he had created, at the moment Napoleon LaRue was leaning against a rain barrel, ankles crossed, indifferent to the challenge. Sourly he contemplated the pearly globe hanging low enough to pluck from the sky with his fingers.

The party at the Guevarra hacienda had begun two hours ago. An engraved invitation for Beaufort Paxton, esquire, was tucked inside LaRue's vest pocket. For three months he'd invested time, energy, and money establishing the identity; for the first time in twenty years, the process had bored, then enraged him.

He should have been in Europe by now, secure from interference by the dogged American authorities. The Petrovna jewels should have been safely tucked away in a German or Austrian bank, where LaRue could have dropped by regularly without drawing undue attention.

Instead, he had been forced to go underground, nursing his frustration while he bided his time in this backwater city. As far as LaRue was concerned, Santa Fe was on the edge of the civilized world. Never mind that it was almost three hundred years old, or that some of the Spanish and Mexican aristos he'd rubbed elbows with these past weeks possessed more pride than a trainload of proper Bostonians.

None of that mattered. At the moment, Santa Fe was a prison.

Abruptly LaRue shoved away from his perch. At least the party would provide momentary diversion, an outlet for the testiness plaguing his every mood. He'd invested time and money, so he might as well get something out of it, though none of the potential pickings equaled even the smallest diamond chip in one jewel-encrusted comb of the Petrovna Parure.

Over the past week he'd also flirted with a flower garden selection of lovely ladies, not only to assess their jewelry, but in an attempt to divert his thoughts from Rosalind Hayes.

He wanted to see her again—and not merely as the means to an end.

He also wanted to kill that interfering detective. Slowly.

With an impatient oath, he tugged down the sleeves of his topcoat and settled his silk top hat firmly in place. The girl had disappeared, doubtless courtesy of the cursed Pinkerton. Until the carefully phrased feelers LaRue had sent out bore fruit, he couldn't risk intensifying the search for her blasted brother— another interfering moron who deserved a slow and painful death.

Of course, he might already be dead, but LaRue knew better than to believe every word Booker Rattray had spoken. Booker . . .

In spite of the betrayal, LaRue still missed the wily old trickster. Booker had been the only person in the world who had known the Catbird was really Napoleon LaRue, a scrawny, scared kid raised in a London orphanage.

Booker had never ridiculed his name. . . . LaRue closed his eyes, remembering the merciless taunts he'd endured as a child. By the time he was eight years old he'd vowed to change his background as well as the now despised moniker. Booker had understood, and had honored that secret for twenty years. He'd been a liar and a cheat, and his betrayal of the Catbird had cost him his life—but he'd understood.

Now only the Hayes girl could identify him as the Catbird, even if she didn't know his real name.

214

Rosalind Hayes. It always came back to Rosalind Hayes.

Jaw muscles quivering, LaRue stalked across the street to his hotel. "I ordered a carriage for ten o'clock," he snapped to the doorman. "Where is it? I'm already late for my evening engagement."

April. He'd wait until the end of April. After that, he'd track her down, no matter where she'd bolted to.

47

Richmond, Virginia
April 1897

". . . SO FIRST YOU DIVIDE IT into three sections, like
this?" Priscilla Bates queried, fumbling with her baby-fine
locks, muttering when strands continued to slither from her
grasp. She made a face. "Fiddle-faddle, Rosalind! Why won't
my hair behave like yours? It's enough to make me plot to shave
your head while you're sleeping, for revenge."

Rosalind smiled. "You have lovely hair, Pris. Here—" She
stuck several long hairpins in her mouth, then deftly wound
and tucked Priscilla's hair into an S-shaped chignon. "A few
curls framing your face is all the rage right now." She stuck in
the final hairpin. "But we're not going to try for that look, since
Jonathan has entered the sticky-fingered grabbing stage."

She stepped back, affecting an obsequious pose and tone.
"Even so, this style will allow Madame to dazzle everyone."

Priscilla giggled. "I love it when you talk as though you're
serious, while your eyes dance like Jonathan's when he grabs
the cat's tail."

"Speaking of Jonathan, I haven't had my daily dose of hugs
this afternoon." Rosalind glanced across at the grandfather
clock dominating Wilhemina's parlor. "It's almost four. He
should be awake from his nap. I'll fetch him for you, before
Aunt Minna returns from her weekly game of bridge whist with
Mrs. Purcell and elbows me aside."

"Please do." Priscilla wandered over to a mirror to admire her new hairstyle. "The two of you spoil him dreadfully." She turned around suddenly and hurried across the room, throwing her arms around the astonished Rosalind. "It's been wonderful these past months, having you for a friend. I wish you would stay here forever."

Throat tight, Rosalind hugged the younger woman back. Stephen and Priscilla Bates lived behind her aunt. Ever since Wilhemina had introduced Rosalind the previous fall, Priscilla had spent almost as much time with Rosalind as she did with her family.

Their friendship soothed the aching wound of uncertainty festering in Rosalind's heart and filled the loneliness of her days. "The feeling is mutual," she replied, swallowing a lump in her throat.

Moments later she returned to the parlor, cuddling the sleepy baby. "Look," she announced with a smile, "not even a whimper."

"I might have known." Priscilla's tone was resigned. "Is there anything you *don't* do well?" Suddenly she lifted both hands to her mouth in a vain attempt to hide a squeak of astonishment.

"She doesn't obey instructions well," a deep voice offered from the entryway.

Rosalind almost dropped the baby. "Adam?" She turned around almost fearfully. "*Adam?*"

She wasn't hallucinating—he was really here, in the flesh. Disbelief and joy caught her up in a dizzying whirl. She clutched Jonathan to her, her gaze never leaving the man posed unmoving in the doorway. "You're here . . ."

He crossed the room in four long strides, looking impossibly healthy. Vitality and masculine assurance infused the air with sparks, exploding the tranquil aura of the staid parlor. The fearful anticipation gatherd itself in a tight knot, just beneath Rosalind's breastbone.

She was almost relieved when he turned his attention to the baby, who was sucking one plump thumb. Amber eyes seemed to gather light. "Hello, little feller. . . ." He lifted his hand to stroke a rosy cheek.

Without warning he caught Rosalind's eye, and she forgot to breathe.

Then he was moving away, across the room. "My name, since Miss Hayes seems to have lost her voice, is Adam Moreaux," he said to Priscilla. "You would be the cherub's mother? He's got your nose, hasn't he?"

Priscilla's head bobbed up and down. She appeared unable to look away from Adam's buckskins. "M-Mr. Moreaux," she stuttered. "Rosalind has mentioned you."

"I'm sure she has." Unabashed, Adam smiled.

Rosalind's mental processes clicked back into place. "Pastor Scrivens. You found him?" She hurriedly handed Jonathan to his mother. "Isaac? What about Isaac? And—"

"All in good time," Adam smoothly interrupted. "Where's your aunt?"

"At a friend's. Adam—" She wanted to mirror his restraint, yet she wanted to hurl herself into his arms. Overwhelmed by conflicting emotions, Rosalind stood like a potted plant and did nothing.

He lifted an inquiring brow, as though sensing her turmoil. "You're looking—" he paused, a slight frown gathering on his forehead, "—drawn," he finished, stepping forward to cup her face, turning her head from side to side.

Without removing the hand he turned to Priscilla. "Are you a friend, or an acquaintance of Rosalind's aunt?"

Astonished, Priscilla looked as though she'd just swallowed a yardstick. "I . . . um—Rosalind, does he treat you with such . . . such familiarity . . . all the time?"

"Pretty much." Flustered by her unguarded response, Rosalind spoke without considering the implications. "Mr. Moreaux believes that etiquette is mostly hypocritical, maidenly sensibilities nothing but posturing. Why, if he'd wanted to—to kiss me, it wouldn't matter a particle if anybody else was in the room—"

"Shall I prove it doesn't matter a particle?" Adam lowered his head as well as his voice.

Priscilla gasped, her eyes round as silver dollars. "I think I should leave."

"Not just yet, please." His voice held a sobering ring of command. "Let's sit down first. Ladies?" Adam's hand dropped to the back of a nearby chair.

The abrupt metamorphosis of the mood, from lighthearted banter to gravity, sent prickles of dread skittering down Rosalind's arms. "What's wrong?" she ventured in a small voice.

Priscilla moved without protest to the Japanese bamboo chair Adam had indicated, settling Jonathan in her lap.

"What is it?" Rosalind whispered again, hardly able to force the words past her constricted throat. But she knew. Deep inside . . . she knew. . . .

Adam didn't respond, instead leading her over to Wilhemina's antique davenport, opposite Priscilla's chair. He dropped down beside Rosalind and took her hands, holding them in a steady, sustaining clasp. "There's no way to do this gently." He drew a long breath. "So I'll do it fast. Last week, I received a cablegram from Jedidiah Scrivens. He's been in England but is returning to Colorado in two weeks."

Adam took a deep breath, then finished bluntly, "Isaac died last October—from blood poisoning. The preacher cared for him until the end. Buried him somewhere up around Cripple Creek."

Rosalind stared without seeing at their clasped hands. She felt removed from the room, borne aloft on a sluggish current of ice-coated air. "I think I've known, for a long time." The words sounded indistinct, stiff. As though they'd been squeezed through a cider press.

"Shall I have the housekeeper bring some water, or hot tea?" Priscilla offered.

Rosalind shook her head. "I'm all right. You . . . just take care of Jonathan." The baby had begun to fret. "Go home, Pris." She lifted her head and looked across at her friend. "Please. It's a shock, but not a surprise."

"Oh, Rosalind . . . I'm so sorry," Priscilla whispered. Jonathan struggled in his mother's arms, then whimpered more loudly. "I . . . I'm not sure I should leave—"

"I'll take care of her," Adam said. He released Rosalind's limp hands and stood. "We're a long ways beyond chaperonage, Rosalind and I. And it seems that Jonathan needs you more. Go home, Mrs. Bates. Here—let me walk you to the door. I'll hold Jonathan while you fetch your hat and cloak. Don't worry. She'll be all right. Rosalind's spine is fashioned from heartwood, not pulp."

"You're a very unusual man, Mr. Moreaux," Rosalind heard Priscilla murmur as Adam ushered mother and baby into the foyer. "No wonder Rosalind . . ." Whatever she was going to say was drowned beneath Jonathan's rising squalls.

Suddenly restless, Rosalind rose on jerky limbs that behaved more like stilts, moving without intent to the window. It was a lovely spring afternoon . . . dogwood trees across the street bursting with frothy pink and white blooms. Wisps of white clouds across a bright blue sky—"mares' tails," Isaac called them.

But now her brother lay in a cold, lonely grave, surrounded by eternal darkness. No more spring days for Isaac. . . .

"Rosalind." Adam's arms folded around her, wrapping her unyielding body in a comforting embrace. "I'm sorry."

Slowly her hands crept around his waist; even more slowly she laid her cheek against his chest. For many moments they remained thus, until gradually Rosalind no longer felt as though she were drifting inside a frozen river. Under Adam's undemanding comfort, the shock of his news receded, and the past six months of separation began to dissolve until it seemed as though only hours had passed. Her senses reawakened to his warmth and strength.

She inhaled, breathing in the scent of leather, man . . . and talcum-sweet baby. Relaxed beneath the calming touch of his fingers massaging away the stiffness in the back of her neck.

Rosalind might not want to put a label on her feelings for Adam. But she did know that, held securely in his arms, she felt safe—and complete. Able to accomplish what she knew she needed to do.

Finally, when resolve firmed her muscles as well as her mind, she stepped back with quiet dignity and looked up into

Adam's face. "It will take me the rest of the afternoon to pack, but I'll be ready to leave in the morning. Will you take me downtown to purchase a ticket?"

One corner of his mouth curled upward. "Won't be necessary," he replied. "I brought it along with me. Our train departs from the Byrd Street Station at 9:22 A.M."

48

"I CAN'T WAIT TO MEET KAT," Rosalind announced, about an hour after they'd left Richmond behind.

Reluctantly Adam laid aside a three-day-old copy of the city's *Daily Dispatch* he'd been reading. He'd hoped they could have enjoyed at least the first day of the long journey west. "Whoa, now. Let's back up a bit," he hedged. "Rosalind . . . there's something I haven't told you."

"Kat? Don't tell me something's happened to Kat, too!"

"No—no. It's nothing to do with Kat. As far as I know, she's fine."

"My . . . family? You told me they were all right, that they had accepted Isaac's death."

She was almost wringing her hands. Adam ground his teeth. "It's nothing to do with your family. Well—" He rapidly assessed the likelihood that she would fall for a red herring. "Perhaps it does, a little. With the Catbird still at large and waiting for a chance to grab you again, your family *is* at risk—if you return to Denver."

"If . . . I return to Denver?" Abruptly she sat up very straight, her eyes narrowing. "There's something you haven't told me, isn't there? Something I'm not going to like."

Adam winced. This was unraveling much too fast. "I'm going to Manitou Springs," he told her flatly. "You're not. The

222

Catbird has had enough time, as well as the resources, to have learned every one of your habits, all the people with whom you've associated for the past ten years, and every member on your family tree. Including your great-aunt, who—as you recall—lives alone."

When Rosalind didn't speak or seem to be visibly upset, he relaxed, hoping the worst was over. "Last week there was a robbery in Santa Fe. Classic Catbird, right down to leaving behind an emerald bracelet from the aborted job at your sister's last October. He's come out of hiding, Rosalind."

The bracelet was the equivalent of a thrown gauntlet. Adam wasn't about to share that. "So . . . you won't be in any of the places he might go hunting for you, and your family won't be endangered because they're in his way. That's why I'm returning to Colorado alone. And you,"—he took her hands and held them between his—"you're going to pay Simon and Elizabeth Kincaid a visit in Montana. It's all been arranged. You and your family will be safe, and there is absolutely no chance the Catbird will find you there."

"All been arranged . . . by you? How thoughtful. How . . . thorough."

Her voice was much too polite; a warning tickle feathered his spine. Just as politely she withdrew her hands, lifting them to pat her hair. "Have you also arranged for a round-the-clock jailer?"

The tickling transformed to a drumroll of thunder. "Rosalind . . ."

"Because that's what you'll need. Either that, or you'll have to keep me locked behind bars."

Moving with Kat-like speed, she rose and planted her hands on the chairback. Her gaze skewered Adam where he sat. "Don't ever try to manipulate me again, Adam Moreaux. I . . . am . . . going . . . to . . . Manitou." She hurled the words like fiery darts. "With or without your help, I will find the treasure my brother lost his life over. Neither you nor any other employee of Pinkerton's Detective Agency can threaten me, or—or blackmail me into abandoning my course. Now, if you'll excuse me, I'm going for a walk." She stalked off down the aisle.

Adam sat in quiet bemusement, feeling a bit as though Kat had lashed out with an angry paw. After a few moments a reluctantly admiring grin inched across his face. "What a woman," he mused aloud.

Perhaps he needed to spend more energy finding a way to protect the rest of the world from Rosalind Hayes.

They pulled into Colorado Springs a little before two on a blustery, sun-shot May afternoon. Rosalind clamped one hand over the crown of her hat as Adam led her through the depot to a spot where passengers waited to board the line to Manitou Springs. Ever since she had refused to fall in with his presumptuous plans, he had treated her with an impersonal courtesy more confusing than hurtful. She searched the uncommunicative features now, feeling the sting of isolation more than ever.

The decision to carry out her brother's dying wish might have been impulsive. Indeed, it was downright foolhardy. But everyone and everything else in Isaac's life had failed him. Rosalind wasn't going to, even though he was dead.

Just before time to board, Adam stiffened. When she looked at him inquiringly, he nodded toward a man hovering on the edge of the crowd.

"Watch the conductor," he tersely instructed her. "I have to talk to that man—he's a fellow operative. This won't take long. And, Rosalind—watch everyone else as well."

Well, Rosalind thought, fuming. Had she risen in his estimation, or been reduced to the level of an aide-de-camp? Still, she tried to adopt the same eye-sweeping circuit of the platform as Adam. She might argue with his philosophical notions, but never his professional expertise. By the time Adam slipped up beside her, Rosalind's disgruntled mood had evaporated.

"The conductor had to settle a fight between two passengers, but he told that woman with the huge black ostrich feather in her hat that we'll be leaving in under four minutes. And there's a shifty-eyed man wearing a jacket that's too big for him, over there where the passengers retrieve their luggage. I think he might be a pickpocket. Perhaps we should—"

"—leave him to the local police. You're impossible, aren't you?" He hustled her onto the trolley, snagging the last two seats just as the conductor leaped aboard and clanged the bell. As they lurched into motion Adam leaned over and whispered in her ear. "Jedidiah Scrivens is taking us to Gustav Wachtler's house, sometime before six this evening."

"Really? Tonight?" The ramifications slammed into her consciousness with the force of a thunderclap. "That means . . . we'll finally know. About Isaac—the Petrovna jewels. . . ."

The trolley jerked into motion, throwing her against Adam's side. "It . . . might sound silly, but I think I'm—" She stopped.

He peered down into her face, and Rosalind ducked her head. "Ah-ah. None of that. Go ahead, say it." He straightened the wrinkled lapel of her traveling suit, and the tenderness of the gesture, so lacking of late, gave her the courage to continue.

"I'm afraid." She tried to smile. "I didn't think I would be, but I am."

"Good."

Her head reared back. "Are you trying to rile me on purpose again? Like you did before, in La Junta?"

"Not entirely. If you're afraid, you might respond with more caution. And Rosalind . . ." He shifted until he was facing her. "It's time. The Catbird might not know what we're up to right now, but he certainly will within the week, when we go after Booker Rattray's stash."

It was almost as though speaking aloud of the Catbird conjured up the image of lightless black eyes, following her every move. Words dripping into her mind like droplets of sleet on a windowpane. *"I can hurt you,"* he'd promised. *"Perhaps it won't be necessary to kill you . . . I'll instruct them to dump you in one of the harlots' bawdy houses . . . you won't last long. . . ."*

"I should have gone to Montana."

Rosalind didn't realize she'd whispered the words aloud until Adam responded. "Yes, you should have. But like I told you earlier, it was your choice—not mine. Now that it's done, we'll just have to deal with the consequences." The words might have been blunt, but compassion finally softened the hard planes of his face. "Besides, you have a point. Isaac was your brother, and Jed did send the Bible to you."

He shifted closer, his presence offering both sanctuary and stability. When long strands of cool black hair brushed her cheek, without thinking Rosalind grabbed the thick queue as if reaching for a lifeline.

Moments later she noticed the couple sitting across from them, their faces frozen in identical expressions of outrage. Inside, Rosalind quailed, but she still refused to let go of Adam's hair.

A tiny smile flickered, and she cut her eyes toward him. "Aunt Minna was right," she announced in a clear voice. "She told me your hair matched you—soft but strong. Under control. So why be intimidated by a creepy little thief who won't even tell me his real name?"

The sound of Adam's deep laughter wrapped her in a warm cloak of confidence. But it was the glowing approval in his face that ignited a flame in her heart.

49

ADAM HAD ARRANGED for them to meet Jedidiah Scrivens on the Cheyenne Mountain trail late in the afternoon, when most of the tourists had left for the day. The elderly preacher reminded Rosalind of a painting of Moses, except that the preacher's unruly white hair haloed in ear-length abandon all over the top of his head.

Homely, burly as an old oaken barrel, Pastor Scrivens wrapped Adam in a bear hug, then turned to Rosalind. "So we finally meet, little sister." His voice rolled through her in a bass rumble. He lifted her hand in two gigantic paws, his fingers roughened with calluses but gentle still. "I see in your face all the strength of character Isaac believed in. How I prayed that his faith in God would come to match his faith in you."

Tears stung Rosalind's eyes, but she blinked them back. "My brother and I understood each other. We always did . . . even though I never would have run away from home." There. She'd betrayed the sentiment that had festered in her soul for the past five years, particularly during these last difficult months.

The sensation of relief was cleansing.

"He told me he regretted both the events that precipitated his leaving home, as well as what followed," the preacher said. "Unfortunately, he never allowed God's grace to carry him beyond regret." He shook his head in a gesture of infinite sorrow.

"Your brother also wished he could have been more like you."

"Sometimes," Rosalind admitted painfully, "I've wished I could be more like Isaac. At least his rebellion was straightforward."

Jedidiah studied her, then glanced across at Adam, who was standing a little ways back, watching them with folded arms and seemingly relaxed posture. "You've snagged yourself an interesting one this time, Panther. I begin to see why the Lord laid His firm hand upon my shoulder and sent me back here. Probably should have heeded the call a trifle sooner."

"You're here now," Adam said. "And we appreciate the help. This situation needs to be resolved."

"You were kind to my brother," Rosalind added. "I'll always be in your debt, Pastor Scrivens."

"Call me Jedidiah, little sister. I haven't deserved the title of Pastor for a long time."

"Oh, I couldn't do that. It would be disrespectful to call you—" She caught herself and rolled her eyes.

The preacher's craggy face softened. "The Lord God deserves your honor and respect, child. But you're not in my debt. I'm just another fallen servant forced to confront the consequences of a grievous sin." He paused, adding gruffly, "I'd like to think my daughter would have been like you."

"Daughter?" Rosalind echoed, bewildered.

A shadow dimmed the luminous expression, but Jedidiah's voice didn't waver. "Your brother isn't the only young man who ever walked away from God. You're familiar with the sad story of King David and Bathsheba?"

"You committed—" Rosalind clapped a hand over her mouth before she mentioned the unmentionable.

"No, not that." He shook his head. "It's a long story, child. But in God's eyes, I'm afraid, I'm guilty. And—like David—the end result was a child. I didn't even know about my daughter until two days after I buried your poor brother."

"How tragic," Rosalind said. "That must have been a dreadful shock."

He nodded. "Little excuse, of course—but that same cablegram also informed me that she was dying. A weakness of the lung. I'm afraid I forgot everything else but trying to reach her in time. God was kind. I was able to remain with her for almost a month—" He looked away, his eyes moist. "Afterward . . . I remained in the place of my birth, mending fences. I'm only sorry Adam's letter didn't catch up with me sooner."

"Jed, leave the timing in God's hands, where it belongs," Adam interrupted brusquely. "Her brother should never have embroiled her in his peccadilloes in the first place."

"Perhaps we should run along to Gustav's," Jedidiah suggested. He lifted a hand to shade his eyes while he gauged the angle of the sun. "It's nearing five o'clock. He'll soon be preparing for an early supper, if his habits haven't changed since I saw him last."

"Are you sure he'll let us in the door?" Rosalind asked, remembering her previous encounter with Mr. Wachtler.

"Probably not. Then again, he might make an exception for me, in order to flay my hide. Only one way to find out, isn't there?"

50

AS PREDICTED, WHILE GUSTAV REFUSED to greet Adam and Rosalind, he hauled Jedidiah into his clock-choked sitting room and proceeded to deliver a lengthy harangue. Jed finally managed to escape, letter in hand. He heaved a sigh of relief as he navigated a path across the littered porch and waved the envelope triumphantly.

"Hurry!" Rosalind demanded. "I've waited for almost a *year*!"

She looked as bright-eyed and inquisitive as a chipmunk. Isaac's sister was light to his shadow. A genuine seeker as opposed to an obstinate rebel, though Jed still feared the consequences of her and Adam's course of action.

"Settle down, now," Adam murmured to Rosalind. The look on his face was a revelation. "Wait until there are not so many listening ears."

Why, he loves her, Jed realized. The legendary Panther, undisputed master of the mountains, was in love with a city gal. *Lord, you do have a wondrous sense of divine humor.*

They began walking back toward town. Jed surreptitiously studied Rosalind, who was sailing down the path some half dozen paces ahead, her frilly parasol twirling in the May sunshine like a bobbing stem of Queen Anne's lace.

"You look far too smug for my peace of mind, Jed."

230

Jed clasped his hands behind his back and tried to look dour. "Does she know you love her?" he asked, just to see what would happen.

Adam scowled. "I've tried my level best to keep it from her."

Jed stopped dead in the path. "Why? She's a lovely, engaging woman, Adam. Strong-minded, of course, but you'd never be satisfied with a timid lass with no opinions of her own."

"She's also a woman whose family weighs around her neck like a millstone. A woman with the moral conservatism of a Puritan and the questioning faith of a Martin Luther." He flicked a baffled look at Jed. "But there's a streak of recklessness there that puts even her brother to shame."

"Ah. I wondered why she was here in the first place." They resumed walking. Jed followed Rosalind Hayes' graceful figure and fervently prayed for counsel. "Adam . . . you know her presence here is not wise."

"It doesn't matter, Jed." For the first time in all the years they'd known each other, Jed saw real fear lurking behind Adam's normally self-possessed countenance. "Because it's more than just the physical threat to Rosalind that I'm worried about. Yes, she's got this notion of filial obligation—but I'm afraid honoring her brother is not her only motivation."

"Oh?"

A muscle twitched in the younger man's jaw. "It's the Catbird, Jed, and the threat is not just to Rosalind's life—but to her soul."

"Adam . . . son, what are you talking about?"

"Even knowing what he is, there's a part of Rosalind that's drawn to the man. I see it in her face, hear it in her voice every time we talk about it. She might loathe his actions, she might fear for her life—but he still fascinates her."

He stopped and turned to Jed, anger and anguish carving deep lines in his face. "I love her. But I won't commit my life to a woman who can't shun evil, no matter how seductive and compelling its form may take."

Jed clasped his hands behind his back, praying as he picked his way through a response. "Adam," he finally said, "Rosalind may be intrigued by the Catbird, but perhaps you should trust her commitment to the Lord a little more. And—forgive me if I cross the line into meddling here—I've seen the way she watches you when you're not looking. I may be a grizzled old eccentric, but I'm a fair hand at reading human emotions. Your headstrong little Puritan cares for you more than you realize. Perhaps more than she herself realizes."

A band of red spread across Adam's forehead and cheeks. "Infatuation isn't love, Jed."

"Mm. I see your point. But it's possible you might be mis-interpreting things."

"What on earth are the two of you talking about?" Rosalind was steaming back down the path at full speed. "Are you hatch-ing some kind of plan to leave me behind, Adam Moreaux?"

Adam's dark brows snapped together and he planted his hands on his hips, but Jed intervened before the pair of them could engage in verbal sparring. "No scheming, my dear. How-ever, now's as good a time as any to confess that the more I think on it, the less I like the idea of opening this Pandora's box of Booker Rattray's. Perhaps a better solution would be to leave the treasure where it is."

"Jed, you're wasting your breath."

"Think, Adam—" he persisted, knowing he was pushing his luck, "what good can come of it? From what Isaac told me, we're talking a fair amount of riches here. Even if you can pro-tect Rosalind from the Catbird, how did you plan to safely re-locate all those sacksful of temptation? Others will be lurking about, hoping to filch a piece or two."

"Maxwell Connelly's sending along some backup. They'll co-ordinate with the marshal. Jed . . . don't fight me on this."

"I wasn't threatening to back out, Adam." Jed had known this man for more than a decade, but even so he found himself backpedaling. "I merely felt it prudent to point out potential hazards."

"If it were just money, I'd agree with you," Rosalind inserted then. "But it's not money the Catbird's after. He's . . . obsessed with recovering those jewels. Talked about them as though they were alive. He'll never give up. And now that Isaac's gone, the Catbird thinks the only obstacle left is . . . me."

"That's why you shouldn't be here," Adam put in roughly.

"Even if I didn't come along," Rosalind finished, her voice starting to wobble, "it no longer matters. I know what he looks like. I even know some of his disguises." She drew a shuddering breath. "I won't be safe until *he's* behind bars—not *me*."

The look on her face as she stared up at Adam was as naked as a newborn baby. Jed took a discreet step back and turned around, feeling as though he were intruding on the most private of scenes.

"Adam," he heard her whisper, "I'm not trying to be blindly stubborn, or hamper your work. I know you don't want me here." Her voice thickened. "It's just that . . . I know I'm not really safe as long as the Catbird's free. But at least when I'm with you, I *feel* safe."

Silence descended. Finally, no longer able to resist, Jed turned back around. Oblivious to his presence, or to other passersby, Adam had surrounded Rosalind in a protective embrace, his cheek resting on the silk flowers decorating her hat. The parasol lay forgotten in the path, for Rosalind's arms were clinging just as hard.

I yield, Lord, Jed silently conceded. *Do with us all as you will. . . .*

51

Manitou Springs, Colorado

FOR THE PAST WEEK LaRue had posed as a photographer's mouthpiece. Every morning he made rounds to all the hotels where Oscar Liebermann, photographer, had secured permission to leave a sign-up list. Any guests who cared to have their likeness made could sign their name, and the photographer would arrange the appointments himself.

LaRue also collected tidbits of information for his own purposes—including the news two days earlier that Panther should be returning soon, with the sister of some young fellow old Jed Scrivens had nursed the previous fall. Local gossip claimed the boy had died.

Soon the ubiquitous detective would join the young fellow, because LaRue had planned a slow, painful end for the infamous Panther.

LaRue had discovered that holding the power of life and death in his hands almost equaled the thrill of holding the cool weight of an exquisitely crafted piece of jewelry. Why, he mused as he trudged along the crowded thoroughfare, hadn't he realized before how satisfying it would be to take someone's life? To plan for it, contemplate the process . . .

He would definitely enjoy Panther's demise.

He still wasn't certain what to do with Rosalind Hayes. For the Catbird's sake, she needed to die. And yet . . .

By the time he reached the tree-lined entrance to the Barker Hotel, he was perspiring and ill-tempered. "Good day to you." He forced a smile for the two busy clerks at the registration office. The prune-faced woman usually treated him like a cockroach, but the spry old gent was a friendly sort who enjoyed a good chat.

LaRue waited while some prissy schoolteachers, then an officious man, signed the register and received their keys. The diamond stickpin winking from the folds of the man's silk cravat would be worth pursuing, LaRue decided. He stood with seeming self-effacement while the clerks answered a spate of questions on the virtues of the various soda springs.

At last, patience was rewarded.

"Glad I was on duty when you stopped by," the old gentleman told him with a conspiratorial wink. "You're the feller trying to convince that Pinkerton detective to sit for a photo, aren't you?"

"That would be my employer," LaRue corrected. Nobody would think to associate a lowly assistant with the death of the Pink. "Says he looks just like an Indian brave, even if his skin's as white as yours and mine. I wouldn't know myself—never saw him before."

"Well, sir, your luck's about to change, maybe. Not two hours gone, he and old Jed Scrivens stopped by to meet up with a young lady. Right comely she was, fresh as paint. Dressed for a trail ride."

He tittered like an old hen. "Don't know for sure where they were headed—most likely Pikes Peak. It's where all the fancy tourists like to go. However,"—he winked at LaRue—"seeing as how old Oscar's got a yen for Panther to sit for him, I'll pass along what I *do* know."

"Makes no difference to me," LaRue mumbled.

"Well, you tell your conniving employer that if he wants that photograph, he'll have to pack his cameras and head up the mountain."

The clerk tapped his nose, then added, "Nope. On second thought, you might catch up with them at the livery. They mentioned stopping by Tim's place to pick up Panther's horse and some mounts for the preacher and the lady."

LaRue missed them at the stable but picked up their trail two hours later. Exultant, he settled back in the saddle, the bitter inertia that had dogged his life for months lifting at last. "Soon," he whispered the word like a refrain. *"Soon now."*

52

Early summer in the Rockies . . .

OVERHEAD, THE BLUE BOWL OF THE SKY fought a shimmering battle with the bright green meadows and deeper forest green of ponderosa pine and Douglas fir. Splashes of scarlet, lavender, and white flowers dotted the landscape. Almost heaven, Adam decided . . . though his father used to tease him that he said the same thing about spring and autumn in the Rockies. Even winter afforded a stark dignity unequaled anywhere else.

When he was up in the mountains, Adam knew he was home. In spite of their tenuous circumstances, with every winding mile upward his spirits soared.

Amazingly, Rosalind had turned out to be a superb traveling companion. Even after four hours of sun and saddle, she hadn't uttered a word of complaint, other than fretting over the fact that Kat was still nowhere to be seen.

Adam was a little concerned about that himself. One of the disturbing reasons Kat might be lying low, he knew, was the presence of someone following them.

"We'll stop for lunch at the top of that meadow ahead," he announced a short while later, twisting in the saddle to make sure his two companions heard. "There's a spring-fed creek with water so clear and cold it's like inhaling a fresh snowfall."

A moment later Rosalind had urged her horse up beside Biscuit. "You love it here, don't you?" she asked, not waiting for his reply. "I can see why. I've never seen anything so beautiful—almost like looking at one of God's own paintings."

Stunned, Adam whipped his head around. "You too?" Never would he have expected a woman like Rosalind to feel the same powerful tug to the heartstrings.

He admired her openly, struggling to reconcile the outer shell with the inner person. She was wearing an elegant riding habit made of some rich-looking brown fabric. Lots of trim and tucks and braiding. Looked expensive. Stylish, too.

Yet she'd met Adam and Jed that morning to proudly display the result of several evenings' worth of alterations: a divided skirt that allowed her to ride comfortably astride.

Back East, Adam knew, she'd have been tarred and feathered for flouting convention. Rosalind, however, had surprised him again. "Any woman silly enough to ride through the mountains sidesaddle," she'd declared, "deserves to fall off into a gorge."

Entranced, Adam had watched her settle her new western hat at a jaunty angle and precede the two men out the door. He longed to announce to the world that he loved her. That she belonged to him—with him. Forever.

But would Rosalind be willing to give up her life in the city for longer than a few days? A small but persistent voice in the back of his mind countered that prickly question with an equally painful one: Could *he* give up his unfettered life in the mountains or his strange but rewarding companionship with a cougar? Wear a suit . . . a *derby*?

"Adam? Is something wrong?"

Rosalind's anxious voice brought him back with a jerk. He needed to keep his mind focused on their present circumstances, or the Catbird could pick them off like ducks in a carnival shooting gallery, and there would be no future at all.

He dredged up a reassuring smile. "Everything's fine. Let's eat lunch." He reined in, waiting for Jed's plodding mare to join them. "The two of you wait here. I'm going to scout out the ridge. The trees offer good cover, but it's still higher than the surrounding terrain, so we're not taking any chances."

He kneed Biscuit up the hill, his spine tingling from the puzzled concern he could feel following him. That he could deal with. It was harder to ignore another, more alarming sensation—the one of fire ants biting the back of his neck.

"Something's worrying him," Rosalind said to Jedidiah, her gaze still following Adam's broad shoulders as his horse loped up a rocky slope studded with aspen, evergreens, and some sort of leafy shrubbery. He looked supremely skilled. Rugged and confident. Even the outrageous black mane of hair blowing in the wind suited him. Rosalind could no longer imagine him wearing a stuffy three-piece suit, starched collar and cuffs.

"There's a fairly deep gorge on the other side of this rise," Jedidiah said, interrupting her girlish moonings. He shifted his considerable bulk in the saddle, grimacing as he pressed his hands to the base of his spine. "Rather be walking," he muttered.

Then he seemed to notice Rosalind's silence. "Adam knows word travels through these parts like the wind," he explained. "As he's warned you, the Catbird's not the only scoundrel out to do the devil's work. By now most folks know Booker Rattray's dead, and his stash has turned up missing. It's a fair guess there are more than tourists and miners prowling these mountains, hoping to find a treasure they won't have to work for. That's why we're not taking a more direct route."

"He told me. But why would anyone except the Catbird think Adam might be tracking Booker Rattray's hoard? I haven't said anything to anyone, and surely the Catbird wouldn't want anyone else to know."

Jedidiah rung out an incredibly wrinkled kerchief and mopped his face. "Child, I don't have a lot of answers." He heaved a deep sigh. "But I do know we're courting trouble, digging up those bags. Adam knows that, too. That's why he didn't want to involve you—"

He stopped and peered up the hillside. A wide, beautiful smile spread across his face. "Praise God for His infinite compassion," he intoned. "Compose yourself, my child. I believe Adam has someone he'd like for you to meet."

Rosalind's gaze flew upward, her heart tumbling with ill-contained excitement. "Kat!" she breathed. "Adam's found Kat."

"Try not to make any sudden moves," Adam counseled moments later, upon reaching Rosalind's side. Kat had halted halfway down the slope, head low, her ears flattened.

"She's beautiful." Rosalind was practically trembling in her eagerness. "Would it be better if I dismounted?"

"Wait until we're at the top. We'll have lunch, give her a chance to adjust to your presence. Jed's, too, since it's been a spell since they've been around each other." He nodded toward the crest of the hill. "This is the territory she marked out for herself some years back—her den's in some boulders just below the crest, on the opposite side."

"Then let's hurry up and eat lunch."

Adam laughed outright. "You're not afraid at all, are you?"

"I know my hands are shaking, but it's because I'm so excited. Kat will know the difference, won't she? According to my research, she can actually smell the odor of fear." Rosalind strained to see around Adam's bulk. "And her vision's extraordinary as well. Did you know scientists speculate that her whiskers—mmph."

Adam's hand, tasting of leather, clamped over her mouth. "Do you want to meet the animal, or quote from a reference book on wildlife?" His eyes danced.

Behind them, Jedidiah cleared his throat. "Since Kat and I enjoy a fleeting acquaintance, how about if I go ahead and set up lunch? I'm afraid I need to feed my body and rest these aching bones."

"We're right behind you, Jed. Aren't we, little wildcat?" he murmured for her ears alone.

Caught up in the joy of his reunion, Rosalind nodded without speaking. *Adam*, she longed to confess, *what I wouldn't give for you to look that way because of me*.

The revelation struck with Damascus-road force, shaking her heart. Blinding her to everything but the revelation.

Aunt Minna was right. She loved Adam. Utterly. Completely.

Without reservation or restriction. She loved an untamed man of the mountains—a man who openly disdained, even despised, Rosalind's world. Who could no more immerse himself in the superficial lifestyle for which Rosalind had been conditioned any more than he could chain Kat with collar and leash.

Well. Rosalind dismounted, feeling as though all of heaven had drawn a collective breath, waiting to see what she planned to do. Even so, she efficiently removed her horse's saddle while Adam fastened a hobble.

"Ready to meet my best friend?" He held out a hand, sounding like an eager young boy. "I'll introduce you from a safe distance. After lunch, we'll . . . see how it goes."

"I've been ready to meet Kat for weeks."

Rosalind placed her hand—and her heart—in his. As effortlessly as a sunrise, her course was determined. Shaken but determined, she clung to the warm fingers as they walked. *I'll fight for your love, Adam Moreaux*, she vowed with every step. Even if she had to exchange every gown she owned for flannel shirts and dungarees . . . even if she lived in a leaky-roofed shack with a dirt floor—she would prove that her love was trustworthy. Forever faithful.

And—*please God*—someday Adam would realize that he could trust her with his love in return.

53

"SIT HERE, BY ME," Adam instructed Rosalind thirty minutes later, patting the grass beside him.

She removed her riding gloves and stuffed them in her pocket. Then she settled in a sun-warmed patch of meadow grass, thankful for every backbreaking hour she'd invested frantically transforming the skirt of her riding costume into two halves. Copying Adam, she sat Indian fashion, her gaze fastened to Kat.

The cougar stood some twenty feet away, beside the trunk of a fallen aspen, the feline expression registering either boredom or curiosity.

Except for Jedidiah's intermittent snoring, the only sound was the rustling sigh of a playful breeze flirting in the tree branches above their heads.

Then Adam spoke in a strange guttural but somehow musical dialect, at the same time lifting his right arm. "Don't flinch," he finished, in English. "I'm going to put my arm around your shoulders. Not only will she see that we're . . . friends"—Rosalind heard the smile in the voice—"some of my scent will transfer to you."

"I hope so," Rosalind murmured dreamily, not realizing she had spoken the thought aloud until the arm draped over her shoulders tightened and a quiet laugh filled her ear.

"Shh—here she comes."

Despite Adam's nearness, Rosalind forgot everything but the big cat's magnificent presence. Muscles rippling, head held low with her tufted ears pricked forward, Kat padded across the space separating them until she reached Adam's side, opposite Rosalind. Sunlight played off the thick tawny coat. This close, Rosalind could see a blue-green tint shimmering in the golden eyes staring at her in unblinking assessment.

Adam began scratching the cougar's chin, tugging on the stiff white whiskers, then sliding his hand up to rub behind her ears. A rumbling purr erupted from the feline's throat. Her eyelids drooped.

"She sounds like a cat!" Rosalind whispered, enchanted.

Adam laughed again. "She *is* a cat. All right, girl. Be a sport for me now. This is my friend Rosalind, remember?" He turned slightly. "Give me your hand, sweetheart."

It took Rosalind the space of three heartbeats to realize that smooth request and accompanying endearment had been spoken to *her*. A blush heated her cheeks as she lifted her hand. With Adam's wrapped around it, guiding her movements, for the first time in her life she experienced the incredible sensation of touching a living, breathing wild creature.

"Oh . . ." she breathed in hushed syllables. "Hello, Kat. You're . . . beautiful."

"She'll love you forever if you scratch behind her ears."

Rosalind obeyed, and was rewarded by more of the noisy purr almost loud enough to be called a growl. "Her fur is soft, but not like a cat's—I mean, a housecat's."

Kat's head lowered, and she began to sniff Rosalind's arm. Rosalind sat quietly, content to let the big animal set the pace. "It's hard to believe people consider cougars either as varmints or monsters," she observed after a while. "Once, when I was about twelve, Papa let me spend the day at the store with him. A man came to buy supplies—a bounty hunter, hired by the federal government to kill mountain lions. He was bragging about how many he'd already bagged."

"One of the many reasons I choose to avoid so-called civilization," Adam said, though the customary bite was absent from his tone. "There's not a whole lot of mountain lions left. I'm afraid mankind hasn't been a very good steward of God's kingdom." He shifted, moving away from Rosalind and Kat. "Keep petting her and talking to her. You're doing fine. A constant surprise, I admit. How on earth did you become who you are, Rosalind Hayes?"

"Mm?" Rosalind wasn't paying attention, having just discovered that stroking the pads of Kat's paws caused the cougar to curl her toes, though she kept the lethal claws sheathed. Utterly captivated, Rosalind's heart swelled with admiration for the creature—and the man sprawled beside them.

When she finally looked up into Adam's face, something about his expression obliterated all thoughts of the cougar.

"How *did* you turn out to be the way you are?" he asked again. "I've never known a woman with your background who understands . . ." He hesitated, then with a shrug, lifted his hand and waved it aloft. "Who understands . . . this," he finished. "All day long, watching you, listening to you, is like watching and hearing myself."

Sensitized by love, Rosalind was able to discern the confusion, the faint vulnerability drifting beneath his stumbling monologue. In all their times together, she'd never known Adam to be at a loss for words. "What happened to make you distrust people—women—like me so much?"

There. She'd said it. Either he would walk away—in the process killing something fragile blooming in her heart—or he would trust her as he trusted the mountain lion at his side. Rosalind kept her head high, but inside she was warm jelly, the thin mountain air she dragged into her lungs feeling more the consistency of Tallulah's navy-bean soup.

A hawk's shrill cry echoed beyond the trees. Beneath their sheltering branches, Jedidiah's snores punctuated the waiting silence in erratic intervals. Butterflies drifted over the meadow like windblown confetti.

Without warning, Adam leaned over, whispered into Kat's ear, and gave her a light nudge. The big cat blinked sleepily, then rose and padded off, muscles rippling and the black-tipped tail undulating in graceful farewell.

Adam searched Rosalind's face and fought the need to leap onto Biscuit's back, losing himself in the roughest, most rugged mountain range in the state. But if he chose the coward's way out, he knew he'd lose someone far more important.

It's time, Adam. Tell the story. She can heal you, change you— if you let her. If you let Me. . . .

He felt a slow unraveling begin, deep within. The Voice was loving, infinitely patient, but Adam sensed the firmness as surely as he sensed the angle of the sun or the waiting silence before a storm. Heard as clearly as he heard Jed's gentle snores.

It was time. Suddenly, the words began to flow.

"My father rescued the woman who became my mother from a band of renegade Utes. Until the day he died, he believed that she loved him when they married. But they had to elope . . . she was one of the San Francisco Tillmans—ah, I see you recognize the name."

Rosalind nodded, her eyes speaking eloquently of her knowledge of the well-known, snobbish family.

"When my mother realized she was expecting, she left my father and threw herself on the mercy of her parents. Said she didn't want to follow him around like a fat squaw . . . or so one of my Shoshoni friends told me many years later."

This was the most difficult part. He'd never shared the story with another living soul—not even Jed. Until Rosalind, he'd never felt the need.

"Some months later a message reached my father, telling him a package had been left for him in Denver. The 'package' turned out to be his six-month-old son. Me."

Rosalind gasped. She reared up, looking so fierce Adam almost laughed. "I don't believe it! She ought to be drawn and quartered! That's despicable—her own child!"

"What a warrior you are," Adam murmured.

Thus buoyed, the rest of his story unfolded, her unrestrained empathy drawing the poison from the lifelong wound. "My father tried several times over the years to reunite us. It was hopeless. The last time, when I was eleven, my mother stood in the open doorway and instructed the butler not to let us in. Then, looking us right in the eye, she told my father her husband was dead. Denied that she had ever had a son. . . ."

Rosalind made a strangled sound.

Adam flipped his hair over his shoulder and stood. "Father gathered me up and we came back out west. He spent the rest of his life trying to help me believe that the lack was in my mother—not in me. Helped me understand the unalterable love of God, who would never discard me, any more than He would His own Son. He also taught me that human beings might be flawed, but that God's purposes never are."

He watched Rosalind's lips move in an effort to speak, saw the dawning awareness light her eyes.

"But you taught yourself that people with money are never to be trusted, didn't you?" she finally said. "You even refused to dress like your mother's people, conform in any fashion to their way of life."

Slowly, giving her every chance to back away, Adam drew her to her feet and then into his embrace. "Rosalind," he whispered, "I know now that I was wrong. I know, because you taught me. Hearing about your parents . . . how your mother still loves and cares for your father in spite of his condition . . . well, you've changed me somehow, inside."

Her face was lifted to his, her gaze luminous with hope—and love.

Now, he thought. *Now's the time*. He couldn't hold the words back another day. Another hour. "Rosalind, I—"

From beyond the crest of the hill an unearthly yowl shattered the silence. Adam whipped around, clamping Rosalind's wrist in a grip that would leave bruises. He didn't notice. "Go up the hill to Jed. Stay there."

Then he was sprinting up the slope with the same silent speed of a hunting cat going for the kill.

54

BREATHLESS, ROSALIND labored up the steep slope toward the preacher, who had been roused from his slumber by the cougar's scream. "Jedidiah!"

He shook his head and pressed a finger to his lips, not speaking until she reached his side. "Kat's trapped something." The deep voice was calming even as his eyes mirrored concern. "Might be an animal, but the way Adam tore off after her—"

"—it might be a human," Rosalind finished, her fear growing. She took two steps, halted. Adam, after all, had ordered her to stay with the preacher. Every muscle in her body rebelled. Whatever was happening down the ridge, Rosalind sensed Adam would need more help than his cougar companion.

"Jedidiah, if it's a man"—*if it's the Catbird*—"he might have a gun. Not even Adam with all his skill or Kat with all her speed can dodge a bullet."

"Neither, my child, can you."

"I can divert attention. Throw a stone. Yell from behind a boulder or tree—"

"You can also divert Adam's attention. Think about that. It's best, I believe, to stay here. Wait."

Frantic now, Rosalind grabbed Jedidiah's arm. "I tell you he needs help."

"The best help we can offer—" He stopped, apparently realizing the futility of further argument. "Very well. I'll go with you then. But, Rosalind—be careful."

Heart in her mouth, she ran down the slope where Adam had disappeared. The silence was almost as alarming as the cougar's electrifying yowl. Dodging from tree to clumps of thick bushes, then to an outcropping of boulders, Rosalind soon outdistanced the preacher. By the time she stopped to catch her breath, he was far behind, no longer in view. Which was why, when she caught sight of a rifle barrel poking out from some brush and aimed at Adam's back, she acted on instinct.

Stooping, gaze fixed on the rifle, she felt along the ground until her hand closed over a pinecone. Its scales were still tightly compressed, giving the prickly object more weight. Not much of a weapon, but it was all she had.

Rosalind stood and threw in a single sweeping motion, hoping to distract the would-be killer. "Adam!" she yelled at the same instant. "Rifle—behind you!" She dived for cover behind some nearby boulders.

Branches rustled in a brief flurry of movement. Then terrifying silence descended again.

She was afraid to move, unwilling to risk even a quick glimpse. She hadn't heard a sound from Adam. Hadn't heard—thankfully—the crack of rifleshot. Had heard nothing but her pulse roaring in her ears like wind blowing down a canyon.

An agony of suspense scorched her nerves. Why didn't *someone* do something, say something?

Another eternity of the scalding silence. Rosalind simply had to move. Cautiously she inched forward, hampered by the heavy weight of her riding skirt. Her labored breaths shrieked like a steam whistle, but she persevered.

At last she reached the edge of the boulder. Panting, she hauled herself into a sitting position.

A dozen paces away a twig snapped. All the hairs at the back of Rosalind's neck lifted in primal warning and she pressed her back against the unforgiving bulk of cold stone. From the corner of her eye, she caught a glimpse of a dark shape. But—the man was moving away from her. *Away?*

She scrambled to her feet. Adam, she wanted to shout.

Where was he? Where was Kat?

There! Only for the flash of a second, but the pitch black queue was unmistakable. Adam—stalking like Kat. Not wounded. Not . . . dead.

She forced her gaze to methodically quarter each foot of terrain, just as she had observed Adam maintain surveillance all day long as they traveled. She spotted her quarry when the sun glinted off his rifle.

Suddenly the man stepped out into the open. It *was* the Catbird! And there was only one reason why he wouldn't bother to conceal his identity—he wasn't planning to leave witnesses behind. Why, oh why did Adam refuse to carry a gun? A blade was worthless against a bullet.

Then she saw the second flash of movement—a fringed sleeve disappearing behind some low-growing yucca. The Catbird had seen, too. He lifted the rifle to his shoulder. Rosalind began to run.

"Don't shoot!" she yelled. "If you kill him I'll never tell you anything! *Never!*"

The Catbird didn't speak, didn't spare her a flickering glance. Horrified, Rosalind watched as he aimed, his finger tightening on the trigger. She was too far away to knock the rifle out of his hands. Too far . . .

A streak of tawny fur erupted from the bushes in front of the Catbird, launched with terrifying speed toward his throat. Mighty paws outstretched, Kat charged the enemy threatening her territory and the man who had taught her to trust him.

The Catbird reacted with equally blinding speed, turning and firing even as he went down beneath the cougar's weight.

Rosalind screamed.

Behind her, an agonized shout of denial. "No!" Adam yelled. "*Kat!*"

The cougar stirred. Rosalind had almost reached her when the Catbird wriggled free and rose, streaked with blood, eyes wild. He lifted the rifle. Kat's paw lashed out again, claws extended, swiping the barrel out of his hands. A feeble growl issued from her throat, but when she tried to rise, her effort was aimless, weak.

"Kat!" Adam yelled again. Rosalind saw him thrashing through shrubbery, vaulting over boulders.

The Catbird's hands clenched at his sides. "It isn't over—not yet." He took a step toward Rosalind. "I'll be back. . . ." Then he plunged into the undergrowth and was swallowed by the woods farther down the slope.

Shaken and unsteady, Rosalind made her way over to Adam. He was kneeling at the cougar's side, his hands moving over her blood-soaked fur. "Kat . . ." he choked, his voice thick. Rosalind dropped down beside him, but he didn't acknowledge her presence. "Kat," he repeated, pleading.

The cougar's tail lifted once. The golden eyes, milky now, were trained on Adam. Her tongue flickered over his trembling hand. Then her head lolled back and her body went slack.

Adam bowed over her, his hands still stroking helplessly. "No . . . please, God. Not Kat . . ."

Weeping herself, Rosalind touched a limp paw. "She saved your life, Adam. . . ."

Shoulders hunched, he gathered the animal's body into his arms, rocking, his face buried in the fur.

"Let him be, child." Jedidiah urged her to her feet. "Come. Right now, Adam needs to say good-bye."

"She saved his life." Rosalind began to sob, too distraught to object when he led her over to the boulders where she had been hiding. "Sh-she d-died, to save his life."

"I know." The pastor sat her down on a rock, then lowered himself beside her and drew her into his comforting embrace. "I know."

Adam abruptly surged to his feet. A howl of inconsolable grief rent the air. "Why, God? *Why?*" Then he hefted the hundred or so pounds of the cougar's weight as though she were straw—and strode off into a stand of evergreens on the other side of the clearing.

"Probably taking her to her den," Jedidiah said.

Rosalind stood, following Adam with her eyes. "I want to help him, Jedidiah. He needs me . . . needs someone. He's so alone. I don't want him to be alone."

Jedidiah's roughhewn face softened, assuming an almost other-worldly glow. "He's not alone, my child. Believe me— Adam's not alone."

55

IT TOOK ADAM TWO HOURS TO BURY Kat inside the shallow cave of her den. A hidden cubbyhole inside an outcropping of jumbled rocks, the hollow was protected from above by a jutting mammoth-sized slab. For twelve years, the loyal cougar had found rest and sanctuary in this haven.

Now her den would serve as her grave.

Twilight stole over the mountains, agonizing red and orange hues bleeding into the sky. Adam worked with the violence of fresh grief, never resting, indifferent to burning muscles and scraped palms. Didn't notice the sweat and caked dirt, the blood matting his hair and clothing.

Finally, in a blind torpor, he laid the last stone over the entrance, tossed a clump of dirt on top—and hurled the collapsible shovel to the ground.

Kat had only been a cougar. A wild animal whose species was a scourge to ranchers, a source of fear and loathing to others. But for Adam she had been companion, partner—a miraculous gift manifesting the power of God.

And with every step he vowed to kill the man who had destroyed her.

"Adam? Adam . . ."

The soft voice was persistent, and after a while he glanced

down. Distantly he noticed the slim white hand wrapped around his aching wrist. Rosalind. A spasm of feeling knifed through him, but this time he didn't look away.

"Jedidiah says his cabin's only a few miles from here. We'll spend the night there, then—" Her voice broke as she touched his cheek. "Please, Adam. Let me help you. Don't carry this alone."

Trancelike, he took her hand, held it in his. She felt so good. So . . . alive. "Rosalind . . ." he whispered her name on a sigh. He was cold all the way to his soul—except for the burning nugget of hatred.

Hesitantly she moved closer, her eyes pleading. "I . . . I don't want to be alone either, Adam. Hold me," she begged, her arms going around his waist with surprising strength. "Adam . . . I love you. I'm so sorry—" Her grip tightened when he would have pulled away, "—but I thank God you're alive," she finished in a rush.

Kat. He squeezed his eyes shut, riding the swell of pain until it passed. Then, too exhausted to resist, he rested his cheek against Rosalind's head, nuzzling the soft hair. "Love you, too," he murmured long moments later. Sounded good, saying it aloud. Sounded . . . right.

But it was too late for them.

He looked down at her, memorizing her features. The shadowed eyes and crooked little nose, the purity of her face despite tear streaks and dried blood and snarled hair.

Almost reverently he lifted his hand to skim the fine-grained skin of her cheek. "My life isn't the only one Kat sacrificed hers for." The nugget of hatred glowed hotter now. "He would have killed you as well. But he's not going to stumble onto a third chance."

"Don't, Adam. Don't hate—it will only hurt us both. I love you. . . ."

"Jed's coming with the horses." He took a deep breath, but it was like inhaling hot wax. "Stay with him. You'll be safe."

"Where are you going?" She reached out, but he easily avoided her grasp. "What are you going to do?"

Adam didn't answer. He walked over to the three hors

little ways up the hill, where Jed patiently waited. "Take care of her, my friend," he said, swinging up into the saddle. "I'll catch up with you later."

"Adam!" Somehow Rosalind was in front of him, lifting her hands to hold Biscuit's head. "Don't go after the Catbird! Don't—you might do something you'll regret for the rest of your life. Adam, please!"

He wouldn't listen to any more. Ruthlessly reining Biscuit out of the way, he kneed the gelding's sides and sent the horse at a headlong canter toward the west, into the rapidly approaching darkness.

Rosalind spent the longest, loneliest night of her life lying sleepless on Jedidiah's lumpy mattress. Her home and her family were a hundred miles and several mountain ranges away, wrapped in luxury and contentment. Much closer—less than five miles, she'd learned—her brother's remains lay in an unmarked grave, wrapped in the cold finality of death.

Snoring in his bedroll, Jedidiah slept outside on the ground. "Closer to God," he'd told Rosalind with an understanding smile. "You'll have privacy, and a chance to allow God to be close to you."

The man she loved with all her heart was—gone.

If God wanted to make His presence known, He would have to do so without Rosalind's help. Her body ached. Her heart ached. Her soul . . . well, her soul seemed to have fled to some vast and distant realm. After a while, weary of spouting words and pleas to the ceiling, still sleepless after counting nails in the boards on the wall next to the bed, she closed her eyes and tried not to think or feel at all.

By ten o'clock the next morning they were ready to leave. The previous night Jedidiah had rewritten the words from each le verse, then selected the phrases that provided directions.

After a breakfast of honeyed pan biscuits and coffee, he'd handed the sheet of paper to Rosalind, telling her to study it while he saddled the horses.

"It's fairly simple, when you string it all together and know where to start," Rosalind said, looking up when he tromped back through the door to tell her everything was ready.

"Pretty good definition of life, too. Start with faith in God's power and presence. After that, everything's simple."

"Sounds good," Rosalind muttered wearily. "But it isn't simple."

"Are you sure you won't change your mind?" he asked, not for the first time.

"Stop asking!" It took tremendous effort to fight back the panic. If Jedidiah didn't lead the way, she'd never find Booker Rattray's stash, even with the clues. She would never have the Petrovna Parure to use as leverage with the Catbird, to convince the thief to take the jewels and run.

Rosalind knew her plans were ill formed, born of desperation. Yet she would do anything to keep Adam from making the costliest mistake of his life. If the price was the Catbird's escape, so be it.

Determinedly she mounted her horse. "Jedidiah, I can't stay here in your cabin and wait. Please try to understand."

"I do." He double-checked the cinch on his horse, then heaved himself into the saddle. "I understand because I knew your brother Isaac." He gathered up the reins. "Let's be off. We've a difficult task ahead of us, and a treacherous path to follow."

56

" 'I WILL SET IN THE DESERT the fir tree, and the pine . . . together.' " She looked up from the paper to scan a tree-covered bump rising above a flat, barren stretch of scrub. "I see them, Jedidiah!"

The early summer morning had dawned crisp and clear. But now the sun burned down from a shimmering sky, and the horses' withers were dark with sweat. Jedidiah drew even with Rosalind and mopped his own beading forehead.

"Amazing," he murmured, half to himself. "Even after almost a year . . ." He shook his head. "What was the next verse?"

Rosalind glanced down. " '. . . there shall be a very great valley, and half the mountain . . . toward the north, and half of it toward the south.' Then you quoted from Ezekiel, which says we're to set our faces toward the mountains." She looked across at Jedidiah. "Wouldn't it have been less trouble just to write down the directions and mail them to me with a letter of explanation?"

"In hindsight, perhaps." They urged their horses forward. "At the time, Isaac was determined to keep the sacks out of Rattray's clutches." He glanced at Rosalind as he stuffed the handkerchief away. "Then, too, there was the matter of keeping you out of danger."

Rosalind almost laughed.

An hour later they had climbed to the top of a small mountain. Halfway down, a narrow canyon divided the peak in half. Somewhere close by, the sound of water splashing over rocks caused both horses to whicker and tug eagerly at the reins.

"Best dismount here, as I recall," Jed instructed. "Horses need a drink and a rest. So do I." He groaned as his feet touched the ground.

"We're close, then?" Rosalind demanded, practically tumbling out of the saddle. "Jedidiah, are we almost there?"

"We should be—did you hear something?"

Rosalind paused from her eager scouting forays and listened. "No. Just the creek, I think." She glanced over her shoulder. Jedidiah was standing with his head tilted to one side, a frown of concentration deepening the lines on his forehead. "Jedidiah, come *on*."

The preacher hesitated, shook his head, then led his mount up the brush-choked rise to where Rosalind was practically dancing in her impatience.

"I hear the water," she repeated. "But I still don't see it."

"Let me double-check the verses."

"Don't you remember?"

"Child, it was a year ago, and I was frankly more concerned about your brother's condition than I was the lay of the land. It took us three days of traipsing back and forth for me to spy out landmarks your bullheaded brother would accept. Like you, Isaac refused to stay behind in the cabin and rest. His stubbornness hastened his death, I'm sorry to say."

Rosalind lifted her chin. "All the more reason to finish this, so he won't have died for nothing. Look"—she pointed—"there! Through those trees and off to the right. I think I see sunlight gleaming off water."

"Careful!" Jedidiah called as she threw him her horse's reins and dashed across the rocky terrain. "Remember that there's a deep gorge at the bottom of this mountain, not to mention untold crevices and hidden caves."

There was also a deep, fast-moving stream that emptied first into a wide pool of water so clear it reflected the fat white clouds floating in the sky like swan feathers. On the other sid of the pool more jumbled boulders blocked the view farther down the mountainside.

"This must be the 'rock into standing water' you underlined in one of the psalms," Rosalind exclaimed, scrambling over the boulders and through thick brush.

Kneeling, she cupped her hands and scooped up water so cold it numbed her fingers in seconds. She drank, and was about to call out to Jedidiah when she heard a faint sound. A bird? Or loose pebbles sliding down a slope? Maybe a miner. Cripple Creek was less than four miles distant, after all.

Rosalind froze, listening hard, but heard nothing beyond the ring of horseshoes against stone and the creak of saddle leather as Jedidiah led the two horses to the pool.

"What is it?" he asked, turning to follow her gaze.

"N-nothing." She shrugged. "I think both of us are a little on the jumpy side."

Jedidiah was still frowning, and he'd turned his attention to the other side of the pool. Rosalind pressed her lips together and listened as well. Waiting. Watching.

Finally the preacher stirred. "Guess it was nothing. We have to cross the pool—I remember now. It's deeper than it looks, so we'd best ride the horses. Are you sure you want to go through with this, Rosalind?"

"It's a little late for cold feet now." She mounted up and guided her horse into the water. "After we cross, the next verse instructs us to climb on some rocks. Do you remember which rocks?"

"I'm afraid so. Courage, child. We're at the mouth of the lion's den."

57

TEN MINUTES LATER JEDIDIAH SIGNALED a halt. "There," he pointed to several large upright chunks of stone that appeared propped together by an enormous hand. A twisted cedar struggled from between the narrow opening, its sparsely needled branches scraping the rocks like arthritic old fingers. "Somehow Isaac dragged every one of those heavy bags up there and through that opening. About fifteen feet down there is a small cave. The bags are inside."

Rosalind was already dismounting, her movements clumsy with haste.

The preacher dismounted more slowly. "The crevice is deep and dangerous. Watch your step."

He wasn't speaking merely about the terrain, Rosalind realized. She lifted her hand in an almost whimsical sweep. "You're a wonderful shepherd, Jedidiah, trailing after another wayward sheep. But you mustn't worry about me. I'm not my brother."

"Try to remember that," Jedidiah countered. "You might also remember that you're not responsible for the choices Adam makes. Only your own." He climbed over the rocky ground until he reached her side. "I'll help you by lifting these sacks of iniquity out of their hiding place. After that, we'll have to wait on Adam—and the Lord."

There were nineteen burlap sacks tossed helter-skelter inside the small burrow, completely concealed behind a pile of rocks. On her own, Rosalind would never have discovered them. Nor, she felt sure, would anyone else, even the Catbird.

Panting, she dragged the eighth heavy bag over to the horses. Jedidiah had manhandled every one of them all the way to the top, where Rosalind took over. How on earth had Isaac managed, alone and in the dark? It had taken all night, he had told Jedidiah, to drag them from the abandoned mine a half mile away, where Booker had stashed them. But Isaac had fallen into an exhausted sleep, using the twentieth sack for a pillow, which was how Rattray had discovered him.

Well, if her brother could handle the job unassisted, the least she could do was to drag the wretched bags across a few feet of ground. Over the past two hours Rosalind had trudged just as doggedly back and forth between the horses and the twisted cedar tree where Jedidiah had fastened a long hemp rope.

The first time Rosalind followed him down the side of the rocky slope, she'd fallen frequently, sustaining a humiliating assortment of scrapes and bruises. After the third attempt, she remained at the top, where she could at least be of some use.

The midday sun was hot. Rosalind dumped the sack next to the others, then fetched a reviving drink of water. After a moment's reflection, she filled the canteen and looped it over her shoulder. This time, she managed to descend, using the rope, without slipping.

Pleased with herself, she handed Jedidiah the canteen. "Thought you might welcome a cool drink."

Groaning, the preacher straightened, swiping a filthy hand over his face. He'd removed his old sack coat, but his shirt was soaked with perspiration, and the hand he reached to take the canteen wasn't quite steady. "Whew. Bless you, child. I'd forgotten what a thankless task it is, digging in the dirt." He drank deeply, then poured water on his head. "Ahh . . . nothing like a ash of spring-fed water to—hey! What are you doing?"

Rosalind had dropped to her knees and crawled halfway inside the dark hole. "I'll do this for a while," she tossed over her shoulder. "You rest." She heard the protest but ignored it.

Moments later she backed out, a lumpy sack in one hand. "This one isn't that heavy," she pronounced. "In fact . . . it feels like—" She paused, then lifted her gaze to stare into Jedidiah's. "It feels like a sackload of jewels."

Jedidiah's mouth tightened. "Go ahead, then. Open it up." The words rang out in the quiet morning. "See for yourself."

Rosalind fumbled with the rough drawstring securing the opening. Finally the knot gave way. Cautiously she stuck her hand inside the bag and pulled out a smaller drawstring pouch made of velvet. Mouth dry, heart thudding against her ribs, she opened the pouch. "Ohh . . . oh, my."

Almost reverently she lifted out a jumble of breathtaking diamonds, emeralds, and bloodred rubies that sorted themselves into an exquisite stomacher. Rosalind carefully arranged the old-fashioned piece of jewelry across the top of one of the other sacks Jedidiah had previously dragged out. Contrasted against the coarse burlap, the intricate filigree work and vivid color of the sparkling gemstones took her breath away.

She reached inside the velvet pouch and pulled out another piece—a matching hair comb encrusted with diamonds, so heavy she wondered how a woman could possibly have kept it in place.

"So that's what the Catbird has sold his soul for," Jedidiah murmured.

"Yes," she replied, her tone subdued. "These match the description of the Petrovna Parure."

Tight-lipped, she returned comb and stomacher to the velvet pouch, then laid the pouch back inside the burlap bag, on top of what appeared to be an assortment of other jewelry. "I'll take this up. It isn't heavy. You stay here and rest. I'll be back in a few moments."

"Rosalind . . . the jewelry is beautiful. Don't be ashamed of admiring the pieces."

"It's not that." She lifted the bag without effort. After tying it to the end of the rope, she turned to Jedidiah. "I was ashame because, for a moment there, I understood why the Catbird would do anything he had to—in order to get them back."

Without waiting for a reply, she grabbed the rough hemp rope and climbed upward. Once at the top, she turned without pausing for breath to haul the queen's ransom in jewels up after her. She had just unknotted the rope when a man's voice spoke from directly behind her.

"Thank you, Miss Hayes. What a tidy job you've made of things for me."

58

CASUALLY, A GLOATING SMILE ON HIS FACE, the Catbird reached down and helped Rosalind to her feet. "Don't spoil it now, trying to escape."

She never had a chance, her hands manacled in seconds in a bone-numbing vise behind her back. With his free hand, the Catbird fumbled the burlap sack open. He retrieved the velvet pouch and tucked it inside his coat pocket. "I'm glad you understand my . . . need for these darlings."

"Understanding isn't agreement." Rosalind gasped when he straightened, jerking her wrists higher. "Don't . . . you're hurting me. . . ."

The vicious hold didn't lessen. "Based on past experience, I'm afraid I can't trust you otherwise. When we reach my horse I'll have some handcuffs for you, courtesy of the sheriff in La Junta."

He began to drag her backward, down a narrow goat path on the other side of the outcropping of boulders. "Wait . . . why are you taking me?" Rosalind stumbled, light-headed with pain. "You've got the jewels. *Run*. You must . . . run."

"Yes, I have my precious darlings. But I've also the problem of a pesky Pinkerton detective. Outwitting Panther these past hours has, I'm afraid, cost me a lot of time and energy . . . mo annoying."

"Please—I won't say anything. Just take the jewels and go. You have to escape. . . ."

"The more you speak, the more suspicious I'm becoming of your motives, my pet. I find it ludicrous that—"

Without warning she tripped. A cry burst from her throat when the Catbird jerked her against him, his grip hardening to iron.

"Careful." His voice was strained. "This stretch of the path's a bit . . . precarious."

Rosalind heard his words, but his meaning didn't register at once—not until her dimming vision focused again. Less than a foot from her right shoe, the ground vanished into clear mountain air. The rocky slope farther up the path that she and Jedidiah had traversed with comparative ease had given way to a steep cliff. Sheer stone walls dropped straight down, forming one side of a deep, narrow gorge. Far below, a sun-sparkled stream of water ribboned along the bottom, splashing merrily over piles of rubble.

A single misstep would send her plunging to instant death.

She went absolutely rigid. All that separated her from eternity was the ruthless hand of the man who had threatened to kill her himself, who didn't believe that she was willing to help him escape.

The Catbird's free arm passed around her waist, and he maneuvered both of them backward, away from the precipice. "I'll give you a second to recover," he said. "Until we get off this path, watch your step."

He wasn't going to release her. The realization burst over Rosalind in a firestorm of bitter regret. She'd been hopelessly naive, imagining that she could negotiate with this man.

"Let me go." The words were scarcely audible. "Let me go— Jedidiah is . . ."

"Trapped halfway down a ravine. I have the rope." He inched them backward. "No help for you there, my pet."

Adam. The longing for him was almost as painful as the ·ands biting into her arms. Adam loved her. No matter how full hatred and grief, his love was stronger. He'd find her, as he the last time. "Adam will come."

The Catbird laughed in her ear. "No chance of that either. Certainly not in time for him to arrange another dramatic rescue. You see, last night someone robbed all the guests at the National Hotel in Cripple Creek. Classic Catbird, complete with his signature style and calling card."

Rosalind began to struggle but was forced to desist when he yanked her arms higher again. "Be still. I haven't told you the best part."

"You're . . ." She couldn't draw a breath, couldn't frame another word.

Another unpleasant laugh floated past her ears. "I left an amethyst dinner ring—nice piece of Cartier, another of the pieces from your sister's reception last fall. Fitting, don't you think? Pity I won't be there to watch your grieving swain stumble around, looking for more clues."

He urged her along the narrow path. "It's just you and me, Miss Hayes. Your fate lies in my hands. This time, nobody but I will determine the course of the rest of your life. Not Panther. Not God. The decision is all *mine*."

Rosalind shook her head. Why couldn't he just take his jewels and run?

"Quite satisfying, I must say—almost as satisfying as my darlings here. You liked them, didn't you? I heard you, saw the way you held them. You're a lot like me . . . you appreciate the finer things—you deserve them, Miss Hayes."

She felt herself falling into the abyss of pitiless black eyes, her will submerged in his absolute confidence. *Think*, she cudgeled her mushy brain as the voice droned on and on.

"I'll keep you with me. Allow you—and only you—to wear them. Adorn you with my most precious possession. The pinnacle of my achievements. Think of it—*Rosalind*. The opportunity of a lifetime. Priceless antique jewelry draping your lovely neck, glowing in your dainty ears, caressing your arms. . . ."

"No."

The oily flow of words stopped.

"I won't wear them . . . unless you—unless you tell me real name." It was the only diversion she could think though it hadn't worked the last time.

Silence stretched between them, taut as a drawn bow. "The only man who knew my name is dead," he finally answered her, his tone reflective. "But . . . I'll think it over. Now move."

Rosalind almost panicked then, but something small and stubborn inside her refused to give up.

Jedidiah would rouse from his nap . . . wonder where she was . . . he was strong . . . could somehow climb to the top without the aid of that rope. . . .

Adam was in Cripple Creek. But at least he was safe. Her courage faltered at the thought of his reaction to her death—so Rosalind shut it out of her mind. As long as Adam was safe, she could fight. Hope. She fixed her gaze on the immovable bulk of some ancient boulders. God would be her rock, her fortress. . . .

Suddenly a tall man, dressed completely in black, appeared at the top of one of those massive boulders. Moccasined feet planted firmly apart, he stood silhouetted against the bright backdrop of an ice blue sky, black hair spilling over one broad shoulder.

A rifle was clenched in both hands.

"Let her go," Adam ordered in a clear, ringing voice as cold as a winter wind. "Let her go, or I'll kill you where you stand."

59

ADAM KEPT HIS GAZE TRAINED ON the Catbird, not on Rosalind, emptying his mind of all emotion. Honing every skill, every lesson learned over the course of his life.

Time stretched, expanding outward in slow-moving ripples. His vision had sharpened so that he could count the number of times the Catbird blinked, see his nostrils flare as he exhaled. His hearing was so acute, the sound of Rosalind's rasping breaths seared his ears.

If his quarry so much as twitched a finger, Adam would strike.

And yet . . . if the Catbird tripped, or panicked, he might fall over the side of the cliff—and take Rosalind with him.

So Adam stood, his mind calm as a glacier while he waited for an opening.

"Do you even know how to use that rifle?" the Catbird taunted.

Adam calmly lifted the weapon and aimed it at the man's temple.

After a stark pause the Catbird sneered, but the vein in his temple was bulging. "My head's not a very large target, but you ladybird here will be hard to miss." He kept Rosalind completely in front of his body. "So go ahead—fire away. Or yet—why not use the knife? Your skill with the bowie is passed. Come on—*Panther*. Impress me."

Still Adam refused to speak. Seemingly relaxed, he kept the rifle primed, his gaze as unblinking as a cougar's.

"Adam, I'm all right!" Rosalind suddenly called. "Please . . . don't kill him. . . ."

Rosalind, begging him to spare the vermin's life? He clenched his jaw. "I won't let him go, Rosalind. Not until he's laid out in a pine box."

"His death won't bring Kat back!" she cried, the words ending in a choked gasp when the Catbird hauled her backward.

Ten feet away the path curved around a bend, and Adam's prey would be safe from a bullet.

In a single bound he leaped from the top of the boulder to the path. "There's nowhere to run," he said. "Jed's with your horse and the gun you bought to replace this one."

He lifted the rifle over his head—and hurled it into the canyon. "If you hurt her again, I won't need to shoot. Or dirty my knife. I'll use my bare hands."

A thick white ridge had formed across the Catbird's sweating brow. His gaze flicked from the shortened distance separating them, to the path behind him. "No matter what happens to me, she'll die. Since you're so set on killing me anyway, what have I got to lose?"

The truth of his statement scored a direct hit. Adam looked into the Catbird's face and read Rosalind's death sentence there. "Let her go, and . . . I'll spare your life." Each word sliced his throat.

A peculiar smile twisted the Catbird's mouth. "But you're not going to let me go, are you? You'll keep dogging my tracks. You won't stop until I'm dead, or behind bars." He glanced toward the edge of the path. "I'd rather be dead."

Adam's mind scrabbled for a solution. He couldn't think of one. Couldn't . . . think. Couldn't even pray. His burning need for vengeance was going to cost him more than he'd ever imag-ed. He swallowed hard. "I'll . . . let you go free," he managed.

-y instinct protested this ultimate betrayal of justice. Of his

"If you let her go—I'll give you twelve hours to lose yourself. And—I'll resign from the Agency. I won't . . . I won't come after you. . . ."

"No!" Rosalind's head twisted until she was looking at the Catbird. Pain had stripped her face of all color. "Can't you see that it's over? We both know who you are. Adam may have promised to let you go in exchange for my freedom—but I will not give you my promise."

"Rosalind, what are you saying?" Appalled, Adam stepped forward. Froze when the Catbird made an abortive move and she choked back a cry.

Then she seemed to collect herself. "*I'll* see that you're hunted down. *I'll* see that you go to jail forever. I will not allow you to destroy the soul of the man I love. So you'll have to kill me if you *don't* surrender."

Unaccountably, the Catbird flinched. "You're a fool." He shook his head. "Nobody dies for someone. Love's about as real as rhinestones."

"You're wrong," Rosalind replied, and the transformation in her voice stunned Adam. "Love is as real as the diamonds in the Petrovna jewels. And Someone *did* die for me, a long time ago."

She lifted her eyes to Adam, and he saw the same transcendent peace flooding her countenance. "Love—when it comes from God—is always more powerful than hate. It covers everything. Grief. Loneliness—even rebellion."

She was telling him good-bye. The numbness of the past twenty-four hours fled, but the pain that followed ripped him apart. He wanted to protest, wanted to plead with her, but no words came.

Then the Catbird was turning Rosalind around so that they were face-to-face. His hands gripped her forearms.

"You really would die for him, wouldn't you?"

Rosalind nodded. "I love him," she declared simply. "Even more than you love those jewels in your pocket."

Adam's heart felt as if it had stopped beating. He half lifted his hand, then let it drop uselessly at his side.

"Ah, yes . . . the Petrovna Parure . . ." The Catbird's voice had softened, sounding almost musing. "I can never hope equal it, can I—the theft of the century? Achieved by the thief of the century—the Catbird."

"What's your given name?" Rosalind asked. Color was seeping delicately back into her cheeks, her lips, lending her an almost unearthly radiance. "Will you tell me your real name, before you—before I die?"

"*No!*" Adam fell to his knees, burying his face in his hands. "Please, God, don't let him kill her. . . ."

The plea drifted away into dead, empty silence.

The Catbird's halting voice broke it. "My name is . . . Napoleon LaRue."

Adam lifted his head, planted a palm on the ground to support his body.

"Nobody ever cared for me like that," the voice continued. "Even Booker . . . he was the only other person to know my name. But I had to kill him—he took my precious darlings." He sounded almost wistful. "Will you call me by my name once, Rosalind? My first name?"

Incredulous, Adam watched as tears welled in Rosalind's eyes. "Napoleon," she responded gently. "A grand and tragic name."

"Always hated it." He shrugged. "I liked 'Catbird' much better." Abruptly he looked up at Adam. "You'd actually let me go? Give me your word? I know your reputation, Panther. Your word's your bond."

"I'd let you go." Adam had to pass his tongue around his dry lips before he could manage the next statement. "But I don't know if Rosalind . . ." His throat closed over the confession.

"I thought that might be the case." Incredibly, LaRue lifted a hand from Rosalind's forearm—and sent Adam a mocking salute. Then the midnight gaze slid back to Rosalind. "I wish I'd met you before. I've never known a woman like you, Rosalind Hayes. Never known a *person* like you, or your man up there."

His mouth twisted in a parody of a smile as he released her and stepped away, sliding one hand in his coat to pull out a small drawstring pouch. "Seeing the two of you . . . makes a man think."

"Napoleon?" Rosalind whispered, a tone in her voice that

sent a warning chill down Adam's back. "Please. Don't—"

Adam sucked in his breath, held it. This was it, then. This was the price he would have to pay for his blindness, his hatred, his reckless stupidity. Agony scored his soul, turned his bones to ash. He couldn't watch.

"Would have liked to see these on you." LaRue took another step. Tossed the pouch in his hand once, twice. "I'll take them with me—but I'll give you a different sort of gift, Rosalind." He shot one last parting look at Adam. "He's not too bad . . . for a Pinkerton detective."

Adam was already up and running—but it was too late.

LaRue swung around, the Petrovna jewels clutched in his fist. He took a single long stride.

And dropped like a stone over the edge of the cliff.

60

DUSK GAUZED THE AIR in mauve and lavender shadows. The restful sound of the stream's silvery gurgle washed through Rosalind, carrying away the last dregs of horror. Wrapped in the cocoon of Adam's arms, she watched dreamily as Jedidiah gathered wood for a campfire.

Beneath a stand of evergreens, fourteen burlap bags waited to be transported to their final destination. After a single shuddering look, Rosalind hadn't glanced their way since, nor did she care about the other five, still hidden. And she refused to think at all about what lay at the bottom of the gorge, beyond reach of hope or help.

Instead, she traced the fringes of Adam's shirt with one finger and thanked God for sparing their lives. "I really could survive the ride to the cabin," she offered once more.

Beneath her shoulder blades Adam's chest expanded, then fell. "I don't know if *I* could," he confessed, hugging her. "If it's all the same, I'd rather stay like this a little longer . . . just holding you."

Rosalind knew he was only half teasing: faint tremors still shook the hands holding her close. A single tear slipped down her cheek. "You can hold me forever, if you like. When I thought I'd never see you again, I . . ." She gave up with a choked laugh.

Adam rose, drawing her with him and cupping her face in

his hands. In the gold-infused light, his expression turned her heart over in her breast. "Is that by any chance a proposal of marriage, Miss Hayes? If so, the answer is yes."

Speechless, Rosalind opened her mouth, shut it, then gave up with a groan and buried her nose in the folds of his shirt-front.

"I believe it's customary to exchange a kiss." He nudged her chin up, brushing her lips in a light, frustratingly *formal* kiss. "You do me great honor, Miss Hayes," he intoned pompously. "I accept."

Jedidiah returned with an armful of kindling, dumped it nearby, then dusted his hands. His eyes gleamed. "How much longer shall I find an excuse to stay away?"

"Jed . . . Rosalind's asked me to marry her," Adam said without shifting his gaze from hers. "I accepted."

Stunned, Jedidiah stared at them. Then, to Rosalind's amazement and relief, he threw back his head in a roar of exultant laughter. "Thank You, Lord!" he bellowed. "It's about time."

Before Rosalind could blink twice, she and Adam were engulfed in a bone-crunching bear hug. Then Jedidiah stepped back, still beaming. "I'll stay away a bit longer, then. Start a fire and rustle in the saddlebags for some supper. . . ." He strode away, singing an impossibly mangled hymn of praise.

"It's official now," Adam said, gently chucking her under her chin with his knuckles. "Too late to change your mind."

Suddenly breathless as well as speechless, Rosalind searched his face. "Adam? Are you—sure? I mean, I'll follow you wherever you need to go, live in a cabin like Jedidiah's. . . . I won't ever do to you what your mother did to you and your father. I don't need a mansion, or—or clothes from Paris—"

The teasing glint switched to a burning intensity. "It's all right, Rosalind. Love, it's all right." He held her close to his heart. "Sometime in this past hour, I realized that the Catbird— that Napoleon LaRue did more than spare your life—though for that alone, I'll always be grateful."

She hugged him tight, hearing the quickening rhythm of h heartbeat beneath her ear. "I suppose I'll always wonder w

A man like that . . . chose death to avoid prison—yet he let me go free."

"He freed us both, because he also freed me from the past. All I want to do is . . . to spend the rest of my life thanking God for the woman I love—and showing her how much she is loved."

Rosalind blinked back fresh tears. "I was so afraid," she confessed at last. "So afraid your hatred toward Napoleon would destroy your soul, because it would have destroyed your relationship with God."

He bowed his head in acknowledgment but lifted it almost immediately. "Will you believe me when I tell you the hatred is gone? I saw his face, just before he—" The hands gripping her shoulders tightened, relaxed. "He was giving you back to me—and he knew it. I saw it in his eyes. And I felt all the hatred vanish. It's gone. Rosalind . . . my love . . . it's gone."

Their lips met in a passionate kiss of affirmation—and absolution.

61

Denver, Colorado
June 1897

"SUN FEELS GOOD ON YOUR FACE, doesn't it, Papa?"
Rosalind asked. She steered the new wheelchair Oliver had personally ordered down the hard-packed dirt path Zeke had laid
the previous fall. Over the winter, Oliver had also hired a nurse
to work with Edward Hayes. His handwriting had improved,
and though his words remained largely unintelligible, his old
spirit had returned.

Just yesterday—for the first time in five years—Ophelia
Hayes had heard her husband whisper, "L—uv . . . you."

It was enough. If he never managed anything else, those
precious words were enough.

A lot of changes, Rosalind thought as she glanced around
the backyard, then down at her father. "Here." She unbuttoned
the top button of his shirt, then tucked the lap robe more securely about him. "Before long, you'll be as brown as Adam."

His left hand lifted, one trembling finger pointing. With a
tolerant smile, Rosalind moved to kneel beside him so he could
look into her face. "You liked Adam, didn't you?" she said, her
smile widening. "Ah-ah. Don't try to scowl, Papa. I know you
too well. Besides, remember what Mamma said to Adam when
he brought me home last week?"

The memory still made Rosalind giggle. " 'Mr. Moreaux,' '
she quoted in her mother's best uppercrust Virginian voice, '

believe I understand why my daughter lost her heart to you.' "

"I'll never live it down, will I?" Ophelia walked up from behind them and bent to drop a discreet kiss on her husband's forehead. "Bit of a rebel's heart beating in all of us, isn't there, dear? I suppose that's why I never minded leaving Virginia for the untamed splendor of the West."

"Who's the letter from?" Rosalind asked, gesturing to a badly crumpled envelope in her mother's hand. "It looks like it's been dropped in the middle of Larimer Street and run over by several trolleys."

"It's addressed to you." She handed it to Rosalind. "There's no return address. Why, it's a wonder it ever got here. Your name's barely legible."

Rosalind opened the tattered envelope and withdrew a slip of cheap, equally wrinkled paper. After a concerned glance at her father, she admitted, "It's from Isaac. Pastor Scrivens had told me that Isaac wrote a letter to me just before he died."

Her father began pounding the arm of the wheelchair. But when her mother tried to clasp it, he shook her free. The expression in his eyes—what was he trying to tell them with his eyes?

Rosalind exchanged a look with her mother. "I'll scan it first."

Ophelia nodded, her hand returning to her husband's. This time, they clung together.

Eyes damp, Rosalind read the uneven flow of sentences, hearing in them everything her dying younger brother should have told them in person. "He was trying to do the honorable thing," she finally said. "He wanted to notify the authorities about the sacks, and only hid them to prevent Booker Rattray from having them. He was never trying to steal—listen. I'll read you this part. 'I know I was a disappointment to our folks. Tell them for me, Rosebud . . . tell them I'm sorry it turned out like this.' "

Her mother stifled a sound of distress.

Oh, Isaac, Rosalind thought in despair. All you needed to do was to come home.

She held the letter out to her mother. "There's a note from

Jedidiah at the bottom, repeating what he told you last month about Isaac's final words, the regret that he wouldn't be able to see his family. I wish—" She felt a tug on the sash of her waist tie and saw that it was her father's hand.

He managed a spasmodic writing motion, and without a word Rosalind rummaged in the cloth sack on the back of the wheelchair and handed him his writing pad and pen. She and her mother waited without moving while Edward laboriously scrawled.

" 'Let your brother go,' " Ophelia read aloud several moments later. " 'Life is for living, not regretting. Leave Isaac to God, as I have.' "

Lump in her throat, Rosalind gave her father a fierce hug. "Thank you, Papa. Knowing you feel that way is the best wedding present in the world."

"Speaking of weddings,"—Ophelia stuffed her hankie in her sleeve and Isaac's letter out of sight—"are you *sure* you won't reconsider? Have it here in Denver at our home church instead of some little chapel in Manitou Springs?"

"Trust me, Mamma. You'll be grateful." She glanced at the watch pinned to her bodice. "I almost forgot. Zeke's driving me into the city."

"Again?" her mother protested. "Rosalind, this is the third time in the past week Zeke's driven you into town, and for what? You've come back empty-handed every time."

"There's something I need before Adam arrives this evening."

For the past week her husband-to-be had been mysteriously busy himself. "Wrapping up loose ends," he'd told Rosalind without elaborating. Two, however, could play that game.

Rosalind kissed both her parents, then hurried down the path.

Hat in hand, Adam waited on the back porch, trying to make conversation with Rosalind's mother while wondering with mounting uneasiness what was going on. Ophelia had met hir at the front door ten minutes earlier, with a peculiar expression on her face and the invitation to join her on the back porch.

"Mrs. Hayes, are you sure Rosalind's all right?"

"Never better. And yourself, Mr. Moreaux?"

Exasperated, he considered the efficacy of lifting his future mother-in-law aside and tracking down his fiancée. Over the past three weeks they'd been separated more often than they'd been together. He hadn't explained any of his own plans, of course. But uncertainty was mounting. The changes would be dramatic for both of them. Still, he was counting on Rosalind's love of adventure to compensate.

He examined Ophelia Hayes' averted face, her skillful but futile effort to hide her nervousness. What was going on here? Why hadn't Rosalind met him, her face alight with joy?

The awful possibility that she might be entertaining doubts—might even have changed her mind, set Adam's heart to pounding in sickening thuds.

If she had, what would he do? He'd given up his career as a Pinkerton operative to pursue a lifelong dream. A home in the mountains. A sanctuary where he would invest his skills and knowledge to aid certain high-level members of Congress in their pursuit to create a system of national parks. But without Rosalind by his side. . . .

Pre-wedding jitters, pal. That's all it was. Simon had even warned him. All right, then. Adam sucked in a calming breath. "Mrs. Hayes," he began, when a strange rusty-hinge screech filled the indigo night.

Hand automatically going to the bowie, Adam tensed, battle-ready and alert to every movement.

The porch door banged open, and Rosalind's graceful figure filled the entrance. She looked rumpled, and a long, thin scratch on her right cheek marred the peaches-and-milk complexion.

"Rosalind!" He leaped onto the porch. Ophelia adroitly stepped out of the way. "Rosalind, what happened? Who's hurt you?"

"Shh . . . don't shout, Adam. You'll scare him."

Adam yanked open the porch door. "You're scaring *me.*

What is all this?" he demanded, his attention swinging suddenly to a box on the floor behind Rosalind. Odd scratching sounds, combined with erratic little jumps, offered the first clue.

His gaze returned to Rosalind's scratched face, the mischievous twinkle in her eyes. "It's your wedding gift," she announced. The twinkle faded, and a love as vast as the universe bathed Adam in its glow. "I know nothing can replace Kat, but Zeke and I have been scrounging alleys all over Denver for the past week." She gestured toward the box. "Go ahead. Open it—but be careful. The last time he got away from me, this happened." She flicked her fingers over the mark on her face.

As though in a dream, Adam knelt by the box. Tentatively, he raked his fingernails across one of the outside panels. Hissing and growling greeted him, along with the sound of claws frantically attacking the noise. A lump lodged somewhere around his breastbone. He lifted incredulous eyes to Rosalind.

"He's not a wildcat," she said, a smile in the words as well as on her face, "but he is most definitely a wild cat. Kitten, to be specific. I thought . . . perhaps you'd enjoy the challenge of taming him?"

Adam rose and engulfed her in a close embrace, lifting her completely off her feet. "I love you," he choked out. "Love you more than you can possibly imagine."

"I wouldn't be so certain of that," his irrepressible wildcat replied. "I have a very active imagination."

Adam laughed, planted a hearty kiss on her unprotesting lips and turned to give the blushing Ophelia a wink. Then he knelt down again and proceeded to introduce himself to his wedding gift.

Epilogue

Manitou Springs, Colorado
June 1897

THE CHURCH WAS PACKED WITH GUESTS, all of them waiting in growing restlessness for the bride and groom to appear. The ceremony, it was clear, was certainly not what most of them had expected from a prominent family like the Hayeses. There were flowers, to be sure, and a lavish reception to follow at the famous Cliff House Hotel.

But the bride was rumored to be walking in unaccompanied, and not even her mother or sister had been permitted to help her into her wedding gown.

"On the other hand," Gladys Hayes, sister-in-law of the bride, huffed, "when has Rosalind ever behaved with proper decorum?"

Two guests seated directly behind her stifled smiles. The man, a tough-looking individual with a pair of glittering green eyes, leaned to whisper in his wife Elizabeth's ear. "I can't wait to see the lady's reaction when Adam comes out in his buckskins."

"Do you think he'll keep the bowie strapped to his side?" Elizabeth whispered back.

Her husband Simon merely shrugged.

"I still don't understand why he refused to let you join him until he and Rosalind are at the altar. You're his best man, after all."

"It's their wedding, my love. We had a few modifications at our own, if you remember." They exchanged indulgent smiles.

A hush fell over the congregation. Then, incredibly, a Scottish bagpiper in full Highland regalia appeared. He began to play a powerful rendition of "Amazing Grace" as Pastor Jedidiah Scrivens and the groom marched from a side door to stand in front of the altar. The haunting melody was unexpected, startling.

But not as startling as the groom.

Mr. Adam Moreaux was impeccably clad—in formal white tie and tails. Instead of the infamous queue, his thick black hair had been cut short, fashionably styled, the epitome of masculine power and sophistication.

He could have graced Queen Victoria's court.

The bagpipe's last haunting notes faded into silence. The groom, looking serene, noble, glowing with anticipation, trained his gaze on the back of the church.

Now the organist began to play, and all heads craned to the rear.

When the bride appeared, a shaft of golden morning sunlight spilled through the high window, bathing her in its radiance. The congregation collectively gasped.

Instead of an exquisite gown of lace and silk and pearls, the bride was dressed—in fringed doeskin. Intricate rows of bead embroidery decorated the bodice and waist, while six-inch strips of leather dangled from hem and arms. Her feet were bound in matching moccasins, and a beaded band circled her forehead. Her unbound chestnut hair streamed halfway down her back in a rich cloud.

The bride and groom stared at each other in astonishment.

The organist launched into the processional, but faltered when bride and groom burst into simultaneous laughter. One by one, the rows of guests joined in, until the joyful sound rang throughout the church.

The music swelled, mingling with the strains of laughter, as Rosalind joined Adam at the altar. Hands entwined, still laughing, they turned to Jedidiah.

"Dearly beloved," he intoned, "we are gathered here toda—

in the sight of God, to join this man and woman in holy matrimony . . . and to celebrate the triumph of His love."

"You will go out in joy and be led forth in peace;
the mountains and hills will burst into song
before you."

Isaiah 55:12, NIV